ANNIE
THE CROW'S INN TRAGEDY

Annie Haynes was born in 1865, the daughter of an ironmonger.

By the first decade of the twentieth century she lived in London and moved in literary and early feminist circles. Her first crime novel, *The Bungalow Mystery*, appeared in 1923, and another nine mysteries were published before her untimely death in 1929.

Who Killed Charmian Karslake? appeared posthumously, and a further partially-finished work, *The Crystal Beads Murder*, was completed with the assistance of an unknown fellow writer, and published in 1930.

Also by Annie Haynes

ANNIE HAYNES

THE
CROW'S INN
TRAGEDY

With an introduction
by Curtis Evans

DEAN STREET PRESS

Published by Dean Street Press 2015

All Rights Reserved

First published in 1927 by The Bodley Head

Cover by DSP

Introduction © Curtis Evans 2015

ISBN 978 1 911095 05 7

www.deanstreetpress.co.uk

THE MYSTERY OF THE MISSING AUTHOR

Annie Haynes and Her Golden Age
Detective Fiction

THE PSYCHOLOGICAL enigma of Agatha Christie's notorious 1926 vanishing has continued to intrigue Golden Age mystery fans to the present day. The Queen of Crime's eleven-day disappearing act is nothing, however, compared to the decades-long disappearance, in terms of public awareness, of between-the-wars mystery writer Annie Haynes (1865-1929), author of a series of detective novels published between 1923 and 1930 by Agatha Christie's original English publisher, The Bodley Head. Haynes's books went out of print in the early Thirties, not long after her death in 1929, and her reputation among classic detective fiction readers, high in her lifetime, did not so much decline as dematerialize. When, in 2013, I first wrote a piece about Annie Haynes' work, I knew of only two other living persons besides myself who had read any of her books. Happily, Dean Street Press once again has come to the rescue of classic mystery fans seeking genre gems from the Golden Age, and is republishing all Haynes' mystery novels. Now that her crime fiction is coming back into print, the question naturally arises: Who Was Annie Haynes? Solving the mystery of this forgotten author's lost life has taken leg work by literary sleuths on two continents (my thanks for their assistance to Carl Woodings and Peter Harris).

Until recent research uncovered new information about Annie Haynes, almost nothing about her was publicly known besides the fact of her authorship of twelve mysteries during the Golden Age of detective fiction. Now we know that she led an altogether intriguing life, too soon cut short by disability and death, which took her from the isolation of the rural English Midlands in the nineteenth century to the cultural high life of Edwardian London. Haynes was born in 1865 in the Leicestershire town of Ashby-de-la-Zouch, the first child of ironmonger Edwin Haynes and Jane (Henderson) Haynes, daughter of Montgomery Henderson, longtime superintendent of the gardens at nearby Coleorton Hall, seat of the Beaumont baronets. After her father left his family, young Annie resided with her grandparents at the gardener's cottage at Coleorton Hall, along with her mother and younger brother. Here Annie doubtlessly obtained an acquaintance with the ways of the country gentry that would serve her well in her career as a genre fiction writer.

We currently know nothing else of Annie Haynes' life in Leicestershire, where she still resided (with her mother) in 1901, but by 1908, when Haynes was in her early forties, she was living in London with Ada Heather-Bigg (1855-1944) at the Heather-Bigg family home, located halfway between Paddington Station and Hyde Park at 14 Radnor Place, London. One of three daughters of Henry Heather-Bigg, a noted pioneer in the development of orthopedics and artificial limbs, Ada Heather-Bigg was a prominent Victorian and Edwardian era feminist and social reformer. In the 1911 British census entry for 14 Radnor Place, Heather-Bigg, a "philanthropist and journalist," is listed as the head of the household and Annie Haynes, a "novelist," as a "visitor," but in fact Haynes would remain there with Ada Heather-Bigg until Haynes' death in 1929.

Haynes' relationship with Ada Heather-Bigg introduced the aspiring author to important social sets in England's great metropolis. Though not a novelist herself, Heather-Bigg was an important figure in the city's intellectual milieu, a well-connected feminist activist of great energy and passion who believed strongly in the idea of women attaining economic independence through remunerative employment. With Ada Heather-Bigg behind her, Annie Haynes's writing career had powerful backing indeed. Although in the 1911 census Heather-Bigg listed Haynes' occupation as "novelist," it appears that Haynes did not publish any novels in book form prior to 1923, the year that saw the appearance of *The Bungalow Mystery*, which Haynes dedicated to Heather-Bigg. However, Haynes was a prolific producer of newspaper serial novels during the second decade of the twentieth century, penning such works as *Lady Carew's Secret, Footprints of Fate, A Pawn of Chance, The Manor Tragedy* and many others.

Haynes' twelve Golden Age mystery novels, which appeared in a tremendous burst of creative endeavor between 1923 and 1930, like the author's serial novels retain, in stripped-down form, the emotionally heady air of the nineteenth-century triple-decker sensation novel, with genteel settings, shocking secrets, stormy passions and eternal love all at the fore, yet they also have the fleetness of Jazz Age detective fiction. Both in their social milieu and narrative pace Annie Haynes' detective novels bear considerable resemblance to contemporary works by Agatha Christie; and it is interesting to note in this regard that Annie Haynes and Agatha Christie were the only female mystery writers published by The Bodley Head, one of the more notable English mystery imprints in the early Golden Age. "A very remarkable feature of recent detective fiction," observed the *Illustrated London News* in 1923, "is the skill displayed by women in this branch of story-telling. Isabel Ostrander, Carolyn Wells, Annie Haynes and last, but very far from least, Agatha Christie, are contesting the laurels of Sherlock Holmes' creator with a great spirit, ingenuity and success." Since Ostrander and Wells were American authors, this left Annie Haynes, in the estimation of the *Illustrated London News*, as the main British female competitor to Agatha Christie. (Dorothy L. Sayers, who, like Haynes, published her debut mystery novel in 1923, goes unmentioned.) Similarly, in 1925 *The Sketch* wryly noted that "[t]ired men, trotting home at the end of an imperfect day, have been known to pop into the library and ask for an Annie Haynes. They have not made a mistake in the street number. It is not a cocktail they are asking for..."

Twenties critical opinion adjudged that Annie Haynes' criminous concoctions held appeal not only for puzzle fiends impressed with the "considerable craftsmanship" of their plots (quoting from the *Sunday Times* review of *The Bungalow Mystery*), but also for more general readers attracted to their purely literary qualities. "Not only a crime story of merit, but also a novel which will interest readers to whom mystery for its own sake has little appeal," avowed *The Nation* of Haynes' *The Secret of Greylands*, while the *New Statesman* declared of *The*

Witness on the Roof that "Miss Haynes has a sense of character; her people are vivid and not the usual puppets of detective fiction." Similarly, the *Bookman* deemed the characters in Haynes' *The Abbey Court Murder* "much truer to life than is the case in many sensational stories" and *The Spectator* concluded of *The Crime at Tattenham Corner*, "Excellent as a detective tale, the book also is a charming novel."

Sadly, Haynes' triumph as a detective novelist proved short lived. Around 1914, about the time of the outbreak of the Great War, Haynes had been stricken with debilitating rheumatoid arthritis that left her in constant pain and hastened her death from heart failure in 1929, when she was only 63. Haynes wrote several of her detective novels on fine days in Kensington Gardens, where she was wheeled from 14 Radnor Place in a bath chair, but in her last years she was able only to travel from her bedroom to her study. All of this was an especially hard blow for a woman who had once been intensely energetic and quite physically active.

In a foreword to *The Crystal Beads Murder*, the second of Haynes' two posthumously published mysteries, Ada Heather-Bigg noted that Haynes' difficult daily physical struggle "was materially lightened by the warmth of friendships" with other authors and by the "sympathetic and friendly relations between her and her publishers." In this latter instance Haynes' experience rather differed from that of her sister Bodleian, Agatha Christie, who left The Bodley Head on account of what she deemed an iniquitous contract that took unjust advantage of a naive young author. Christie moved, along with her landmark detective novel *The Murder of Roger Ackroyd* (1926), to Collins and never looked back, enjoying ever greater success with the passing years.

At the time Christie crossed over to Collins, Annie Haynes had only a few years of life left. After she died at 14 Radnor Place on 30 March 1929, it was reported in the press that "many people well-known in the literary world" attended the author's funeral at St. Michaels and All Angels Church, Paddington, where her sermon was delivered by the eloquent vicar, Paul Nichols, brother of the writer Beverley Nichols and dedicatee of Haynes' mystery novel *The Master of the Priory*; yet by the time of her companion Ada Heather-Bigg's death in 1944, Haynes and her once highly-praised mysteries were forgotten. (Contrastingly, Ada Heather-Bigg's name survives today in the University College of London's Ada Heather-Bigg Prize in Economics.) Only three of Haynes' novels were ever published in the United States, and she passed away less than a year before the formation of the Detection Club, missing any chance of being invited to join this august body of distinguished British detective novelists. Fortunately, we have today entered, when it comes to classic mystery, a period of rediscovery and revival, giving a reading audience a chance once again, after over eighty years, to savor the detective fiction fare of Annie Haynes. *Bon appétit!*

Curtis Evans

CHAPTER I

THE OFFICES of Messrs. Bechcombe and Turner took up the whole of the first floor of the corner house of Crow's Inn Square. Bechcombe and Turner was one of the oldest legal firms in London. Their offices were dingy, not to say grimy-looking. The doors and windows had evidently not had a coat of paint for years. There were no lifts in Crow's Inn. Any such modern innovation would have been out of place in the tall, narrow-casemented houses that stood square round the grass—grass which was bound and crossed by stone flagged walks. The front door of the corner house stood open; the tessellated floor of the hall was dulled by the passing of numberless footsteps. The narrow, uncarpeted stairs went up just opposite the door.

A tall, grey-haired clergyman, who was carefully scrutinizing the almost illegible doorplate, glanced round in some distaste as he went up the worn stairs. At the top he was faced by a door with the legend "Inquiries" written large upon it. After a moment's hesitation he knocked loudly. Instantly a panel in the middle of the door shot aside and a small, curiously wrinkled face looked out inquisitively.

"Mr. Bechcombe?" the caller said inquiringly. "Please tell him that Mr. Collyer has called, but that he will wait."

The message was repeated by a boyish voice, the panel was pushed into its place again, a door by the side opened and Mr. Collyer was beckoned in. He found himself in a small ante-room; a door before him stood open and he could see into an office containing a row of desks on each side and several clerks apparently writing busily away. Nearer to him was another open door evidently leading into a waiting-room, furnished with a round centre-table and heavy leather chairs—all with the same indescribable air of gloom that seemed to pervade Messrs. Bechcombe and Turner's establishment.

The boy who had admitted Mr. Collyer now stood aside for him to pass in, and then departed, vouchsafing the information that Mr. Bechcombe would be at leisure in a few minutes.

With a sigh of relief the clergyman let himself down into one of the capacious arm-chairs, moving stiffly like a man afflicted with chronic rheumatism. Then he laid his head against the back of it as if thoroughly tired out. Seen thus in repose, the deep lines graven on his clean-shaven face were very noticeable, his mouth had a weary droop, and his kind, grey eyes with the tiny network of wrinkles round them were sad and worried.

The minutes were very few indeed before a bell rang close at hand, a door sprang open as if by magic and the same boy beckoned him into a farther room.

Luke Bechcombe was standing on the hearthrug with his back to the open fireplace. The head, and in fact the sole representative, of the firm of Bechcombe and Turner, since Turner had retired to a villa at Streatham, Luke Bechcombe was a small, spare man with grey hair already growing very thin near the temples and on the crown, and a small, neatly trimmed, grey beard. His keen, pale eyes were hidden from sight by a pair of horn-rimmed spectacles. His general appearance was remarkably spick and span.

He came forward with outstretched hand as the clergyman entered somewhat hesitatingly.

"Why, Jim, this is an unexpected pleasure! What has brought you up to town?"

The clergyman looked at him doubtfully as their hands met.

"The usual thing—worry! I came up to consult you, to ask if you could help me."

The solicitor glanced at him keenly, then he turned to the revolving chair before his desk and motioned his visitor to the one opposite.

"Tony again?" he questioned, as his visitor seated himself.

The clergyman waited a minute, twirling his soft hat about in his hands as he held it between his knees.

"Tony again!" he assented at last. "It isn't the lad's fault, Luke, I truly believe. He can't get a job that suits him. Those two years at the War played ruination with the young men just beginning life. Tony would make a good soldier. But he doesn't seem to fit in anywhere else."

"Then why doesn't he enlist?" Luke Bechcombe snapped out.

"His mother," Mr. Collyer said quietly. "She would never have a moment's peace."

Luke Bechcombe pushed back his glasses and stared at his brother-in-law for a moment. Then he nodded his head slowly. The Rev. James Collyer's statement was true enough he knew—none better. Mrs. Collyer was his sister; the terrible anxiety of those last dreadful days of the Great War, when her only son had been reported wounded and missing for months, had played havoc with her heart. Tony Collyer had had a hot time of it in one of the prisoners' camps in Germany; he had been gassed as well as badly wounded, and he had come back a shadow of his old self. His mother had nursed him back to health and sanity, but the price had been the invalid couch that had stood ever since in the Rectory morning-room. No. Tony Collyer could never enlist in his mother's lifetime. The same applied to emigration. Tony must get a job at home, and England, the home of heroes, had no use for her heroes now. There had been times when Tony envied those comrades of his whose graves lay in Flanders' soil.

They, at any rate, had not lived to know that they were little better than nuisances in the land for which they had fought and died. He had had several jobs, but in every one of them he had been a square peg in a round hole. They had all been clerkships of one kind or another and Tony had hated them all. Nevertheless he had conscientiously done his best for some time. Latterly, however, Tony had taken to slacking. He had met with some of his old companions of the Great War and had spent more money than he could afford. Three times already his father had paid his debts, taxing his resources to the utmost to do so. Each time Tony had promised reformation and amendment, but each time the result had been the same. Small wonder that the rector's hair was rapidly whitening, that every day seemed to make new lines on his fresh-coloured, pleasant face.

His brother-in-law glanced at him sympathetically now.

"What is Tony doing just at present?"

"Nothing, most of the time," his father said bitterly. "But I hear this morning that he has been offered a post as bear-leader to the younger brother of a friend of his. I gather the lad is a trifle defective."

"Must be, I should think. His friends too, I imagine," Luke Bechcombe barked gruffly.

The implication was unmistakable. The rector sighed uneasily.

"I have faith, you know, Luke, that the boy will come right in the end. He is the child of many prayers."

"Umph!" Mr. Bechcombe sat drumming his fingers on the writing-pad before him. "Why don't you let him pay his debts out of his salary?"

The clergyman stirred uneasily.

"He couldn't. And there are things that must be met at once—debts of honour, he calls them. But that is enough, Luke. I mean to give the boy a clean start this time, and I think he will go straight. He has an inducement now that he has never had before."

"Good heavens! Not a girl?" Luke Bechcombe ejaculated.

Mr. Collyer bent his head.

"Yes, I hope so. A very charming girl too, I believe."

"Who is she?"

"I do not suppose I shall be betraying confidence if I tell you," the clergyman debated. "You will have to know soon, I expect. Her name is Cecily Hoyle."

"Good heavens!" The lawyer sat back and stared at him. "Do you mean my secretary?"

"Your secretary," Mr. Collyer acquiesced. "She is a nice girl, isn't she, Luke?"

"Niceness doesn't matter in a secretary, the solicitor said gruffly. "She types and takes shorthand notes very satisfactorily. As for looks she is nothing particular. Madeline took care of that—always does! In fact she engaged her for me. Still, she is a taking little thing. How the deuce did Tony get hold of her?"

The clergyman shook his head.

"I don't know. He only spoke of her the other day. But it will be good for the lad, Luke. I believe it is the genuine thing."

"Genuine thing! Good for the lad!" Luke Bechcombe repeated scornfully. "Tony can't keep himself. How is he going to keep my secretary?"

"Tony can work if he likes," his father maintained stoutly. "And if he has some one to work for I think he will."

"Girl won't take him. She has too much sense," growled the solicitor.

"Oh, I think she has given Tony some reason to hope."

"She is as big a fool as he is then," Mr. Bechcombe said with asperity. "But Tony isn't the only one of the family on matrimony bent. What do you think of Aubrey Todmarsh?"

"Aubrey Todmarsh!" repeated the rector of Wexbridge in amazed accents. "I should have thought matrimony would have been the last thing to enter his head. His whole life seems to be bound up in that community of his."

"Not so bound up but that he still has a very good eye to the main chance," retorted Luke Bechcombe. "He is not thinking of a penniless secretary! He's after money, is Mr. Aubrey. What do you think of Mrs. Phillimore?"

"Mrs. Phillimore! The rich American widow! She must be much too old for him."

"Old enough to be his mother, I dare say. She is pretty well made up, though, and that doesn't matter to Aubrey as long as she has got the money. She has been financing these wildcat schemes of his lately. But I suppose he thinks the whole would suit him better than part."

"But are they really engaged?"

"Oh, nothing quite so definite yet. But I am expecting the announcement every day. Hello!"—as an intermittent clicking made itself heard—"there's your future daughter-in-law at work. That's the typewriter."

Mr. Collyer started.

"You don't mean that she has been able to hear what we have been saying?"

Mr. Bechcombe laughed.

"Hardly! That would be delightful in a solicitor's office. She sits in that little room at the side, but there is no communicating door and of course she can't hear what goes on here. The door is in the top passage, past my private entrance. I didn't expect to hear her machine, but there is something particularly penetrating about a typewriter. However, it is really very faint and I have got quite used to it. Would you like to see her?"

The clergyman looked undecided for a moment; then he shook his head.

"No, I shouldn't care to do anything that might look like spying. Time enough for me to see her when there is anything decided."

"Please yourself!" Luke Bechcombe said gruffly. "Anyway if I had to choose between Tony and Aubrey Todmarsh I should take Tony."

"I wouldn't," Tony's father said. "The lad is a good lad when he is away from these friends of his. But he is weak—terribly weak. Now Aubrey Todmarsh—though I haven't always approved of him—is doing wonderful work in that East End settlement of his. He is marvellously successful in dealing with a class of men that we clergy are seldom able to reach."

"Umph! Well, he is always out for money for something," said the solicitor. "He invades this office sometimes almost demanding subscriptions. Will he expect his wife to go and live down at his Community house, I wonder? However, I believe the settlement is an attraction to some silly women, and to my mind he will want all the attraction he can get. I can't stand Aubrey myself. I have no use for conscientious objectors—never had!"

"There I am with you," assented the clergyman. "But I think Aubrey is hardly to be judged by ordinary standards. He is a visionary, an enthusiast. Of course I hold him to have been mistaken about the War, but honestly mistaken. With his dreams of reforming mankind I can understand—"

Mr. Bechcombe snorted.

"Can you? I can't! I am jolly glad your Tony didn't dream such dreams. Two conscientious objectors in the family would have been too much for me. I never could stand old Todmarsh. Aubrey is the very spit of him, as we used to say in Leicestershire."

"Oh, I don't see any resemblance between Aubrey and his father," the rector dissented. "Old Aubrey Todmarsh was a thoroughly self-indulgent man. I don't believe he ever gave a thought to anyone else in the world. Now Aubrey with his visions and his dreams—"

"Which he does his best to get other people to pay for," the solicitor interposed. "No use. You won't get me to enthuse over Aubrey, James. I remember him too well as a boy—a selfish, self-seeking little beast."

"Yes, I was not fond of him as a child. But I believe it to be a case of genuine conversion. He spends himself and his little patrimony for others. Next week he goes to Geneva, he tells me, to attend a sitting of the League of Nations, to explain the workings of—"

"Damn the League of Nations!" uttered the solicitor, banging his fist upon his writing-pad with an energy that rattled his inkstand. "I beg your pardon, James. Not but what it went out of fashion to apologize to parsons for swearing in the War. Most of them do it themselves nowadays—eh, what?" with a chuckle at his own wit that threatened to choke him.

The rector did not smile.

"I look upon the League of Nations as our great hope for the future."

"Do you? I don't," contradicted his brother-in-law flatly. "I look to a largely augmented Air Force with plenty of practice in bomb-throwing as my hope for the future. It will be worth fifty of that rotten League of Nations. Aubrey Todmarsh addressing the League of Nations! It makes me sick. I suppose they will knight *him* next. No, no more of that, please, James. When I think of the League of Nations I get excited and that is bad for my heart. But now to business. You say you want money for Tony—how do you propose to get it? I should say you have exhausted all ways of doing it by now."

"How about a further mortgage on my little farm at Halvers?"

The solicitor shook his head.

"No use thinking of it. Farm is mortgaged up to the hilt already—rather past it, in fact."

"And I can't raise any more on my life insurance." Mr. Collyer sighed. "Well, it must be—there is nothing else—the emerald cross."

"Oh, but that would be a thousand pities—an heirloom with a history such as that. Oh, you can't part with it."

"What else am I to do?" questioned the clergyman. "You said yourself that I had exhausted all my resources. No. I had practically made up my mind to it when I came here. I had just a forlorn hope that you might be able to suggest something else, though as a matter of fact I want your assistance still. I am deplorably ignorant on such matters. How does one set about selling jewellery? Can you tell me a good place to go to?"

"Um!" The solicitor pursed up his lips. "If you have really made up your mind, how would you like to put the matter in my hands? First, of course, I must have the emeralds valued—then I can see what offers we get, and you can decide which, if any, you care to accept. Not but what I think you are quite wrong, mind you!"

"I shall be enormously obliged to you," the clergyman said haltingly. "But do you know anything of selling jewellery yourself, Luke?"

Mr. Bechcombe smiled. "A man in my position and profession has to know a bit of everything. As a matter of fact I have a job of this kind on hand just now, and I might work the two together. I will do my best if you like to entrust me with the emeralds."

The clergyman rose.

"You are very good, Luke. All my life long you have been the one to help me out of any difficulty. Here are the emeralds," fumbling in his breast pocket. "I brought them with me in case of any emergency such as this that has arisen."

"You surely don't mean that you have put them in your pocket?" exclaimed the solicitor.

Mr. Collyer looked surprised.

"They are quite safe. See, I button my coat when I am outside. No one could possibly take them from me."

Mr. Bechcombe coughed.

"Oh, James, nothing will ever alter you! Don't you know that there have been as many jewels stolen in the past year in London as in twenty years previously? People say there is a regular gang at work—they call it the Yellow Gang, and the head of it goes by the name of the Yellow Dog. If it had been known you were carrying the emeralds in that careless fashion they would never have got here. However, all's well that ends well. You had better leave them in my safe."

The rector brought an ancient leather case out of his pocket.

Mr. Bechcombe held his hand out for the case.

"Here it is."

"So this is the Collyer cross! I haven't seen it for years." He was opening the case as he spoke. Inside the cross lay on its satin bed, gleaming with baleful, green fire. As Mr. Bechcombe looked at it his expression changed. "Where have you kept the cross, James?"

The rector blinked.

"In the secret drawer in my writing-table. Why do you ask?"

Mr. Bechcombe groaned.

"A secret drawer that is no secret at all, since all the household, not to say the parish, knows it. As for why I asked, I know enough about precious stones to see"—he raised the cross and peered at it in a ray of sunlight that slanted in through the dust-dimmed window—"to fear that these so-called emeralds are only paste."

"What!" The rector stared at him. "The Collyer emeralds—paste! Why, they have been admired by experts!"

"No. Not the Collyer emeralds," Mr. Bechcombe contradicted. "The Collyer emeralds were magnificent gems. This worthless paste has been substituted."

"Impossible! Who would do such a thing?" Mr. Collyer asked.

"Ah! That," said Luke Bechcombe grimly, "we have got to find out."

CHAPTER II

THE SETTLEMENT of the Confraternity of St. Philip was situated in one of the most unsavoury districts in South London. It faced the river, but between it and the water lay a dreary waste of debatable land, strewn with the wreckage and rubbish thrown out by the small boat-building firms that existed on either side.

Originally the Settlement had been two or three tenement houses that had remained as a relic of the days when some better class folk had lived there to be near the river, then one of London's great highways. At the back the Settlement had annexed a big barnlike building formerly used as a storehouse. It made a capital room for the meetings that Aubrey Todmarsh and his assistants were continually organizing. In the matter of cleanliness, even externally, the Settlement set an example to the neighbourhood. No dingy paint or glass there. The windows literally shone, the front was washed over as soon as there was the faintest suspicion of grime by some of Todmarsh's numerous protégés. The door plate, inscribed "South London Settlement of the Confraternity of St. Philip," was as bright as polish and willing hands could make it.

The Rev. James Collyer looked at it approvingly as he stood on the doorstep.

"Just the sort of work I should have loved when I was young," he soliloquized as he rang the door bell.

It was answered at once by a man who wore the dark blue serge short coat and plus fours with blue bone buttons, which was the uniform of the Confraternity. In addition he had on the white overall which was *de rigueur* for those members of the Community who did the housework. This was generally understood to be undertaken by all the members in turn.

But Mr. Collyer did not feel much impressed with this particular member. He was a rather short man with coal-black hair contrasting oddly with his unhealthily white face, deep-set dark eyes that seemed to look away from the rector and yet to give him a quick, furtive glance every now and then from beneath his lowered lids. He was clean-shaven, showing an abnormally large chin, and he had a curious habit of opening and shutting his mouth silently in fish-like fashion.

"Mr. Todmarsh?" the rector inquired.

The man held the door wider open and stood aside. Interpreting this as an invitation to enter, Mr. Collyer walked in. The man closed the door and with a silent gesture invited the clergyman to follow him.

The Community House of St. Philip was just as conspicuously clean inside as out. Mr. Collyer had time to note that the stone floor of the hall had just been cleaned, that the scanty furniture, consisting of a big oak chest under the window and a couple of Windsor chairs at the ends, was as clean as furniture polish and elbow-grease could make them. His guide opened a door at the side and motioned him in.

A man who was writing at the long centre table got up quickly to meet him and came forward with outstretched hands.

"My dear uncle, this is a pleasure!"

"One to which I have long been looking forward," Mr. Collyer responded warmly. "My dear Aubrey, the reports I have heard of the Settlement have been in no way exaggerated. And so far as I can see this is an ideal Community house."

Todmarsh held his uncle's hand for a minute in his firm clasp, looking the elder man squarely in the eyes the while.

"There is nothing ideal about us, Uncle James. We are just a handful of very ordinary men, all trying to make our own bit of the world brighter and happier. It sounds very simple, but it isn't always easy to do things. Sometimes life is nothing but disappointments. But I know you realize just how it feels when one spends everything in striving to cleanse one's own bit of this great Augean mass that is called London—and fails."

His voice dropped as he spoke, and the bright look of enthusiasm faded from his face, leaving it prematurely old and tired. For it was above all things his enthusiasm, a sort of exalted look as of one who dreamed dreams and saw visions not vouchsafed to ordinary men, that made Aubrey Todmarsh's face attractive. Momentarily stripped of its bright expression it was merely a thin rather overjowled face, with deep-set, dark eyes, noticeably low forehead, and thick dark hair brushed sleekly backwards, hair that was worn rather longer than most men's.

The clergyman looked at him pityingly.

"Oh, my dear Aubrey, this is only nerves, a very natural depression. We parsons know it only too well. It is especially liable to recur when we are beginning work. Later one learns that all one can do is to sow in faith, and then be content to wait the issue in patience, leaving everything to Him whose gracious powers can alone give the increase." Todmarsh did not speak for a moment, then he drew a long breath and, laying his hand on the rector's shoulder, looked at him with the bright smile with which his friends were familiar.

"You always give me comfort, Uncle James. Somehow you always know just what to say to heal when one has been stricken sorely. That idea of sowing and waiting—somehow one gets hold of that."

"It isn't original, dear Aubrey," his uncle said modestly. "But for all Christian work I have found it most helpful. But you, my dear Aubrey, the founder of this—er—splendid effort—might rather have cause for—er—spiritual exaltation than depression."

"There is cause enough for depression sometimes, I assure you," Aubrey returned gloomily. "Much of our work is done among the discharged prisoners, you know, Uncle James. Different members of our Community look after those bound over under the First Offenders' Act, and those undergoing terms of imprisonment. With those who have had longer sentences and the habitual offenders I try to deal as much as possible myself with the valuable help of my second-in-command."

"I know. I have heard how you attend at police courts and meet the prisoners when they come out. I can hardly imagine a more saintly work or one more certain to carry with it a blessing."

"It doesn't seem to," Todmarsh said, his face clouding over again. "There is this man, Michael Farmore, the case I was speaking of. He was convicted of burglary and served his five years. We got hold of him when he came out and brought him here. In time he became one of our most trusted members. If ever there was a case of genuine conversion I believed his to be one. Yet—"

"Yes?" Mr. Collyer prompted as he paused.

"Yet last night he was arrested attempting to break into General Craven's house in Mortimer Square."

Todmarsh blew his nose vigorously. His voice was distinctly shaky as he broke off. His uncle glanced at him sympathetically.

"You must not take it too much to heart, my dear Aubrey. Think of your many successes, and even in this case that seems so terrible I feel sure that your labour has not really been wasted. You have cast your bread upon the waters, and you will assuredly find it again. You are fighting against the forces of the arch-enemy, remember."

"We are fighting against a gang of criminals," Aubrey said shortly. "We hear of them every now and then in our work. The Yellow Gang they call them in the underworld—they form regular organizations of their own, working on a system, and appear to carry out the orders of one man. Sometimes I think he is the arch-fiend himself, for it seems impossible to circumvent him."

"But who is he?" the rector inquired innocently.

Aubrey Todmarsh permitted himself a slight smile.

"If we knew that, my dear uncle, it wouldn't be long before this wave of crime that is sweeping over the Metropolis was checked. But I have heard that even the rank and file of his own followers do not know who he is, though he is spoken of sometimes as the Yellow Dog. Anyway, he has a genius for organization. But now we must think of something more cheerful, Uncle James. I want you to see our refectory and the recreation rooms, and our little rooms, cells, kitchens. Through here"—throwing open a glass door—"we go to our playground as you see."

Mr. Collyer peered forth. In front of him was a wide, open space, partly grass, partly concrete. On the grass a game of cricket was proceeding, the players being youths apparently all under twenty. On the concrete older men were having a game at racquets. All round the open space at the foot of the high wall that surrounded the Community grounds there ran a flower border, just now gay with crocuses and great clumps of arabis—white and purple and gold. The walls themselves were covered with creepers that later on would blossom into sweetness. Here and there men were at work. It was a pleasant and a peaceful scene and the Rev. James Collyer's eyes rested on it approvingly.

"There are always some of us at play," Aubrey smiled. "These men have been on night work—porters, etc. You know we undertake all sorts of things and our record is such—we have never had a case of our trust being betrayed—that our men are in constant request."

"I do not wonder," his uncle said cordially. "It is—I must say it again, Aubrey—wonderful work that you are carrying on. Now what have these men been before they came to you?"

Todmarsh was leading the way to the other part of the house.

"Wastrels; drunkards most of them," he said shortly. "Discharged prisoners, sentenced for some minor offence. I told you that we meet prisoners on their release. Many of them are the wreckage—the aftermath of the War."

The rector sighed.

"I know. It is deplorable. That terrible War—and yet, a most righteous War."

"No war is righteous," Aubrey said quickly. Then his expression changed, the rapt look came back to his eyes. They looked right over his uncle's head. "No war can be anything but cruel and wicked. That is why we have made up our minds that war shall stop."

Mr. Collyer shook his head.

"War will never stop, my boy, while men and women remain what they are—while human nature remains what it is, I should say."

Todmarsh's eyes looked right in front of him over the Community playing fields.

"Yes, it will! Quarrelling there will be—must be while the world shall last. But all disputes shall be settled not by bloodshed and horrible carnage, but by arbitration. Every day the

League of Nations' labours are being quietly and ceaselessly directed to this end, and I think very few people realize how enormously the world is progressing."

"Your Uncle Luke does not think so. He does not believe in the League of Nations," Mr. Collyer dissented. "He, I regret to say, used a lamentably strong expression—'damned rot,' he called it!"

"Oh, Uncle Luke is hopeless," Aubrey returned, shrugging his shoulders. "The League of Nations means nothing to him. He is one of the regular fire-eating, jingo-shouting Britons that plunged us all into that horrible carnage of 1914. But his type is becoming scarcer every day as the world grows nearer the Christian ideal, thank Heaven!"

"Sometimes it seems to me to be growing farther from the Christian ideal instead of nearer." The clergyman sighed. "I am going through a terrible experience now, Aubrey. I must confess it is a great trial to my faith."

Instantly Todmarsh's face assumed its most sympathetic expression.

"I am so sorry to hear it, Uncle James. Do tell me about it, if it would be any relief to you. Sit down"—as they entered the refectory—"what is it? Tony?"

But the rector put aside the proffered chair.

"No, no. I must see all I can of the Settlement. No, it has nothing to do with Tony, I am thankful to say. He is to the full as much bewildered as I am myself. It is the emeralds—the cross!"

"The Collyer cross?" Aubrey exclaimed. "What of that?"

"Well—er, circumstances arose that made it—er—desirable that I should ascertain its value. I took it to your Uncle Luke, thinking that he might be able to help me, and he discovered that the stones were paste."

"Impossible!" Aubrey stared at his uncle. "I cannot believe it. But, pardon me, Uncle James, I don't think that either you or Uncle Luke are very learned with regard to precious stones. I expect it is all a mistake. The Collyer emeralds are genuine enough!"

"Oh, there is no mistake," Mr. Collyer said positively. "I had them examined by a well-known expert this morning. They are paste—not particularly good paste, either. If I had known rather more about such things, I might have discovered the substitution sooner. Not that it would have made much difference! You are wrong about your Uncle Luke, though, Aubrey. He has an immense fund of information about precious stones. He told me that he was about to dispose of—"

"Hush! Don't mention it!" Aubrey interrupted sharply. "I beg your pardon, Uncle James, but it is so much safer not to mention names, especially in a place like this. But what in the world can have become of the emeralds? One would have been inclined to think it was the work of the Yellow Gang. But they seem to confine their activities to London. And how could it have been effected in peaceful little Wexbridge? Now—what is that?" as a loud knock and ring resounded simultaneously through the house. "Tony, I declare!" as after a pause they heard voices in the hall outside.

A moment later Hopkins opened the door and announced "Mr. Anthony Collyer."

"Hello, dad, I guessed I should find you here," the new-comer began genially. "Aubrey, old chap, is the gentleman who announced me one of your hopefuls? Because if so I can't congratulate you on his phiz. Sort of thing the late Madame Tussaud would have loved for her Chamber of Horrors, don't you know!"

"Hopkins is a most worthy fellow," Aubrey returned impressively. "One of the most absolutely trustworthy men I have. There is nothing more unsafe than taking a prejudice at first sight, Tony. If you would only—"

"Dare say there isn't," Tony returned nonchalantly. "You needn't pull up your socks over the chap, Aubrey. I'll take your word for it that he possesses all the virtues under the sun. I only say, he don't look it! Come along, dad, I have ordered a morsel of lunch at a little pub I know of, and while you are eating it I will a scheme unfold that I know will meet with your approval."

The rector did not look as if he shared this conviction.

"Well, my boy, I have been telling my troubles to Aubrey. The emeralds—"

"Oh, bother the emeralds, dad! It is the business of the police to find them, not yours and mine or Aubrey's."

Anthony Collyer was just a very ordinary type of the young Englishman of to-day, well-groomed, well set up. There was little likeness to his father about his clear-cut features, his merry, blue eyes or his lithe, active form. The pity of it was that the last few years of idleness had blurred the clearness of his skin, had dulled his eyes and added just a suspicion of heaviness to the figure which ought to have been in the very pink of condition. Tony Collyer had let himself run to seed of late and looked it and knew it. To-day, however, there was a new look of purpose about his face. His mouth was set in fresh, strong lines, and his eyes met his father's firmly.

"I hoped you would both lunch with me," Aubrey interposed hastily. "I am sure if you could throw your trouble aside you would enjoy one of our Community meals, Uncle James. The fare is plain, but abundant, and the spirit that prevails seems to bless it all. You would find it truly interesting."

"I am sure I should, my boy. I really think, Tony—"

"That is all very well, Aubrey," Tony interrupted, "I'm jolly well sure your meals are interesting. But it isn't exactly the sort of feast I mean to set the Dad down to when he does get a few days off from his little old parish. No, I think we will stick to my pub—thank you all the same, Aubrey."

"Oh, well, if you put it that way—" Todmarsh shook hands with his visitors.

The rector's expression was rather wistful as they went out. He would have liked to share the simple meal Aubrey had spoken of. But Tony wanted him and Tony came first.

At the front door they paused a minute. Tony looked at his cousin with a wicked snigger.

"I'm really taking the Dad away out of kindness, Aubrey. There is a car standing a little way down the road, and a certain bewitching widow is leaning out talking to a couple of interesting-looking gentlemen. Converts of yours, recent ones, I should say by the cut of them."

"Mrs. Phillimore!" Aubrey came to the door and looked out. "It is her day for visiting our laundry just down the road."

Mr. Collyer smiled.

"Well, she is a good woman, Aubrey. We are dining with your Uncle Luke to-night. Shall we meet you there?"

"Oh, dear, no! My time for dining out is strictly limited," Aubrey responded. "Besides, I do not think that Uncle Luke and I are in much sympathy. It is months since I saw him."

CHAPTER III

FOR A WONDER the clerks in Messrs. Bechcombe and Turner's offices were all hard at work. The articled clerks were in a smaller office to the right of the large one with a partition partly glass between. Through it their heads could be seen bent over their work, their pens flying over their paper with commendable celerity.

The managing clerk had left his desk and was standing in the gangway in the larger office opposite the door leading into the ante-room. Beyond that again was the door opening into the principal's particular sanctum. Most unusually his door stood open this morning. Through the doorway the principal could plainly be seen bending over his letters and papers on the writing-table, while a little farther back stood his secretary, apparently waiting his instructions. Presently he spoke a few words to her in an undertone, pushed his papers all away together and came into the outer office.

"I find it is as I thought, Thompson. I have only two appointments this morning—Mr. Geary and Mr. Pound. The last is for 11.45. After Mr. Pound has been shown out you will admit no one until I ring, which will probably be about one o'clock. Then, hold yourself in readiness to accompany me to the Bank."

"Yes, sir."

The managing clerk at Messrs. Bechcombe and Turner's glanced keenly at his chief as he spoke.

"It is quite possible that a special messenger from the Bank may be sent here in the course of the morning," Mr. Bechcombe pursued. "Unless he comes before twelve he will have to wait until one o'clock as no one—*no one* is to disturb me until then. You understand this, Thompson?" He turned back sharply to his office.

"Quite so, sir."

The managing clerk had a curious, puzzled look as he glanced after the principal. Amos Thompson had been many years with Messrs. Bechcombe and Turner, and it was said that he enjoyed Mr. Bechcombe's confidence to the fullest degree. Be that as it may, it was evident that he knew nothing of the special business of this morning. He was a thin man of middle height with a reddish-grey beard, sunken-looking, grey eyes, like those of his principal usually concealed by a pair of horn-rimmed, smoke-coloured glasses; his teeth were irregular—one or two in front were missing. He had the habitual stoop of a man whose life is spent bending over a desk, and his faintly grey hair was already thinning at the top. As he went back to his desk both communicating doors in turn banged loudly behind Mr. Bechcombe. Instantly a change passed over his clerks; as if moved by one spring all the heads were raised, the pens slackened, most of them were thrown hastily on the desk.

Percy Johnson, one of the articled pupils, emitted a low whistle.

"What is the governor up to, Mr. Thompson?" he questioned daringly. "Casting the glad eye on some fair lady; not to be disturbed for an hour will give them plenty of time for—er—endearments."

Thompson turned his severe eyes upon him.

"This is neither the place nor the subject for such jokes, Mr. Johnson. May I trouble you to get on with your work? We are waiting for that deed." Mr. Johnson applied himself to his labours afresh.

"It is nice to know that one is really useful!"

The morning wore on. The two clients mentioned by Mr. Bechcombe—Mr. Geary and Mr. Pound—duly arrived and were shown in to Mr. Bechcombe, in each case remaining only a short time. Then there came a few minutes' quiet. The eyes of the clerks wandered to the clock. At twelve o'clock the first batch of them would depart to luncheon.

Amos Thompson's thoughts were busy with his chief. Some very important business must be about to be transacted in Mr. Bechcombe's private room, and the managing clerk, though usually fully cognizant of all the ins and outs of the affairs of the firm, had no notion what it might be. He would have been more or less than mortal if his speculations with regard to the mysterious visitor had not risen high. Just as the clock struck twelve there was a knock and ring at the outer door, and he heard a loud colloquy going on with the office boy. In a minute Tony Collyer came through into the clerks' office. It showed the upset to the general aspect of the managing clerk's ideas that he should go forward to meet him.

"Good morning, Mr. Anthony. I am sorry that Mr. Bechcombe is engaged."

"So am I," said Tony, shaking him heartily by the hand. "Because I want to see him particularly and my time is limited this morning. But I suppose I must wait a bit. Get me in as soon as you can, there's a good old chap!"

Thompson shook his head.

"It won't be any good your waiting this morning, Mr. Anthony. We have orders that no one is to disturb Mr. Bechcombe. It would be as much as my place is worth to knock at the door."

"And how much is your place worth, old boy?" Tony questioned with a laugh, at the same time bringing down his hand with friendly heartiness on the managing clerk's back. "Come, I tell you I must see my uncle—honour bright, it is important."

"It's no use, Mr. Anthony," Thompson said firmly. "You can't see Mr. Bechcombe this morning. And, pardon me, but it may be as well in your own interests that you should wait until later in the day."

Anthony laughed.

"What a quaint old bird you are, Thompson! Well, since my business is important, and I don't want you to lose your berth—wouldn't miss the chance of seeing your old phiz for anything—I shall go round and try what I can make of my uncle at his private door. I'll bet the old sport has some game on that he don't want you to know about, but he may be pleased to see his dear nephew."

"Mr. Anthony—you must not, indeed—I cannot allow—"

Anthony put up his hand.

"Hush—sh! You will know nothing about it! Keep your hair on, Thompson!" With a laughing nod round at the grinning clerks he vanished, pulling the door to behind him with a cheerful bang.

A titter ran round the office. Anthony Collyer with his D.S.O. and his gay, irresponsible manners was somewhat of a hero to the younger clerks.

Amos Thompson looked grave. He knew that Luke Bechcombe had been intensely proud of his nephew's prowess in the War, he guessed that his patience had been sorely tried of late, and he feared that the young man might be doing himself serious harm with his uncle this morning. But he was powerless. There was no holding Tony Collyer back in this mood. Presently Thompson, listening intently, caught the sound of a distant knocking at his chief's door, twice repeated, then there was silence.

He shrugged his shoulders, imagining Mr. Bechcombe's wrath at the intrusion. After a smothered laugh or two the clerks applied themselves to their work again and silence reigned in the office. The managing clerk watched the clock anxiously. He could imagine Mr. Bechcombe's reception of his nephew, but, knowing Tony as he did, he felt surprised that he had not returned to report proceedings. Then just as the office clock was nearing the half-hour a messenger from the Bank arrived. The waiting-room was reserved for clients, so the Bank clerk was shown into a little office that Amos Thompson used sometimes when there was a press of work, and the managing clerk went to him there.

"Is there anything I can do? Mr. Bechcombe is unfortunately engaged until one o'clock."

"No, thank you!" the young man returned. "I was charged most particularly to give my message to no one but Mr. Bechcombe himself. I suppose I must wait till one o'clock if you are sure I cannot see him before."

The managing clerk looked undecided. His eyes wandered from side to side beneath his horn-rimmed spectacles.

"I will see what I can do," he said at last.

He went back to his own desk, selected a couple of papers, put them in his pocket, and went through the outer office. In the lobby he picked up his hat, then after one long backward glance he went towards the outer door.

The time wore on. The first contingent of clerks returned from their luncheon. Their place was taken by a second band. The clock struck half-past one; and still there was no sign of either the principal or his managing clerk. The messenger from the Bank went away, came back, and waited.

At last the senior clerks began to look uncomfortable. John Walls, the second in command, went over to one of his confrères.

"I understood the governor said he was not to be disturbed until one o'clock, Spencer, but it's a good bit after two now, and Mr. Thompson isn't here either. The waiting-room is full and here's this man from the Bank back again. What are we to do?"

Mr. Spencer rubbed the side of his nose reflectively.

"How would it be to knock at the governor's door, Walls? He couldn't be annoyed after all this time."

John Walls was of the opinion that he couldn't either. Together they made up their minds to beard the lion in his den. They went through the anteroom and knocked gently at Mr. Bechcombe's door. There came no response.

After a moment's pause Mr. Walls applied his knuckles more loudly, again without reply.

He turned to his companion.

"He must have gone out."

The fact seemed obvious, and yet Spencer hesitated.

"You didn't hear anyone moving about when you first knocked?"

"No, I didn't," responded John Walls, staring at him. "Did you?"

"Well, I expect it was just fancy, because why shouldn't the governor answer if he was there? But I did think I heard a slight sound—a sort of stealthy movement just on the other side of the door," Spencer said slowly.

"I don't believe you could hear any movement except a pretty loud one through that door," the other said unbelievingly. "But it is very awkward, Mr. Thompson going out too. I don't know what to do."

"The governor did say something about Mr. Thompson going to the Bank with him," Spencer went on. "I wonder now if Mr. Bechcombe went out by the private door, and Mr. Thompson and he met in the passage and they went off to the Bank together."

"I don't know," John Walls said slowly. "It is a funny sort of thing anyway. I tell you what, Spencer, I shall go round and knock at the private door."

"What's the good of that?" Spencer objected sensibly. "If he's out it will make no difference. And if he is in and won't answer at one door he won't at the other."

"Well, anyway, I shall try," John Walls persisted. His rather florid face was several degrees paler than usual as he went through the clerks' office. Man and boy, all his working life had been spent in the Bechcombes' office, and he had become through long years of association personally attached to Luke Bechcombe. Within the last few minutes, though there seemed no tangible ground for it, he had become oppressed by a strange feeling, a prevision of some evil, a certainty that all was not well with his chief.

The private door into Mr. Bechcombe's office opened into a passage at right angles with the door by which clients were admitted to the waiting-rooms and to the clerks' offices.

John Walls knocked first tentatively, then louder, still without the slightest response.

By this time he had been joined by Spencer, who seemed to have caught the infection of the elder man's pallor. He looked at the keyhole.

"Of course the governor has gone out. But I wonder whether the key is in its place?"

He stooped and somewhat gingerly applied his eye to the hole. Then he jerked his head up with an inaudible exclamation.

"What—what do you see?" Walls questioned with unconscious impatience. Then as he gazed at the bent back of his junior that queer foreboding of his grew stronger.

At last Spencer raised himself.

"No, the key isn't in its hole," he said slowly. "But I thought—I thought—"

"Yes, yes; you thought what?"

Both men's voices had instinctively sunk to a whisper.

Spencer was shorter than his senior. As he looked up his eyes were dark with fear, his words came with an odd little stutter between them.

"I—I expect I was mistaken—I must have been. You look yourself, Walls. But I thought I saw a queer-looking heap over there by the window."

"A queer-looking heap!" Without further ado the other man pushed him aside.

As he knelt down Spencer went on:

"It—there is something sticking out at the side—it looks like a leg—a leg in a grey trouser—do you see?"

There was a moment's tense silence. Then Mr. Walls raised himself.

"It is a leg. Suppose—suppose it is the governor's leg! Suppose that heap is the governor! He may have had a fit. We shall have to break into the room. Just see if Thompson has come back. If he hasn't get hold of two of the juniors quietly. Send another as fast as he can go to the nearest doctor, and get some brandy ready. It's a strong door, but together we ought to manage it."

There was no sign of Thompson in the office, but one of the articled pupils was a Rugby half back. Spencer returned with him and one of his fellows and the Rugby man attacked the door with a vigour that had brought him through many a scrum. It soon yielded to their combined efforts, and then with one accord all the men stood back. There was something at first sight about the everyday aspect of the room into which they gazed that seemed oddly at variance with their fears. Then slowly all their eyes turned from Mr. Bechcombe's writing-table with his own chair standing before it, just as they had seen it hundreds of times, to that ominous heap near the window.

John Walls bent over it, then he looked up with shocked eyes.

"He—I am afraid it is all over."

"Not dead!" Spencer ejaculated; but one look at that ghastly face upon the floor, at the staring eyes, and wide open mouth with the protruding tongue, drove every drop of colour from his face. He turned to Walls with chattering teeth. "It—it must have been a fit, Walls. He looks terrible."

"Is there anything wrong?"

It was a woman's voice. With one consent the men moved nearer the private door so as to shut out the sight of that ghastly heap.

"Is there anything wrong?" There was an undertone of fear about the voice now.

John Walls turned.

"Mr. Bechcombe has been taken ill, Miss Hoyle—very ill, I am afraid."

The sight of his white, stricken face was more eloquent than his words. Cecily Hoyle's own colour faded slowly.

"What is it?" she questioned, looking from one to the other. She was a tall, thin slip of a girl with clear brown eyes, a nose that turned up and a mouth that was too wide, a reasonably fair complexion and a quantity of pretty, curly, nut-brown hair that waved all over her head and low down over her ears, and that somehow conveyed the impression of being bobbed when it wasn't. Ordinarily it was a winsome, attractive little face, but just now, catching the fear in Walls's voice, the brown eyes were full of dread and the mobile lips were twitching. "Can't I do anything?" she questioned. "It must be something very sudden. Mr. Bechcombe was quite well when I went out."

John Walls laid his hand on her shoulder.

"You can't do anything, Miss Hoyle. We can none of us do anything. It is too late."

Cecily shrank from him with a cry.

"No, no! He can't be—dead!"

A strong hand put both her and John Walls aside.

"Let me pass. I am a doctor. What is the matter here?"

John Walls recognized the speaker as a medical man who had rooms close at hand.

"I think Mr. Bechcombe has had a fit, sir. I am afraid it is all over."

"Stand aside, please. Let us have all the air we can."

The doctor bent over the man on the floor, but one look was sufficient. He touched the wrist, laid his hand over the heart. Then he stood up quickly.

"There is nothing to be done here. He has been dead, I should say, an hour or more. We must ring up the police, at once. You will understand that nothing is to be moved until their arrival."

"Police!" echoed John Walls with shaking lips.

"Yes, police!" the doctor said impatiently. "My good man, can't you see that this is no natural death? Mr. Bechcombe has been murdered—strangled!"

CHAPTER IV

THE FIRST FLOOR of 21 Crow's Inn was entirely in the hands of the police. Two plain clothes men guarded the entrance of the corridor, others were stationed farther along. Both the big waiting-rooms were filled, one with indignant clients anxious to go home, the other with the clerks and employees of the firm.

Two men came slowly down the passage. Inspector Furnival of Scotland Yard was a man of middle height with a keen, foxy-looking face, at present clean-shaven, and sharp grey eyes whose clearness of vision had earned him in the Force the sobriquet of "The Ferret." His companion, Dr. Hackett, carried his occupation writ plain on his large-featured face and his strictly professional attire.

Both men were looking grave and preoccupied as they entered the smaller office which had been little used since Mr. Bechcombe's partner retired. Inspector Furnival took the revolving chair and drew it up to the office table in the middle of the room. Then he produced a notebook.

"Now, Dr. Hackett, will you give me the details of this affair as far as you know them?"

"I can only tell you that I was summoned about two o'clock this afternoon by a clerk—Winter, I fancy his name is. He told me that his employer was locked up in his office, that they thought he had had a fit and were breaking the door open, and wanted me to be there in readiness as soon as they had forced their way in. I hastily put a few things that I thought might be wanted into my bag and hurried here. I arrived just as the door gave way and found matters as you know."

The inspector scratched the side of his nose reflectively with the handle of his fountain pen.

"Mr. Bechcombe was quite dead?"

"Quite dead. Had been dead at least two hours, I should say," Dr. Hackett assented.

"And the cause?" the inspector continued, suspending his pen over the paper.

"You will understand that you will have to wait until after the post-mortem for a definitely full and detailed opinion. But, as far as I can tell you after the examination which was all I could make this afternoon, I feel no doubt that the cause of death was strangulation."

"It seems inconceivable that a man should be strangled in his own office, within earshot of his own clerks," debated the inspector. "Still, it is quite evident even at a casual glance that it has been done here. But I cannot understand why Mr. Bechcombe apparently offered no resistance. His hand-bell, his speaking-tube, the telephone—all were close at hand. It looks as though he had recognized his assassin and had no fear of him."

"I think on the contrary that it was a sudden attack," Dr. Hackett dissented. "Probably Mr. Bechcombe had no opportunity of recognizing his murderer. The assassin sprang forward and—did you notice a sweet sickly smell that seemed to emanate from the body?"

The inspector nodded.

"That was the first thing I noticed. Chloroform, I suppose?"

"Yes," said the doctor slowly. "I should say the assassin sprang forward with the chloroform, or perhaps approached his victim unobserved, and attempted to stupefy him, and then strangled him. That is how it looks to me. For anything more definite we must wait for the post-mortem."

The inspector made a few hieroglyphics in his notebook, then he looked up.

"You say that death took place probably about two hours before you saw the body, doctor? and you were called in about two o'clock. Therefore, Mr. Bechcombe must have died about twelve o'clock. You are quite definite about this?"

"I cannot be more exact as to the time," Dr. Hackett said slowly. "I should say about twelve o'clock—certainly not much after. More probably a little before."

The inspector stroked his clean-shaven chin and glanced over his notes.

"Just one more question, Dr. Hackett. Can you tell me just who was in the room when you got there?"

Dr. Hackett hesitated a moment.

"Well, there was Mr. Walls, who seems to be managing things in Thompson's absence, and three other men whose names I do not of course know, and the late Mr. Bechcombe's secretary, whose name I understand to be Hoyle—Miss Hoyle."

The inspector pricked up his ears.

"I have not seen Miss Hoyle. What sort of a woman?"

"Oh, just a girl," the doctor said vaguely. "Just an ordinary-looking girl. I did not notice her much, except that I thought she looked white and shocked, as no doubt she was, poor girl!"

"No doubt!" the inspector assented. "How was she dressed, doctor?"

"Dressed?" the doctor echoed in some surprise. "Well, I don't take much notice of dress myself. Just a dark gown, I think."

"No hat?"

"No, I don't think so. No, I am sure she hadn't."

"Do you know where she works?"

"Didn't know such a person existed until this afternoon. I know nothing about her," the doctor said, shaking his head.

The inspector coughed.

"Um! Well, that will be all for the present, doctor. It is probable that you may be wanted later, and of course possible that Mrs. Bechcombe may wish to see you."

"I suppose she has been told?"

"Of course," the inspector assented. "We phoned to the house at once, and I gather she was informed of the death, not of course of the cause, by a relative who was there—a Mr. Collyer, a clergyman. I shall go round to see her when I have finished here. I hear that she collapsed altogether on hearing of her loss."

"Poor thing! Poor thing!" the doctor murmured. "Well, inspector, I shall hold myself at your disposal."

Left alone, the inspector looked over his notes once more and then sounded the electric bell twice. One of his subordinates opened the door at once.

"Tell Moore and Carter to take the names and addresses of all the clients. Verify them on the phone and then allow them to go home. If any of them are not capable of verification, have them shadowed. Now send John Walls to me."

The clerk did not keep Inspector Furnival waiting. He came in hesitatingly, dragging his feet like a man who has had a stroke. His face was colourless, his eyes were dark with fear.

"You sent for me, inspector?" he said, his teeth chattering as if with ague.

"Naturally!" the inspector assented, glancing at him keenly. "I want to hear all you know about Mr. Bechcombe's death. But, first, has Amos Thompson returned?"

"N—o!" quavered Walls.

"Can you account for his absence in any way?" the inspector questioned shortly.

"No, I have no idea where he is," Walls answered, gathering up his courage. "But then he is the managing clerk. I am not. I very seldom know anything of his work."

The inspector did not answer this. He drew his brows together.

"When did you see him last?"

"About half-past twelve, it would be. He went out of the office, I have not seen him since. But he did go out to lunch early sometimes. And he may have gone somewhere on business for Mr. Bechcombe." Walls wiped the sweat from his brow as he spoke.

The inspector looked at him.

"I understand that Mr. Bechcombe was heard to tell him to be in readiness to go with him to the Bank at one o'clock?"

"I—I believe Spencer said something about that," Walls stammered. "But I did not hear what Mr. Bechcombe said myself. My desk is farther away than Spencer's and I was busy with my work. All I heard was that Mr. Bechcombe was not to be disturbed on any account. He slightly raised his voice when he said that."

"Did you gather that Mr. Bechcombe had business of an important nature with a mysterious client?"

"I didn't gather anything," said Walls with some warmth. "It wasn't my business to. If Mr. Bechcombe did have an important client he must have admitted him himself by the private door. The last one that went to him in an ordinary way came out in a very few minutes."

"Before twelve o'clock?" questioned the inspector sharply.

"Oh, yes. Some minutes before the clock struck—about a quarter to, I should say. I noticed that."

"Because—" Inspector Furnival prompted.

"Oh, well, because I heard it strike afterwards, I suppose," Walls answered lamely. "There are days when I don't notice it."

"Um!" the inspector glanced at him. "Do you know the name of the last client who saw Mr. Bechcombe?"

"Pound—Mr. Pound, of Gosforth and Pound, the big haberdashers. He came about the lease of some fresh premises they are taking. I happen to know that."

"Ah, yes." The inspector looked him full in the face. "But you don't happen to know why Mr. Anthony Collyer wanted to see his uncle, perhaps?"

The sweat broke out afresh on Mr. Walls's forehead.

"I don't know anything about it."

"You know that Mr. Collyer came," the inspector said with some asperity. "Why did you not mention it?"

Walls glanced at him doubtfully.

"There wasn't anything to mention. Mr. Anthony wanted to see Mr. Bechcombe, and he couldn't, so he went away. He talked to Mr. Thompson, not to me."

"You did not hear what he said when he went away? Your desk seems to be most inconveniently placed, Mr. Walls."

"I heard him talking a lot of nonsense to Mr. Thompson."

"Such as—" The inspector paused.

"Oh, well, he said he must see Mr. Bechcombe and he said he would, and Mr. Thompson—"

"Be careful!" warned the inspector. "Don't make any mistakes, Mr. Walls, I want to know what Mr. Anthony Collyer said."

"He said—he said—if Mr. Thompson didn't let him in he would go round to Mr. Bechcombe's private door," the man said, then hesitated. "But it—it was just nonsense."

"Did he try to get into the room through the private door?"

"I don't know," Walls said helplessly. "I didn't see him any more."

The inspector drew a small parcel wrapped in tissue paper from his breast pocket and, opening it, displayed to the clerk's astonished eyes a long, white suede glove.

"Have you ever seen this before?"

John Walls peered at it.

"No. I can't say that I have. It—It is a lady's glove, inspector."

"It *is* a lady's glove," the inspector assented. "Where do you imagine it was found, Mr. Walls?"

"I'm sure I don't know," Walls said, staring at him. "It—I think a good many ladies wear gloves like that nowadays, Mr. Furnival. I know Mrs. Walls—"

"This particular glove," the inspector went on, "I found beside Mr. Bechcombe's writing-table this afternoon."

"Did you?" Mr. Walls looked amazed. "Well, I don't know how it came there. All Mr. Bechcombe's clients were men that came to-day."

"Except perhaps the one that came to the private door," suggested the inspector.

"I don't know anything about that," Walls said in a puzzled tone. "I never heard anything of a lady coming to-day."

The inspector folded the glove up and put it away again.

"That will do for the present, Mr. Walls. I should like to see Mr. Thompson if he returns, and now please send Miss Hoyle to me."

Walls looked uncomfortably surprised.

"Miss Hoyle?"

"Yes, Miss Hoyle—Mr. Bechcombe's secretary!" the inspector said sharply. "I suppose you know her, Mr. Walls?"

"Oh, yes," Walls stammered. "At least, I couldn't say I know her. I have spoken to her once or twice. But she didn't make any friends among us. And her office was quite apart. She didn't come through our door, or anything. She is a lady—quite a lady, you understand, and her office is next to Mr. Bechcombe's own."

"Indeed!" For once the inspector looked really interested. "Well, I should like to see Miss Hoyle without delay, Mr. Walls."

"Very well, I will tell her at once."

Miss Hoyle did not keep the inspector waiting. He glanced at her keenly as he placed a chair for her.

"Your name, please?"

"Cecily Frances Hoyle."

"How long have you been with Mr. Bechcombe?"

"Just over a month."

"Where were you previously?"

"At school. Miss Arnold Watson's at Putney. I stayed there until I was nineteen as a governess-pupil. Then—I hadn't any real gift for teaching—I took a course in shorthand and typing. Mr. Bechcombe wanted a secretary and I was fortunate enough to get the job."

"Um!" The inspector turned over a new page in his notebook. "Now will you tell me all you know about Mr. Bechcombe's death?"

Cecily stared at him.

"But I don't know anything," she said helplessly. "I never saw Mr. Bechcombe after he called me into his office about a quarter to twelve."

"A quarter to twelve!" The inspector pricked up his ears. "You saw Mr. Bechcombe at a quarter to twelve?"

"At a quarter to twelve, she confirmed. "He sounded the electric bell which rings in my office, and I went in to him. He told me that he should have some important work for me later in the day, but that at present there was nothing and that I could go out to lunch when I liked. When I came back there were some letters to be attended to, and then he said I was to wait until he rang for me. That was all."

"You saw and heard nothing more of Mr. Bechcombe until you came on the scene when the door was broken open by the clerks?"

"I did not see anything."

The slight emphasis on the verb did not escape the inspector.

"Or hear anything?" he demanded sharply. "Be very careful please, Miss Hoyle."

"I heard him speak to some one outside very soon after I had gone back to my office, and I heard him moving about his room after I came from lunch," Cecily said, her colour rising a little.

The inspector looked at her searchingly. "To whom did you hear Mr. Bechcombe speak?"

Cecily hesitated, the colour that was creeping back slowly into her cheeks deepening perceptibly.

"Some one was knocking at the door," she stammered. "I think Mr. Bechcombe spoke to him. I heard him say he was engaged."

"Who was he speaking to?"

The girl twisted her hands together.

"It was his nephew, Mr. Anthony Collyer."

"How do you know?" The inspector fired his questions at her rather as if they had been pistol shots.

Cecily looked round her in an agony of confusion.

"He came to my office—Mr. Anthony, I mean."

"Why should he come to your office?"

"He asked me to go out to lunch with him," Cecily faltered. Then seeing the look on the inspector's face, she gathered up her courage with both hands and faced him with sudden resolution. "We are engaged," she said simply. "We—I mean it hasn't been announced yet, but his father knows; and we shall tell mine as soon as he comes home—he is abroad now—we are engaged, Anthony Collyer and I."

The inspector might have smiled but that the thing was too serious.

"Did Mr. Bechcombe know?"

The girl hesitated a moment.

"I think he guessed. From the way he smiled when he mentioned Mr. Collyer in the morning."

The inspector looked over his notes. He was inclined to think that Cecily Hoyle's evidence, if it could be relied on, would put Anthony Collyer off his list of suspects. Still, he was not going to take any chances.

"I see. So you went out with Mr. Anthony Collyer. Where did you lunch?"

"I said he asked me," Cecily corrected. "But I didn't say I would go. However, we were talking about it and walking down—the passage together when Mr. Bechcombe called Tony back—'I want you a minute, Tony,' he said."

"Well?" the inspector prompted as she paused.

"Tony did not want to go back," the girl said slowly. "But I persuaded him. 'I will wait for you in St. Philip's Field of Rest,' I said. He ran back, promising not to keep me waiting for a minute."

"Field of Rest," the inspector repeated. "What is a Field of Rest?"

"At the back of St. Philip's Church—just over the way. It is the old graveyard really, you know," Cecily explained. "But they have levelled the stones and put seats there, and it is a sort of quiet recreation ground. I often take sandwiches with me and eat them there."

The inspector nodded. There were many such places in London he knew.

"And I suppose Mr. Anthony Collyer soon overtook you?"

"No. He didn't. He—I had to wait in the Field of Rest."

"How long?"

"I don't really know," Cecily said uncertainly. "Perhaps it wasn't very long. But it seemed a long time to me."

The inspector looked at her.

"This is important. Please think, Miss Hoyle. This is very important. How long approximately do you think it was before Mr. Anthony Collyer joined you in the Field of Rest?"

"Twenty minutes perhaps—or it might have been half an hour."

The inspector looked surprised.

"Half an hour! But that's a long time. What excuse did Mr. Collyer make for being so long?"

"He said he couldn't find the Field of Rest. He hadn't been there before, you know."

The inspector made no rejoinder. He turned back to his notes.

"What time did you come back to the office, Miss Hoyle?"

"We were a little over an hour," Cecily confessed. "After half-past one, it would be."

"Did Mr. Collyer go back with you?"

Cecily shook her head.

"Oh, no. He walked as far as Crow's Inn—up to the archway with me."

The inspector was drawing a small parcel from his pocket. Laying back the tissue paper he slowly shook out the white glove he shown to John Wallis.

"Have you ever seen this before, Miss Hoyle?"

The girl leaned forward and looked at it more closely.

"No, I am sure I have not."

"It is not yours?"

Cecily shook her head.

"I could not afford anything like that. It is a very expensive glove—French I should say."

"That glove was found beside the writing-table in Mr. Bechcombe's private room this afternoon," the inspector said impressively.

Cecily looked amazed.

"What an extraordinary thing! I don't believe it was there when I was in this morning. I wonder who could have dropped it?"

"Possibly the murderer or murderess," the inspector suggested dryly.

Cecily shivered back in her chair with a little cry.

"It cannot be true! Who would hurt Mr. Bechcombe? He must have had a fit!"

"Miss Hoyle"—the inspector leaned forward—"it was no fit. Mr. Bechcombe was certainly murdered, and Dr. Hackett says that death must have overtaken him either a few minutes before twelve or a few minutes after."

"What!" Cecily's face became ghastly as the full significance of the words dawned upon her. "It couldn't—" she said, catching her breath in a sob. "He—he was quite well at twelve o'clock, and when I came back from my lunch I heard him moving about."

"Could you hear what went on in his room in yours?"

"Oh, no. Absolutely nothing. But as I passed his door when I came back from lunch I distinctly heard him moving about. I was rather surprised at this, because I don't remember ever hearing any sound from Mr. Bechcombe's room before."

"What did you do after you went back?"

"I finished some letters that had to be ready for Mr. Bechcombe's signature before he went home. I was still busy with them when I heard them breaking into Mr. Bechcombe's room."

"Now one more question, Miss Hoyle. Did you notice anything particular about Mr. Anthony Collyer's hands when you first saw him?"

Cecily stared.

"Certainly I did not. Why?"

"He did not wear gloves?"

"Oh, dear, no!" Cecily almost smiled, "I should certainly have noticed if he had. I have never seen Tony in gloves since I knew him."

The inspector's stylo was moving quickly in his notebook.

"You are prepared to swear to all this, Miss Hoyle?"

"Certainly I am!" Cecily said at once. "It is absolutely true."

"Your address, please."

"Hobart Residence, Windover Square. It is a club for girls," she added.

"But your permanent home address," the detective went on.

There was a pause. The girl's long eyelashes flickered.

"My father is away on some business abroad; when he comes back we shall look for a cottage in the country."

"Oh!" The inspector asked no more questions, but there was a curious look in his eyes as he scrawled another entry in his book.

"That is all for the present, then, Miss Hoyle. The inquest will be opened to-morrow, and you may be wanted. I cannot say."

He rose. Cecily got up at once and with a little farewell bow went out of the room.

The inspector stood still for a minute or two, then he opened the door again.

"Call Mr. William Spencer, please."

Ordinarily Mr. Spencer was a jaunty; self-satisfied young man, but to-day both the jauntiness and the self-satisfaction were gone and it was with a very white and subdued face that he came up to the inspector.

"Well, Mr. Spencer, and what have you to tell me about this terrible affair?" the inspector began conversationally.

"Nothing; except what you know. I heard the governor tell Mr. Thompson not to let anyone into his room, and I heard no more until Mr. Walls asked me to go round to the private door."

"You were the first to see the body, I understand."

"Well, looking through the keyhole, I saw a heap and I told Mr. Walls I thought it was the governor."

"Exactly!" The inspector looked at his notes. "You were right, unfortunately. Now, Mr. Spencer, have you ever seen this?" suddenly displaying the white glove he had previously shown.

Mr. Spencer's eyes grew round.

"I—I don't know."

"What do you mean by that?" the inspector questioned. "Have you any reason to suppose you have done so?"

Spencer stared at it.

"I met a lady with long gloves like that coming up the stairs when I went out to lunch."

"What time was that?"

"About half-past twelve, it would be, or a little later, I think," debated Spencer.

"Ah!" the inspector made a note in his book. "What was she like—the woman you met?"

"Well, she was tall with rather bright yellow hair and—and she had powder all over her face. The curious thing about her was," Spencer went on meditatively, "that I had an odd feeling that in some way her face was familiar. Yet I couldn't remember having seen her before."

"Did you notice where she went?"

"No, I couldn't. It was just where the stairs turn that I stood aside to let her pass, and you can't see much from there. But I thought I heard—"

"Well?"

"I did think at the time that I heard her stop on our landing and go along the passage—"

"To Mr. Bechcombe's room?" said the inspector quickly.

"Well, it would be to his room, of course," Spencer said, his face paling again. "But I dare say I was wrong about her going down the passage. I didn't listen particularly."

"Do you know that I found this glove beside Mr. Bechcombe's writing-table when I went into the room?" questioned the inspector.

Spencer shivered.

"No. I didn't see it."

"Nevertheless it was there," said the inspector. "Mr. Spencer, I think you will have to try to remember why that lady's face was familiar to you. Had you ever seen her here before?"

"No, I don't think so. I seem to—" Spencer was beginning when there was an interruption, a loud knock at the door. Spencer turned to it eagerly. "Mr. Thompson has come back, I expect."

The inspector was before him, but it was not Amos Thompson who stood outside, or any messenger; it was a tall, thin clergyman with a white, shocked face—the rector of Wexbridge to wit. He stepped aside.

"I must apologize for interrupting you, Mr. Inspector. But I represent my sister-in-law, Mrs. Luke Bechcombe. I had just called and was present when the sad news was broken to her. I came here to make inquiries and also to arrange for the removal of the body. And here I was met by these terrible tidings. Is it—can it be really true that my unfortunate brother-in-law has been murdered?"

"Quite true," the inspector confirmed in a matter-of-fact fashion in contrast with the clergyman's agitated tone.

"But how and by whom?" Mr. Collyer demanded.

"Mr. Bechcombe appears to have been attacked, possibly chloroformed, deliberately, and strangled. His body was found in his private office."

The rector subsided into the nearest chair.

"I cannot believe it. Poor Luke had not an enemy in the world. What could have been the motive for so horrible a crime?"

"That I am endeavouring to find out," the inspector said quietly.

"I can't understand it," the clergyman said, raising his hand to his head. "Nobody would wilfully have hurt poor Luke, I am sure."

"It is tolerably evident that somebody did," the inspector commented dryly.

Mr. Collyer was silent for a minute; putting his elbow on the table, he rested his aching head upon his hand.

"But who could have done it?" he questioned brokenly at last.

The inspector coughed.

"That also I am trying to discover, sir. When did you see Mr. Bechcombe last, Mr. Collyer?"

"Last night. I dined with him at his house in Carlsford Square. Just a few hours ago, and poor Luke seemed so well and happy with us all, making jokes. And now—I can't believe it."

He blew his nose vigorously.

"Was your son one of the dinner party?" the inspector questioned.

Mr. Collyer looked surprised.

"Oh, er—yes, of course Tony was there. He is a favourite with his uncle and aunt."

"Did you know that he was here this morning?"

Mr. Collyer's astonishment appeared to increase.

"Certainly I did not. I do not think he has been. I fancy you are making a mistake."

"I think not," the inspector said firmly. "Your son was here this morning just before twelve o'clock. He appears to have caused quite a commotion, demanding to see his uncle and announcing his intention of going to the private door and knocking at it himself."

Mr. Collyer dropped his arm upon the table.

"But—Good—good heavens! Did he go?"

"He did. He also saw his uncle," said the inspector. "And now I am rather anxious to hear your son's account of that interview, Mr. Collyer."

CHAPTER V

"IT IS THE aftermath of the War," said Aubrey Todmarsh, shaking his head. "You take a man away from his usual occupation and for four years you let him do nothing but kill other men and try to kill other men, and then you are surprised when he comes home and still goes on killing."

"Don't you think, Aubrey, that you had better say straight out that you believe I killed Uncle Luke?" Tony Collyer inquired very quietly, yet with a look in his eyes that his men had known well in the Great War, and had labelled dangerous.

Instinctively Aubrey drew back. "My dear Tony," he said, with what was meant to be an indulgent smile and only succeeded in looking distinctly scared, "why will you turn everything into personalities? I was speaking generally."

"Well, as I happen to be the only man who went to the War and who profits by my uncle's will, and who was at the office the day he was murdered, I will thank you not to speak generally in that fashion," retorted Anthony.

His father lifted up his hand.

"Boys, boys! This terrible crime is no time for unseemly bickering," he said, in much the same tone as he would have used to them twenty years ago at Wexbridge Rectory.

The three were in the dining-room of Mr. Bechcombe's house in Carlsford Square. They had been brought there by an urgent summons from the widow of the dead man. Mrs. Bechcombe, prostrated at first by the news of her husband's death, had been roused by learning how that death had been brought about, and, in her determination that it should be immediately avenged, she had insisted on her husband's brother-in-law and his two nephews coming together to consult with her as to the best steps to be taken to discover the assassin.

In appearance the last twenty-four hours had aged the rector by as many years. His shoulders were bent as he leaned forward in his chair—the very chair in which Luke Bechcombe had sat at the bottom of his table only the night before last. There were new lines that sorrow and horror had scored upon James Collyer's face, even his hair looked whiter. Glancing round the familiar room it seemed to him impossible that he could never see again the brother-in-law upon whose advice he had unconsciously leaned all his married life. He was just about to speak when the door opened and Mrs. Bechcombe entered. She was a tall, almost a regal-looking woman, with flashing dark eyes and regular, aquiline features. To-day her beautifully formed lips were closely compressed and there was a very sombre light in her dark eyes, and there were great blue marks under them.

Mr. Collyer got up, raising himself slowly. "My dear Madeleine, I wish I could help you," he said, taking her hands in his, "but only Our Heavenly Father can do that, and since it is His Will—"

"It was not His Will!" Mrs. Bechcombe contradicted passionately. She tore her hands from his. "My husband was murdered. He did not die by the Will of God, but by the wickedness of man."

"My dear aunt, nothing happens but by the Will of God—" Aubrey Todmarsh was beginning, when the door opened to admit a spare, short, altogether undistinguished-looking man of middle age.

Mrs. Bechcombe turned to him eagerly.

"This is my cousin, John Steadman. You have heard me speak of him, I know, James. He is a barrister, and, though he does not practise now, he is a great criminologist. And I know if anyone can help us it will be he."

"I hope so, I am sure," Mr. Steadman said as he shook hands. "This is a most terrible and mysterious crime, but there are several valuable clues. I do not think it should remain undiscovered long."

"I hope not!" the rector sighed. "And yet we cannot bring poor Luke back, we can only punish his murderer."

"And that I mean to do!" Mrs. Bechcombe said passionately. "I have sworn to devote every penny of my money and every moment of my life to avenging my husband."

"Vengeance is mine, I will repay," murmured Aubrey Todmarsh.

"Yes, I never professed to be of your way of thinking," Mrs. Bechcombe returned with unveiled contempt. "I prefer to undertake the vengeance myself, thank you."

Mr. Steadman looked at Anthony. "I understand that you called at the office yesterday morning."

"Yes, I did," returned Anthony defiantly. "And, when old Thompson told me I couldn't see Mr. Bechcombe, I was fool enough to say I would go round to the private door and get in to him that way."

"And did you?" questioned Mr. Steadman quietly.

"Yes, I did, but I did not go in and murder my uncle," returned Anthony in the same loud, passionate tone.

"Did you see him?" Mr. Steadman inquired.

"Yes. He came to the door and told me to go away. He was expecting an important client."

"Tony, you did not ask him for money?" his father said piteously.

Anthony's face softened as he looked at him. "I was going to, but I didn't get the chance. He wouldn't listen to me. I went on to ask a friend of mine in the next room to come out to lunch with me. As we were passing my uncle's room he came to the door. 'I want you, Tony,' he said sharply. My friend went on, telling me to follow to the Field of Rest. Uncle Luke kept me a few minutes talking. He told me that if I had a really good opening he would go into it, if it were really promising the lack of money should not stand in the way. He said I was to come and see him that night and talk things over. I meant to go, of course. But then I heard this—" and Anthony gulped down something in his throat.

"Did you keep your friend waiting?" inquired Mr. Steadman.

"Yes, I did!" Tony answered, staring at him. "Uncle Luke kept me a minute or two. But then I missed my way to the Field of Rest, and was wandering about the best part of half an hour. I suppose you don't call that a very satisfactory alibi," he added truculently.

"Oh, don't be silly, Tony!" Mrs. Bechcombe interposed fretfully. "Of course we are all sure that you would not have hurt your uncle. We want to know if you saw anyone—if you met this wicked woman."

"What wicked woman? What do you mean, Aunt Madeleine?"

"The woman who left her glove in his room, the woman who killed my husband," Mrs. Bechcombe returned, her breath coming quickly and nervously, her hands clenching and unclenching themselves.

"My dear Madeleine," Mr. Steadman interrupted her, "I do not think it possible that the crime could have been committed by a woman."

"And I am sure that it was," she contradicted stormily. "Women are as powerful as men nowadays and Luke was not strong. He had a weak heart." And with the last words she burst into a very tempest of tears.

Her cousin looked at her pityingly.

"Well, well, my dear girl! At any rate the police are searching everywhere for this woman. The finding her can only be a matter of a few days now. I am going to send your maid to you." He signed to the other men and they followed him out of the room. "Do her all the good in the world to cry it out," he remarked confidentially when he had closed the door. "I haven't seen her shed a tear yet. Now I am going to see Inspector Furnival before the inquest opens. That, of course, will be absolutely formal, at first. Can I give any of you a lift?"

"I think not, thank you," Mr. Collyer responded. "There must be some—er—arrangements to be made here and it's quite possible we may be of some real service."

Both young men looked inclined to dissent, but the barrister proffered no further invitation and a minute or two later they saw him drive off.

He was shown in at once to Inspector Furnival, who was writing at his office table, briskly making notes in a large parchment bound book. He got up as the door opened.

Mr. Steadman shook hands. "You haven't forgotten me, I hope, inspector?"

The inspector permitted himself a slight smile. "I haven't forgotten how you helped me to catch John Basil."

"Um! Well, my cousin—Mrs. Bechcombe is my cousin, you know—has insisted on my coming to you this morning," Mr. Steadman went on, taking the chair the inspector placed by the table. "This is a terrible business, inspector. It looks fairly plain sailing at first sight, but I don't know."

The inspector glanced at him. "You think it looks like plain sailing, sir? Well, it may be, but I confess I don't see it quite in that way myself."

Mr. Steadman met the detective's eyes with a curious look in his own. "What of Thompson's disappearance?"

The inspector blotted the page in his ledger at which he had been writing and left the blotting-paper on.

"Ay, as usual you have put your finger on the spot, Mr. Steadman. What has become of Thompson? He walked out of the office and apparently disappeared into space. For from that moment we have not been able to find anyone who has seen him."

"The inference being—?" Mr. Steadman raised his eyebrows.

The inspector laid his hand on a parcel of papers lying on the table at his elbow.

"There wasn't much about the case in the papers this morning," he said, replying indirectly to the barrister's question, "but the one that comes out at ten o'clock—Racing Special they call it: selections on the back page, don't you know—in almost every case gives a large space on its front page to 'The Murder of a Solicitor in his Office,' and every one of them mentions the disappearance of his managing clerk. The inference, though the paragraphs are naturally guarded in the extreme, is unmistakable."

Mr. Steadman reached over for one of the papers.

"Don't take any notice of these things myself; they have to write up the sensation. Um! Yes! No doubt what they're hinting at, but they're generally wrong. What should Thompson want to kill his employer for, unless—"

"Ay, exactly; unless—" the inspector said dryly. "That was one of my first thoughts, sir. John Walls is going through the books with an auditor this morning. And Mr. Turner, who was in the firm until last year, is going over the contents of the safe. When we get their reports we shall know more."

The barrister nodded. "Thompson had been with the firm for many years."

"Eighteen, I believe," assented the inspector. "He seems to have been a great favourite with Mr. Bechcombe, but it is astonishing how little his fellow-clerks know of him. Only two of them have ever seen him out of the office, and none of them appear to have the least idea where he lives."

Mr. Steadman did not speak for a moment, then he said slowly:

"The fact that so little is known seems in itself curious. Is there no way of ascertaining his address?"

"One would imagine that there must be a note of it somewhere at the office," the inspector remarked, "but so far we have not been able to find it."

"How about the woman visitor?" the barrister inquired, changing the subject suddenly.

"We haven't been able to identify her at present." The inspector opened the top drawer at his right hand, and took the white glove that had been found by the murdered man's desk from its wrapping of tissue paper. The most cursory glance showed that it was an expensive glove, even if the maker's name had not been known as one of the most famous in London and Paris. About it there still clung the vague elusive scent that always seems to linger about the belongings of a woman who is attracted by and attractive to the other sex.

Mr. Steadman handled it carefully and inspected it thoroughly through his eyeglasses. "Yes. We ought to be able to find the mysterious woman with the aid of this."

"Ah, yes. We shall find the wearer," the inspector said confidently. "But will that be very much help in solving the mystery of Luke Bechcombe's death?"

The barrister looked at him.

"I don't know that it will. Still, why doesn't she come forward and say 'I saw Mr. Bechcombe the morning he was murdered. My business with him was urgent and I saw him by special appointment.' She is much more likely to be suspected of the crime if she refuses to come forward. Mrs. Bechcombe seems certain of her guilt, and women do have intuitions."

"I'm not much of a believer in them myself," remarked Inspector Furnival, shrugging his shoulders. "I would rather have a penn'orth of direct evidence than a pound's worth of intuition. And I don't believe that Mr. Bechcombe was murdered by a woman. A woman doesn't spring at a man and strangle him. She may stab him or shoot him, the weapons being to hand, but strangle him with her hands—no. Besides, this was a premeditated crime. There was an unmistakable smell of chloroform about the body, faint, I grant you, but unmistakable. No, no! It wasn't a woman. As to why she doesn't speak—well, there may be a dozen reasons. In the first place she may not have heard of the murder at all. It doesn't occupy a very conspicuous place in the morning's papers. It will be a different matter to-night. Then, she might not want her business known. And, above all, many a woman—and man too—hates to be mixed up in a murder case, and won't speak out till she is driven to it."

"Quite so!"

The barrister sat silent for a minute or two, his eyes staring straight in front of him at nothing in particular. Inspector Furnival took another glance at his notes.

"Spencer, the only person we have been able to trace so far who has seen this mysterious woman, fancies that her face is familiar to him, but does not know in what connection. I have suggested to him that she is possibly an actress, and he is inclined to think that it may be so. I have sent him up a quantity of photographs to see if he can identify any of them. But don't you see, Mr. Steadman, Mr. Spencer's evidence tends rather to exonerate Thompson. Spencer went out after Thompson and met this woman. It therefore appears probable that Thompson was off the premises before the woman came on."

Mr. Steadman shook his head.

"It isn't safe to assume anything in a case of this kind. We do not know that Thompson went off the premises. We do not know where he went or where he is."

"Very true! I wish we did," asserted the inspector. "At the same time—"

The telephone bell was ringing sharply over his desk. He took up the receiver.

"That you, Jones? Yes, what is it? Inspector Furnival speaking."

"Thompson's address has been found in one of Mr. Bechcombe's books. There are several other of the clerks' addresses there all entered in Mr. Bechcombe's writing, and all the others we have verified."

"What is it?"

"Number 10 Brooklyn Terrace, North Kensington."

"Um! I will see to it at once." And the inspector rang off sharply.

CHAPTER VI

"CAN'T HEAR of Brooklyn Terrace anywhere, sir." The speaker was Mr. Steadman's chauffeur.

He had been going slowly the last few minutes, making ineffectual inquiries of the passers-by. Inside the car Mr. Steadman had Inspector Furnival seated beside him.

"Better drive to the nearest post-office and ask there. They will be sure to know."

"Call this North Kensington, do they?" the barrister grumbled, as the car started again. "Seems to me in my young days it used to be called Notting Hill."

The inspector laughed. "Think North Kensington sounds a bit more classy, I expect. Not but what there are some very decent old houses hereabouts. Oh, by Jove! Is this Brooklyn Terrace?" as the car turned into a side street that had apparently fallen on evil days. Each house evidently contained several tenants. In some cases slatternly women stood on the doorsteps, shouting remarks to their neighbours, while grubby faced children played about in the gutter or crawled about on the doorsteps of their different establishments. It scarcely seemed the place in which would be found the missing managing clerk of Messrs. Bechcombe and Turner's establishment.

No. 10 was a little tidier than its neighbours, that is to say, the door was shut and there were no children on the doorstep.

The chauffeur pulled up.

"This is it, sir."

Mr. Steadman eyed it doubtfully.

"Well, inspector, I expect this really is the place."

"It is the address in Mr. Bechcombe's book right enough, sir. As to whether Mr. Amos Thompson lives here—well, we shall soon see."

He got out first and knocked at the door, the barrister following meekly. The car waiting at the side was the object of enormous interest to the denizens of the street. There was no response to the knock for some time. At last a small child in the next area called out:

"You'll have to go down, they don't never come to that there door!"

Mr. Steadman put up his glass and peered over the palings. A slatternly-looking woman was just looking out of the back door.

"Can you let us in, my good woman?" the barrister called out. "We want Mr. Thompson."

The woman muttered something, probably scenting a tip, and presently they heard her clattering along the passage.

"Mr. Thompson, is it?" she said as she admitted them. "His room is up at the top."

"Is he at home?" Inspector Furnival questioned.

The woman stared at him. "I don't know. If you just like to walk up you will find out."

The stairs were wide, for the house had seen better days, but indescribably dirty. Up at the very top it was a little cleaner. There were several doors on the landing but nothing to show which, if any, was Thompson's. As they stood there, wondering which it could be, an old man came up behind them.

"Were you looking for anyone, gentlemen?" he asked, in a weak, quavering voice that told that, like the house, he had fallen on evil times.

The inspector turned to him. "I want Mr. Amos Thompson."

The old man pointed to the door just in front of them.

"That is his door, but I doubt if you will find him in. I haven't seen him since yesterday morning. I don't think he slept here."

"Do you often see him?" the inspector questioned as he applied his knuckles to the door.

The old man looked surprised at the question.

"Why, yes, sir, I have only been here a month, but I have found Mr. Thompson a remarkably pleasant gentleman. He always passes the time of day with me and often stops for a word over the day's news. An uncommonly nice man is Mr. Thompson. It has often crossed my mind to wonder why he stayed here, where there is no comfort to speak of for the likes of him."

The inspector and Mr. Steadman wondered too, as they waited there, while no answer came to the former's repeated knocking.

A room in No. 10 Brooklyn Terrace certainly seemed no fitting home for Amos Thompson with his handsome salary.

"We must get in somehow," the inspector said to Mr. Steadman. Then he turned to the old man opposite who was watching them with frightened eyes. "Has anyone else a key to these rooms, a charwoman or anybody?"

The man shook his head.

"We all do for ourselves, here, sir. We don't afford char-women and such-like. As for getting in—well, I expect the landlord has keys. He is on the first floor. But I do not think he would open Mr. Thompson's door without—"

"Is this landlord likely to be at home now?" the inspector interrupted.

"He is at home, sir. I saw him as I came upstairs."

The inspector took out his card. "Will you show him this and say that Mr. Thompson cannot be found. He disappeared under peculiar circumstances yesterday and, since he is not here, we must enter his room to see whether we can find any clue to his whereabouts."

The man visibly paled as he read the name on the card. Then he rapidly disappeared down the stairs. Mr. Steadman looked across at the inspector.

"Queer affair this! What the deuce does the fellow mean by putting up at a place like this?"

"Well, he isn't extravagant in the living line!" the inspector said with a grin.

John Steadman raised his eyebrows. "Not here!"

At this moment the landlord arrived with the keys. Quite evidently his curiosity had been excited by the advent of the visitors to his lodger. Probably he had been expecting his summons. He held Inspector Furnival's card in his hand.

"I understand I have no choice, gentlemen."

"None!" the inspector said grimly.

The landlord made no further demur, but unlocking the door he flung it open and stood back. The others waited for a minute in the doorway and looked round. At first sight nothing could have been less likely to give away the occupier's secrets than this room. It was quite a good size with a couple of windows, and a small bed in a recess with a curtain hung over it, an oil lamp stood before the fireplace. The floor was covered with linoleum, there was no carpet, not even a rug. A solid square oak table stood in the middle of the room and there were three equally solid-looking chairs. The only other piece of furniture in the room was a movable corner cupboard standing at the side of the window. The inspector went over and threw the door open. Inside there was a cup and saucer, a teapot and tea-caddy, a bottle of ink, and a book upon which the inspector immediately pounced. He went through it from end to end, he shook it, he banged it on the table; a post card fell from it; the inspector stared at it, then with a puzzled frown he handed it to Mr. Steadman. The barrister glanced at it curiously. On the back was a portrait of a girl—evidently the work of an amateur.

"Do you know who that is?" questioned the inspector.

Mr. Steadman shook his head. "It is no one that I have ever seen before. Do you mean that you do?"

"That is a likeness—very badly taken, I grant you—but an unmistakable likeness of Miss Hoyle, the late Mr. Bechcombe's secretary."

Mr. Steadman was startled for once. "Good Lord! Do you mean that he was in love with her too?"

"Oh, I don't know," said the inspector, taking possession of the post card once more. "Elderly men take queer fancies sometimes, but I haven't had any hint of this hitherto. However, I will make a few inquiries with a view to ascertaining whether Mr. Tony Collyer has a rival."

"Poor Tony!" said the barrister indulgently.

He took up the book which the inspector had thrown down. It was a detective novel of the lightest and most lurid kind, and it bore the label of a big and fashionable library. He made a note of it at once. The inspector went on with his survey. Beside the bedstead, behind the curtain, there stood a small tripod washing-stand with the usual apparatus. The bed in itself was enough to arouse their curiosity. Upon the chain mattress lay one of hard flock with one hard pillow, and an eiderdown quilt rolled up at the bottom. Of other bedclothing there was not a vestige, neither was there any sign of any clothing found about the room, with the exception of a pair of very old slippers originally worked in cross stitch, the pattern of which was now indecipherable. The inspector peered round everywhere. He turned over the top mattress, he felt it all over. He moved the wash-stand and the corner cupboard, he looked in the open fireplace which apparently had not been used for years, but not so much as the very tiniest scrap of paper rewarded him. At last he turned to the barrister.

"Nothing more to be done here, I think, sir." He took up the book and the slippers and moved to the door.

John Steadman followed him silently. His strong face bore a very worried, harassed expression.

Outside the landlord stopped them.

"Gentlemen, I hope it is understood that I have no responsibility with regard to this raid on Mr. Thompson's property?"

"Quite, quite!" assented the inspector. "Refer Mr. Thompson to me if you should see him again."

"Which I hope I shall," the landlord pursued, following them down the stairs. "For a better tenant I never had; punctual with his rent, and always quiet and quite the gentleman."

Inspector Furnival stopped short. "How long has he lived with you?"

The man scratched his head. "A matter of four years or more, and always brought the rent to me, I never had to ask for it. I wish there were more like him."

"Did you see much of him?"

"Only passing the time of day on the stairs, and when he came to pay his rent which he did regularly every Saturday morning."

"That room does not look as if it had been slept in or eaten in," John Steadman said abruptly.

The landlord stared at him.

"Well, we don't bother about our neighbour's business in Brooklyn Terrace, sir. But, if he didn't want the room to sleep in or live in, why did he rent it?"

"Oh," said the barrister warily, "that is just what we should like to know."

With a nod of farewell the two men went on. They got into the waiting car in silence. With a glance at the inspector John Steadman gave the address of the library from which Thompson's book had been procured. Then as the car started and he threw himself back on his seat he observed:

"Admirably stage managed!"

The inspector raised his eyebrows. "As how?"

"Do you imagine those people know no more than they say of Thompson?"

"They may. On the other hand it is quite possible they do not," the inspector answered doubtfully.

"That room had been arranged for some such emergency as has arisen," Steadman went on. "Thompson has never lived there. But he came there for letters or something. He has some place of concealment very likely quite near. I have no doubt that either of those men could have told us more. I expect they will give the show away if a reward is offered."

"If—" the inspector repeated. "I don't quite agree with you, Mr. Steadman. I think those men were speaking the truth, and I doubt whether they knew any more of Thompson than they said. The man, who as you say, has so admirably stage managed that room would hardly be likely to give himself away by making unnecessary confidants. But now I wonder for whose benefit this scene was originally staged?"

The barrister drew in his lips. "Don't you think Luke Bechcombe's murder answers your question?"

"No, I don't!" said the inspector bluntly. "Thompson was a wrong 'un, but at present I do not see any connection with the murder at all! They are at it now, full swing!" For as they neared Notting Hill Gate they could hear the voices of the newsboys calling out their papers—"Murder of a well-known Solicitor. Missing Clerk!" Up by the station the newsboys exhibited lurid headlines.

They bought a handful of papers and unfolded them as they bowled swiftly across to the library. In most cases the murder of the solicitor occupied the greater part of the front page. The disappearance of the managing clerk was made the most of. But in several there were hints of the mysterious visitor, veiled surmises as to her business and identity. Altogether the Crow's Inn Tragedy, as the papers were beginning to call it, seemed to contain all the materials for a modern sensational drama.

At the library they both got out. The section devoted to 'T's was at the farther end. A pleasant-looking girl was handing out books. Seizing his opportunity the inspector went forward and held out the volume.

"I have found this book under rather peculiar circumstances. Can you tell me by whom it was borrowed?"

For a moment the girl seemed undecided; then, murmuring a few unintelligible words, she went round to the manager's desk. That functionary came back with her.

"I hear you want to know who borrowed this book, but it is not our custom to give particulars—"

"I know it is not." The inspector held out his card. "But I think you will have to make an exception in my case."

The manager put up his pince-nez and glanced at the card, and then at the inspector. Then he signed to an assistant to bring him the book in which subscribers' names were entered, and spoke to her in a low tone. She looked frightened as she glanced at the inspector.

"It was borrowed by a Mr. Thompson, sir, address 10 Brooklyn Terrace, North Kensington. He is an old subscriber."

"Did he come for the books himself?" the inspector questioned. "Can you describe him?"

"There—there wasn't much to describe," the girl faltered. "He had a brown beard and some of his front teeth were missing, and he nearly always wore those big, horn-rimmed glasses."

"Height?" questioned the inspector sharply.

"Well, he wasn't very tall nor very short," was the unsatisfactory reply.

"Thin or stout?"

"Not much of either!" The girl twisted her hands about, evidently wishing herself far away.

The inspector deserted the topic of Mr. Thompson's appearance. He held up the book.

"When was this taken out?"

The manager glanced at a list of volumes opposite the subscribers' names.

"Last Thursday. I may say that Mr. Thompson always wanted books of this class—detective fiction, and he literally devoured them. He always expected a new one to be ready for him, and he was inclined to be unpleasant if he had for the time being exhausted the supply. He generally called here every day. This is an unusually long interval if he has not called since Thursday."

"Um!" The inspector glanced at Mr. Steadman. Then he turned back to the manager. "I am obliged by your courtesy, sir. Would you add to it, should Mr. Thompson call or send again, by ringing me up at Scotland Yard? The book we will leave with you."

CHAPTER VII

"EXTENSIVE DEFALCATIONS. A system of fraud that must have been carried on for many years," repeated Aubrey Todmarsh. "Well, that pretty well settles the matter as far as Thompson is concerned."

"I don't see it," contradicted Tony Collyer. "Thompson is a defaulter. That doesn't prove he is a murderer. I don't believe he is. Old chap didn't look like a murderer."

"My dear Tony, don't be childish!" responded Todmarsh. "A man that commits a murder never does look like a murderer. He wouldn't be so successful if he did."

"Anyway, if Thompson is guilty, it pretty well knocks the stuffing out of your pet theory," retorted Tony. "Thompson didn't go to the War."

"No, but the lust for killing spread over the entire country," Todmarsh went on, his face assuming a rapt expression as he gazed over Anthony's head at the little clouds scudding across the patch of sky which he could see through the windows above. "Besides, there were murders before the War, and there will be murders when, if ever, it is forgotten. But I do maintain that there have been many more brutal crimes since the War than ever before in the history of the country. Teach a man through all the most impressionable years of his life that there is nothing worth doing but killing his fellow-creatures and trying to kill them, and he will—"

"Oh, stow that—we have heard it all before," Tony interrupted irritably. "According to your own showing the murder might just as well have been committed by one of your own dear conchies as anyone else. Anyway, I don't believe Thompson killed Uncle Luke. Why should he? He had got the money. He had only to make off with it. Why should he kill the old chap?"

"Well, Uncle Luke may have taxed him with his shortcomings and threatened to prosecute him, perhaps he tried to phone or something of that sort. And Thompson may have sprung at him and throttled him."

"Don't believe it!" Tony said obstinately.

Todmarsh's eyes narrowed.

"I wouldn't proclaim my faith in Thompson's innocence quite so loudly if I were you, Tony. I imagine you have no idea who the world is saying must be guilty if Thompson is innocent."

"I imagine I have," Tony returned, his tone growing violent. "I am quite aware that the world"—laying stress on the noun—"is saying that, if Thompson didn't murder Uncle Luke, I did, to gain the money my uncle left. But I am not going to try to hang Thompson to save my own neck. By the way, I come into some more money when Aunt Madeleine dies. You will be expecting me to murder her next! You had something left you too. You may have done it to get that!"

Aubrey Todmarsh shook his head.

"My legacy is a mere flea-bite compared with yours. And I trust that my life and aims are sufficiently well known—"

Tony turned his back on him deliberately.

"Bosh! Don't trouble to put it on for me, Aubrey. I have known your life and aims fairly well for a good while. Take care of your own skin, and let everything else go to the wall. That's your aim."

His cousin's dark eyes held no spark of resentment.

"You do not think that, I know, Tony. But, if the world should misjudge my motives, I cannot help it."

The cousins were standing in the smaller of the two adjoining waiting-rooms in the late Luke Bechcombe's flat offices. The inquest had been held that morning and the auditors' report on the books that had been in Thompson's charge and the contents of the safe had been taken. Their statement that there had been a system of fraud carried on probably for years had not come as a surprise. The public had from the first decided that Thompson's disappearance could only be accounted for as a flight from the charge of embezzlement that was hanging over him. Ever logical, rumour did not trouble to account for the chloroform and the covered finger-prints or the lady with the white gloves.

The auditors' report had brought both Aubrey Todmarsh and Tony to the office this afternoon, and as usual the cousins could not meet without contradicting one another or quarrelling. Inspector Furnival and Mr. Steadman had also given their account of their visit to Thompson's room and the mystery mongers were more than ever intrigued thereby. There could be no doubt that, whatever might be their opinion of his guilt, Thompson's disappearance was becoming more and more of an enigma to the police. Not the faintest trace of him could be discovered. When he left the clerks' office in Crow's Inn, he apparently disappeared from the face of the earth; no one had met him on the stairs, no one had seen him in the vicinity of the square. After an enormous amount of inquiry the police had at last discovered a small restaurant where he generally lunched, but he had neither been there on the day of the murder nor since, and the railway stations had been watched so far without success. In fact, Inspector Furnival had been heard to state that but that they could not find the body he would have thought that Thompson had been murdered as well as his chief.

Thompson was described at the restaurant as always taking his meals by himself and speaking to no one, and always at the same table. Then the waitress who had waited on him for the last two years had never heard him say more than good morning, or good afternoon. He always lunched *à la carte*, so that there was no ordering to be done. Still with the precautions taken, with his description circulated through the country, it seemed that his capture could only be a matter of time.

But the inspector was frankly puzzled. At every point he was baffled in his attempt to discover anything of the real man. The very mystery about him was in itself suspicious.

The inspector and Mr. Steadman were in Mr. Bechcombe's private room this afternoon. Everything remained just as it had been when the murder was discovered, except that the body had been removed to the nearest mortuary now that the inquest had been adjourned, and the funeral was to take place at once.

The inspector had been over the room already with the most meticulous care. To-day he was trying to reconstruct the crime. The dead man's writing-table table was opposite the door into the anteroom, and from there into the clerks' room. The door into the passage opened upon Mr. Bechcombe's usual seat. Supposing that to have been unlocked, it seemed to the inspector that, when Mr. Bechcombe had received his expected visitor, he might have been thinking over some communication that had been made to him, and the assassin might have entered the room silently from behind, and strangled him before he was aware of his danger. But there seemed no motive for such a crime, and the inspector was frankly puzzled. There was no view from the window, the lower panes being of frosted glass, the upper looking straight across to a blank wall. The safe was locked again now as it had been in Mr. Bechcombe's lifetime. Mr. Turner had finished his examination. But, try as the inspector would to reconstruct the crime, he could not build up any hypothesis which could not be instantly demolished, or so it seemed to him. Mr. Steadman stood on the hearthrug with his back to the ashes of Luke Bechcombe's last fire. For the lawyer had been old-fashioned—he had disliked central heating and gas and electric contrivances. In spite of strikes and increasing prices he had adhered to coal fires.

At last the silence was broken by Mr. Steadman:

"You have the experts' opinion of the fingerprints, I presume?"

The inspector bent his head.

"It came this morning. It was not put in at the inquest, for it is just as well not to take all the world into our confidence at first, you know, Mr. Steadman."

"Quite so," the barrister assented. "Do you mean that you were able to identify them?"

"No," growled the inspector. "They will never be identified. The murderer wore those thin rubber gloves that some of the first-class crooks have taken to of late."

"Phew!" Mr. Steadman gave a low whistle. "That—that puts a very different complexion on the matter."

The inspector raised his eyebrows. "As how?"

"Well, for one thing it settles the question of premeditation."

The inspector coughed.

"I have never believed Mr. Bechcombe's murder to have been unpremeditated. Neither have you, I think, sir."

"Well, no," the other conceded. "The crime has always looked to me like a carefully planned and skilfully executed murder. And yet—I don't know."

"It is the most absolutely baffling affair I have come across for years," Inspector Furnival observed slowly. "It is the question of motive that is so puzzling. Once we have discovered that I do not think the identity of the murderer will remain a secret long."

"The public seems to have made up its mind that Thompson is guilty."

"I know." Inspector Furnival stroked his clean-shaven chin thoughtfully. "But why should Thompson, having robbed his master systematically for years, suddenly make up his mind to murder him? For he didn't have the rubber gloves and the chloroform by accident you know, sir."

"Obviously not." Mr. Steadman studied his finger nails in silence for a minute, then he looked up suddenly. "Inspector, to my mind absolute frankness is always best. Now, we do not know that Thompson went to Mr. Bechcombe's room at all on the morning of the murder. But there is another whose name is being freely canvassed who certainly did go to the room."

"Ay, Mr. Tony Collyer," the inspector said, frowning as he looked over his notes again. "The obvious suspect. Motive and opportunity—neither lacking. But here the question of premeditation comes in again. Young Collyer would not have known he would have the excellent opportunity that really did occur. Would he have come on chance provided with chloroform and rubber gloves? Would he not have fixed up an opportunity when he could have been certain of finding Mr. Bechcombe in? And also when his fiancée, Miss Cecily Hoyle, was out of the way? Then, when he did put his rubber gloves on is a question. According to Miss Hoyle's testimony he had not got them on when she left him. He could hardly bring them out while Mr. Bechcombe was talking to him. No, so far as I can see nothing conclusive with regard to either of these two is to be found, Mr. Steadman. What do you think yourself?"

"Personally I shall find it always a very difficult matter to believe Tony Collyer guilty, strong though the evidence seems against him," Mr. Steadman said frankly. "Thompson, I must confess, seems a very different proposition. Then we must remember the third person in the case, the lady of the white gloves."

"The owner of the white glove did not strangle Mr. Bechcombe," Inspector Furnival said positively. "Though she may have been an accomplice. The experts' evidence decided that the fingers of the hand that killed Mr. Bechcombe were considerably too large to have gone into that white glove."

"So that's that!" said the barrister. "Well, it is a curious case. It seemed bristling with clues at first. And yet they all seem to lead nowhere."

"One of them will in time, though," the inspector remarked confidently. "The thread is in our hands right enough, Mr. Steadman. We shall find the other end before long."

"You don't mean—" the barrister was beginning when there was an interruption.

There was a knock at the door. Mr. Steadman put up his pince-nez as the inspector opened the door. To their surprise Aubrey Todmarsh stood in the passage. He stepped inside, his face paling as he glanced round the room in which his uncle had met his death.

"Ugh!" He shivered. "There is a terrible atmosphere about this room, inspector. Even if one did not know it, I think one would unconsciously sense the fact that some horrible crime had been committed here."

"Um, I am not much of a believer in that sort of thing," Mr. Steadman answered. "It is easy enough to sense crime, as you call it, when you know that it has been committed."

Aubrey shrugged his shoulders.

"Well, I don't know. You may be right, but I shall stick to my convictions. There are subtler emotions that cannot be shared by anyone. But I am here on business to-day. One of my men, my most trusted man—Hopkins by name—has been doing some work in the East End up by the docks. He met with a man whom he believes to have been Thompson."

"When?" Mr. Steadman questioned sharply.

"Two days ago."

"Then why didn't he speak out sooner?"

"He did not see any description of Thompson until this morning. Then he saw one outside a police-station and he remembered."

"Remembered what?"

"This man," Aubrey responded impatiently. "A man that answered to Thompson's description. He came down to the docks and tried to get a job on some distant cargo boat. Said he could do anything; but Hopkins noticed that his hands were smooth and carefully manicured. Like a gentleman's hands, Hopkins described them."

"Did he get his job on the cargo boat?"

"Hopkins thinks that he did, or, at any rate, if not that he managed to get taken as a passenger. He went off somewhere."

"Where was the cargo boat bound for?" Mr. Steadman seemed more interested than the inspector who was making notes in a desultory fashion.

Aubrey shook his head.

"Hopkins doesn't know. You see he had no particular reason to notice anything about the man. He would not have done so at all but for the hands, I think."

"You said just now that Hopkins recognized him from the description when he saw it," Mr. Steadman pursued. "I must say I thought it delightfully vague. A study in negatives, I should call it."

"It wasn't very definite, of course. And Hopkins may have been entirely mistaken. But he said he particularly noticed the short brown beard and the defective teeth."

"Um!" Mr. Steadman stuck his hands in his pockets. "I am inclined to think Hopkins' identification a flight of the imagination. The police-station description tells what Thompson was like when he left here. I should look out for a clean-shaven man with regular teeth now."

Todmarsh did not look pleased.

"I suppose I am particularly stupid, but I really fail to understand why the police should circulate a description when they want something entirely opposite."

"My dear man, you don't imagine that a man who could hide his traces as Thompson did would be foolish enough to leave his personal appearance unprovided for? No. We must have every cargo boat that left the docks overhauled at its first stopping-place, but I don't fancy we shall find Thompson on any of them."

"Well, he has managed to get away somehow, and I thought you might be glad to hear of something that is a possible clue," Todmarsh said sulkily.

At this moment the telephone bell, Mr. Luke Bechcombe's own telephone bell, rang sharply. Todmarsh stopped and started violently, staring at the telephone as if he expected to see his uncle answer it.

The inspector took up the receiver; the other men watched him breathlessly.

"Yes, yes, Inspector Furnival speaking," they heard him say. "Yes, I will be with you as soon as it is possible. Detain her at all hazards until I come."

He rang off and turned.

"What do you think that was?"

"Thompson caught at the docks," Aubrey Todmarsh suggested.

Mr. Steadman said nothing, but a faint smile crossed his lips as he glanced at the inspector.

"The message is that a lady is at Scotland Yard asking to see the official who is in charge of the Bechcombe case," Inspector Furnival said, glancing from one to the other of his auditors as if to note the effect of his words on them. "A lady, who refused to give her name, but who says that she saw the late Mr. Luke Bechcombe on the day of his death."

His words had the force of a bombshell thrown between the others.

Aubrey Todmarsh did not speak, but his face turned visibly whiter. He moistened his lips with his tongue. Even the impassive Mr. Steadman started violently.

"The lady of the glove!" he exclaimed.

The inspector caught up his hat.

"I don't know. I must ascertain without delay, Mr. Steadman."

CHAPTER VIII

DISMISSING his taxi at the Archway, Inspector Furnival made the best of his way to his office. Outside a man was standing. He touched his forehead respectfully.

"Glad to see you, sir. The lady has just been to the door to say she can't wait more than five minutes longer."

The inspector paused.

"What is her name, Jones?"

The man shook his head.

"She wouldn't give one, sir. She said her business was with the detective in charge of the Bechcombe case, and with him alone. I was on tenterhooks all the time, sir, fearing that she would be gone before you came."

The inspector nodded and went on.

He turned the handle of his door quietly and entered the room as quickly and noiselessly as possible. If he had hoped to surprise his visitor, however, he found himself disappointed.

She was standing immediately opposite the door with her back to the window. She did not wait for him to speak.

"Are you in charge of the Bechcombe case?" she demanded, and he noticed that her voice was powerful and rather hard in tone.

The inspector glanced keenly at her as he walked to the chair behind his office table. Standing thus with her back to the light he could see little of his visitor's face, which was also concealed by the hat which was crushed down upon her forehead and overshadowed by an uncurled feather mount. But he could tell that she was fashionably gowned, that the furs she had thrown back from her shoulders were costly.

He answered her question and asked another.

"I am Inspector Furnival, and I am inquiring into the circumstances of Mr. Bechcombe's death. May I ask why you want to know?"

His interlocutor took a few steps forward, clasping her hands nervously together.

"You know that a white glove was found by Mr. Bechcombe's desk?"

"Yes."

"It was my glove. I left it there!"

The inspector did not speak for a minute. He unlocked a drawer and took out an official-looking notebook.

"Your name and address, madam?"

"Is that necessary?" There was a quiver in the clear tones. "I have told you that I was there—that the glove is mine. Is not that enough?"

"Scarcely, madam. But"—waiving the subject of the name for a moment—"why have you not spoken before?"

"I didn't hear at first." She hesitated a moment, her foot tapping the floor impatiently.

And now she was nearer to him he could see that her make-up was extensive, that complexion and eyes owed much of their brilliancy to art, and that the red-gold hair probably came off entirely. But it was a handsome face, though not that of a woman in her first youth. The features, though large, were well formed, and the big blue eyes would have been more beautiful without the black lines with which they were embellished.

"I don't read the papers much, at least only the society news and about the theatres—never murders or horrors of that kind, and it was not until I heard some people talking about it, and they mentioned Mr. Bechcombe's name, that I knew what had happened. I did not realize at first that it—the murder had taken place on the very day on which I had been to the office, and that it was my glove that had been found beside the desk. Even then I made up my mind not to speak out if I could help it. Mr. Bechcombe was alive and well when I saw him. I couldn't tell you anything about the murder. And I couldn't have my name mixed up in a murder trial, or let the papers, or certain—er—people get to know what I had been doing at Mr. Bechcombe's office."

"Then why have you come to us now?"

"Because I thought, if I didn't tell you, you would be sure to find out," was the candid reply. "And—and if I came myself I thought you might call me Madame X, or something like that. They do, you know, and then perhaps—er—people might never know."

The inspector smiled.

"I am afraid you are too well known and the illustrated papers are too ubiquitous for that, Mrs. Carnthwacke."

She emitted a slight scream.

"Oh! How did you know?"

The inspector's smile became more apparent.

"I was a great admirer of Miss Bella Laymond on the Variety stage. I had the pleasure of 'assisting' at her marriage with the American millionaire, Cyril B. Carnthwacke—that is to say, I was passing a fashionable church, saw a large waiting crowd, and was lucky enough to get in the first rank and obtain a good view of the beautiful bride. I could not help remembering a face like that, Mrs. Carnthwacke. And now I want you to forget that I am a detective, and just think that I am a friend who is anxious to help you, and tell me all the story of your visit to Mr. Bechcombe."

He pushed forward a chair as he spoke.

She looked from it to him undecidedly for a minute. Then, as if coming to a sudden resolution, she sat down and pulled the chair nearer to his desk.

"You promise not to tell my—husband what I am going to tell you?"

"I promise," the inspector said reassuringly. "Now, first please, why did you come to Luke Bechcombe's office on the day of his death?"

"Well, I dare say you know my husband is very rich?"

The inspector nodded. Cyril B. Carnthwacke's name and his millions were well known to the man in the street.

"When we were married he gave the most gorgeous jewels," Mrs. Carnthwacke went on. "And he made me an enormous allowance. Americans are always generous—bless you, I thought I was going to have the time of my life. But I—I had never been rich. Even when I got on on the stage and had a big salary I was always in debt. I suppose I am extravagant by nature. Anyway, when I was married it seemed to me that I had an inexhaustible store to fall back upon. I spent money like water with the result that after a time I had to go for more to my husband. He gave it to me, but I could see that he was astonished and displeased. Still, I could not change my nature. I gambled at cards, on the racecourse, on the Stock Exchange, and I staked high to give myself a new excitement. Sometimes I won, but more often I lost and my husband helped me again and again. But more and more I could see I was disappointing him. At last he told me that he would pay no more for me; he hated and mistrusted all gambling and I must make my huge allowance do. I couldn't—I mean I couldn't give up gambling. It was in my blood. And just as I was in a horrible hole the worst happened. A—a man who had been my lover years ago began to blackmail me. I gave him all I could but nothing satisfied him." She stopped and passed a tiny lace-trimmed handkerchief over her lips.

"Why did you not tell your husband?" the inspector inquired. "I guess Mr. Carnthwacke would have settled him pretty soon."

"I—I daren't," she confessed. "And I have been an awful ass. He—this man—had letters. They were silly enough, goodness knows, and they might have been read to mean more than they did, and my husband is jealous—terribly, wickedly jealous of my past. At last he—the man—said that if I would pay him a large, an enormous sum, he would go abroad and I should never hear of him again. If I did not he swore he would send the letters to my husband in such a fashion that the worst construction would be placed upon them. What was I to do? I hadn't any money. I dared not tell my husband. I made several attempts to pull off a grand *coup*, and only got worse in the mire. I made up my mind to sell my diamonds and substitute paste. A friend of mine had done so and apparently had never been suspected. But I couldn't take them to the shop myself—we were too well known in London. And, when I was at my wit's end to know what to do with them, I happened to hear a woman saying how she had disposed of hers quite legitimately and openly through a solicitor, Mr. Luke Bechcombe. I thought perhaps he might do something for me, and I rang him up."

"Well?" the detective said interrogatively; his face was as expressionless as ever, but there was a veiled eagerness in his deep-set eyes as they watched Mrs. Carnthwacke's every movement.

"I told him what I wanted. And he said it would be necessary to have them valued. We talked it over and made an appointment for two days later, the very day he was murdered. I was to take them to him myself. And he told me to go down the passage to his private door so that none of his clients should see me, because I explained that it must be kept a real dead secret."

"What time was your appointment for?" the inspector asked.

"A quarter past twelve," Mrs. Carnthwacke answered. "But I was late—it must have been quite half-past when I got there. He looked at the diamonds and said that they were very fine and he would have them valued at once and get them disposed of for me if I approved of the price. He was to ring me up at twelve o'clock the next day. But of course he didn't, and I couldn't think what had happened, until I saw this dreadful thing in the papers. Oh, you will keep my name out of it, won't you?"

She broke off and looked appealingly at the inspector. He did not answer. For once in his long experience he was thoroughly taken aback. The woman had told her story calmly and convincingly enough, but—and as the inspector looked at her he wondered if she had no idea of the horrible danger in which she stood.

"I will do my best for you in every way," he said at last. "But you must first answer all my questions straightforwardly. You have at least done the right thing in coming to us now, though it might have been better if you had come earlier. Now first will you tell me exactly what time you reached Mr. Bechcombe's office?"

"Well, as I say, I ought to have been there at a quarter past twelve, but I dare say it was half-past, or it might have been a quarter to one."

The inspector kept his keen eyes upon her face; not one change in her expression could escape him.

"Mrs. Carnthwacke, do you know that the doctors have stated that Mr. Bechcombe died about twelve o'clock—sooner rather than later?"

"Twelve o'clock!" Her face turned almost livid in spite of its make-up, but her blue eyes met the inspector's steadily. "It's no use, inspector. I suppose doctors make mistakes like other folks sometimes. Luke Bechcombe was alive, very much alive, when I went in about half-past twelve."

The inspector did not argue the question, but his eyes did not relax their watchful gaze for one second as he went on.

"How did Mr. Bechcombe seem when you saw him? Did you notice anything peculiar about his manner?"

"Well, I had never seen him before, so I couldn't notice any difference. He just seemed an ordinary, pleasant sort of man. He admired my diamonds very much and said we ought to get a high price for them. He was to have had them valued the next day. Now—now I am in pressing need of money and I want to have them valued myself if you will give them back to me."

For once Inspector Furnival was shaken out of his usual passivity.

"You—do you mean that you left the diamonds there?"

"Well, of course! Haven't I been telling you so all this time?" Mrs. Carnthwacke said impatiently. "Mr. Bechcombe gave me a receipt for them, and locked them up in his safe—like that one!"

She pointed to the wall where a large cupboard was built into it.

"The—the executors will give them to me, won't they?"

The inspector went over and stood near the door.

"Mrs. Carnthwacke, when the door of the safe was opened in the presence of Mr. Bechcombe's executors and of the police, there were no diamonds there."

"What! You do not—you cannot mean that my diamonds are lost!" Mrs. Carnthwacke started to her feet. "Mr. Bechcombe put them in the safe himself, I tell you."

"That was not a safe. It is just an ordinary cupboard in which papers and documents of no particular importance were kept. And when the safe was opened there was no sign of diamonds there," the inspector said positively. "It may be possible that Mr. Bechcombe moved them before, otherwise—"

"Otherwise what?" she demanded. "Heavens, man, speak out! My diamonds are worth thousands of pounds. Otherwise what?"

"Otherwise they may have provided a motive for the crime," the inspector said slowly. "But no—that is impossible, if you saw him lock them up."

"Of course I did, you may bet I watched that." Mrs. Carnthwacke calmed down a little. "Besides, I have got the receipt. That makes him, or his executors, liable for the diamonds, doesn't it?"

"Have you the receipt here?" the inspector asked quickly.

"Of course. I thought it might be wanted to get back my diamonds. The fact that your firm might deny having them never entered my head."

She opened the vanity bag which hung at her side and took out a piece of paper crushed with much folding.

"There! You can't get away from that!"

The inspector read it.

"Mrs. Carnthwacke has entrusted her diamonds to me for valuation and I have deposited them in my safe. Signed—Luke Francis Bechcombe," he read.

The paper on which it was written was Luke Bechcombe's. There was no doubt of that. The inspector had seen its counterpart in Mr. Bechcombe's private room. But his face altered curiously as he looked at it.

"Certainly, if this receipt was given you by Mr. Bechcombe, the estate is liable for the value of the diamonds," he finished up.

"Well, Mr. Bechcombe gave it me, safe enough," Mrs. Carnthwacke declared. "I put it in this same little bag and went off, little thinking what was going to happen. It struck one as I came out."

"One o'clock!" The inspector was looking puzzled. If Mrs. Carnthwacke's story were true it was in direct contradiction to the doctors'. "Did you meet anyone on the stairs?"

Mrs. Carnthwacke looked undecided.

"I don't remember. Yes, I think I did—some young man or another. I didn't notice him much."

"And you didn't notice anything peculiar in Mr. Bechcombe's manner?"

"Nothing much," Mrs. Carnthwacke said, holding out her hand for the receipt. "I'll have that back, please. You bet I don't part with it till I have got my diamonds back. The only thing I thought was that Mr. Bechcombe seemed in rather a hurry—sort of wanted me to quit."

The inspector felt inclined to smile. Half an hour in the busiest time of the day seemed a fairly liberal allowance even for a millionaire's wife.

"Now, can you tell me how many people knew that you were bringing the diamonds to Mr. Bechcombe?"

"Not one. What do you take me for? A first-class idiot?" Mrs. Carnthwacke demanded indignantly. "Nobody knew that I had the diamonds at all—not even my maid. I kept them in a little safe in my bedroom—one my husband had specially made for me. Great Scott, I was a bit too anxious to keep the whole business quiet to go talking about it."

"Not even to the friend that told you that Mr. Bechcombe had helped her out of a similar difficulty?"

"No, not a word! I didn't think of asking Mr. Bechcombe while she was with me, and the next day she went off to Cannes and I haven't seen her since. The receipt, please?"

The inspector did not relax his hold.

"You will understand that this is a most valuable piece of evidence, madam. You will have to entrust it to me. I will of course give you a written acknowledgment that I have it."

The colour flashed into Mrs. Carnthwacke's face.

"Do you mean that you will not let me have it back?"

"I am afraid I cannot, madam."

She sprang forward with outstretched hands—just missed it by half an inch. The inspector quietly put it in his notebook and snapping the elastic round it returned it to his pocket.

"You may rely upon me to do my best for you, madam. I shall make every possible search for the diamonds and will communicate with the executors, who will of course recognize their responsibility if the jewels are not found. And now will you let me give you one piece of advice?"

"I don't know. I guess I am not a good person to give advice to."

Evidently Mrs. Carnthwacke was not to be placated. Her eyes flashed, and one foot beat an impatient tattoo on the floor.

The inspector was unruffled.

"Nevertheless, I think I will venture upon it. Tell your husband yourself what has happened. He will help you more efficiently than anyone else in the whole world can. And Mr. Carnthwacke's advice is worth having."

CHAPTER IX

"Good morning, Miss Hoyle." Inspector Furnival rose and placed a chair for the girl, scrutinizing her pale face keenly as he did so.

Cecily sat down.

"You sent for me," she said nervously.

The inspector took the chair at the top of the table that had been Luke Bechcombe's favourite seat.

His interview with Cecily Hoyle was taking place by special arrangement in the library of the murdered man's private house, where, by special desire of Mrs. Bechcombe, Cecily was now installed as secretary to her late employer's widow.

The canny inspector had taken care to place the girl's chair so that the light from the near window fell full upon her face. As he drew his papers towards him and opened a capacious notebook he was thinking how white and worn the girl was looking, and there was a frightened glance in her brown eyes as she sat down that did not escape him.

The door opened to admit John Steadman. After a slight bow to Cecily he sat down at the inspector's right.

"Yes," the inspector said, glancing across a Cecily, "I want to ask you a few questions, Miss Hoyle. It may make matters easier for you at the adjourned inquest if you answer them now."

"I will do my best," Cecily said, looking at him with big, alarmed eyes. "But, really, I have told you everything I know."

John Steadman watched her from beneath his lowered eyes. She would be a good witness with the jury, he thought, this slim, pale girl, with her great appealing eyes and her pathetic, trembling lips.

"A few curious sidelights have arisen in connection with Mr. Bechcombe's death," the inspector pursued. "And I think you may be able to help me more than you realize. First, you recognize this, of course?" He took from its envelope of tissue paper the picture post card he had found in Amos Thompson's room in Brooklyn Terrace and handed it to her.

Cecily gazed at it in growing amazement.

"It—it looks like me! It *is* me, I believe," she said ungrammatically. "But how in the world did you get it?"

"I found it," the inspector said slowly, watching every change in her mobile face as he spoke, "in Amos Thompson's room in Brooklyn Terrace."

Cecily stared at him.

"Impossible! You couldn't have! Why should Mr. Thompson have my photograph? And where was this taken, anyway?"

"That is what I am hoping you may tell us."

"But I can't! I don't know!" Cecily said, still gazing in a species of stupefaction at her presentment. "It—it is a snapshot, of course, but I never saw it before, I never knew when it was taken."

"You did not give it to Amos Thompson, then?" the inspector questioned.

"Good heavens, no! I knew nothing about Mr. Thompson. I have just seen him at a distance in the office. But I have never spoken to him in my life. I should not have known him had I met him in the street."

"You can give no explanation of his treasuring your photograph then?"

Cecily shook her head. "I can't indeed. I should have thought it a most unlikely thing to happen. I cannot bring myself to believe that it did. This thing"—flicking the card with her forefinger—"must have got into his room by accident."

The inspector permitted himself a slight smile.

"I really do not think so."

Cecily shrugged her shoulders. "Well, I give it up. Unless—unless"—an accent of fear creeping into her voice—"he wanted to implicate me, to make you think that I had been helping him to rob Mr. Bechcombe."

"In that case he would surely have thought of some rather more sure plan than leaving your photograph about in his room," said the inspector. "You do not think it likely that seeing you so much in the office, he has taken a fancy to you—fallen in love with you, in fact, as people say."

"I do not, indeed!" Cecily said impatiently. "As I tell you, I know nothing of Mr. Thompson, and he did not see much of me in the office. I never went in to Mr. Bechcombe's room through the clerks' office. I never had occasion to go there at all. My business concerned Mr. Bechcombe, and Mr. Bechcombe only, and by his wish I always went to him by the private door."

"I see." The inspector studied the photograph in silence. "You know where this was taken?" he said at last.

Cecily looked at it again.

"It looks—I believe I am sitting in my favourite seat in the Field of Rest. I suppose I must have been snapshotted without my knowing it—by some amateur probably."

"Mr. Thompson?" the inspector suggested.

"I do not know!" Cecily tip-tilted her chin scornfully. "It was a mean thing to do, anyway."

The inspector wrapped the photograph in its paper. "No use bothering about that any more," he said, somewhat contradictorily, putting it away carefully in his pocket as he did so. "Now, Miss Hoyle, once more, you adhere to your statement that you heard some one moving about in Mr. Bechcombe's room when you passed the door on your return from lunch— that return being some little time after one o'clock."

"Half-past one, I dare say," Cecily corrected. "As I came down the passage I heard the door into Mr. Bechcombe's room close rather softly, as I have heard Mr. Bechcombe close it heaps of times. Then just as I passed I heard some one move inside the room distinctly. It was a sound like a chair being moved and catching against something hard—table leg or something of that sort."

"And you are aware that the doctors say that Mr. Bechcombe's death must have occurred about twelve o'clock?"

"I have heard so. You told me so," Cecily murmured, then gathering up her courage, "but doctors make mistakes very often."

"Scarcely over a thing of this kind," the inspector remarked. "I suppose you realize the inference that will be drawn from your testimony?" he went on.

A little frown came between Cecily's straight eyebrows.

"Inference? No, I don't!" she said bluntly.

"If Mr. Bechcombe died at twelve o'clock, and you heard some one moving about when you came back about half-past one o'clock," the inspector said very slowly, giving due weight to each word, "the inference is that the person you heard moving about when you came back was the murderer."

Cecily shivered as she stared at him.

"Oh, no, no, surely it could not have been! I do not believe it could!"

The inspector made no rejoinder. He glanced at his notebook again.

"Most probably you will be among the first witnesses called at the adjourned inquest on Friday, Miss Hoyle. I think that is all for to-day. Your name and address, please."

"Cecily Frances Hoyle, Hobart Residence, Windover Square."

The detective wrote it down.

"I think that is only a temporary address, though, you said, Miss Hoyle. Will you let me have your permanent one, please?"

Cecily hesitated in obvious confusion.

"I—I—that is my only address—the only one I have at present. I came to Mr. Bechcombe straight from school."

The inspector scratched the side of his nose with his pencil.

"That is rather awkward. It will be necessary that we should be in touch with you for some time. And you might leave Hobart Residence at any moment."

"Then I could let you know," Cecily suggested.

"That would not quite do," the inspector said mildly. "No. Just give me some address from which letters could be forwarded to you. Some relatives, perhaps!"

"I don't know any of my relatives—yet," Cecily faltered, a streak of red coming in her pale cheeks. "But Miss Cochrane,

Morley House, Beesford, Meadshire, would always forward letters."

The inspector wrote the address down without further comment.

Cecily got up. "If that is all, I think Mrs. Bechcombe wants me, inspector."

"Yes, thank you." The inspector and Mr. Steadman rose too. John Steadman moved to the door.

"I must introduce myself, Miss Hoyle," he said courteously. "I am the late Mr. Bechcombe's cousin and, as your post with Mrs. Bechcombe is of course only temporary, it has struck me that you might possibly be looking out for another engagement. Now, a friend of mine is in urgent need of a secretary, and we thought you might like the post."

The red streak in Cecily's cheeks deepened to crimson.

"I—I don't mean to do anything else at present, thank you."

John Steadman looked disappointed.

"Oh, well! Then there is no more to be said. Should you change your mind perhaps you will let us know," he said politely.

When he had closed the door behind Cecily he looked across at the inspector.

"Well, you were right."

"I was pretty sure of my ground," returned the inspector. "What do you think of young Mr. Collyer's choice, Mr. Steadman?"

"Well, she looks a nice girl enough," the barrister returned somewhat dubiously.

"It is easier to look nice than to be nice nowadays," the inspector returned enigmatically. "What do you make of this, Mr. Steadman?" throwing a torn telegram form on the table. "And this, and this," placing several odd pieces of writing paper beside it.

The barrister bent over them. The used telegraph form had been torn across and crumpled, but as the inspector smoothed it out the writing was perfectly legible.

"Do not mention home address. Father."

"Um!" John Steadman drew in his lips. "Handed in at Edgware Road Post Office at 12.30, March 4th," he said. "Well!"

He turned to the scraps of paper. The inspector leaned forward and pieced them together. The whole made part of a letter.

"Will see you as soon as possible. In the meantime be very careful. A chance word of yours may do untold harm. Say as little as possible—all will be explained later. Further instructions will reach you soon." Then came a piece that was torn away, and it ended in the corner—"5 o'clock, Physical Energy."

John Steadman's face was very stern as he looked up.

"It is obvious the girl knows—something. How did you get these scraps of paper, inspector?"

"One of our most trustworthy women agents has been doing casual work in Hobart Residence," said Inspector Furnival with a quiet smile. "These were found in Miss Cecily's Hoyle's room there, in the waste-paper-basket."

"Have you taken any steps in the matter?"

"Not yet! Of course we have had 'Physical Energy'—the statue in Kensington Gardens, you know—watched since yesterday morning, but so far there has been no sign of Miss Cecily Hoyle, or of anyone who could be identified as the writer of that letter."

"Have you any idea who that is likely to be?"

"Well, ideas are not much use, are they, sir? It is not young Mr. Collyer's writing, so much is certain, I think."

Was the inspector's reply evasive? Used to weighing evidence, John Steadman decided that it was. He made no comment, however, but bent his brows over the paper once more.

"Of course the temporary help has been chatting with the regular staff at Hobart Residence," the inspector pursued. "But there is little enough to be learned of Miss Hoyle there. Hobart Residence is a sort of hostel, you know, sir; all the inmates are supposed to be ladies in some sort of a job. They have a bedroom varying in price according to its position, and there is a general dining-room in which meals are served at a very reasonable price. Miss Hoyle usually took her breakfast and dinner there and was very seldom absent from either meal. She was looked upon as a very quiet, well-conducted girl, but she made no friends—and nothing was known of her private life. It was impossible to get at her home address there. Then I rang up Miss Watson, her old schoolmistress, but found that Cecily Hoyle's father had always paid her school bills in advance. He is an artist and has never given any settled address; sometimes he took his daughter away in the vacation. If he did not Miss Watson was asked to arrange a seaside or country holiday for her. Miss Watson only knew the Hobart Residence address."

"Extraordinary! I should have thought Cecily Hoyle one of the last girls about whom there would be any mystery," was the barrister's comment.

"Well, having drawn both those coverts blank, yesterday I made an exhaustive search of her room at Mr. Bechcombe's offices," the inspector proceeded. "For a long time I thought I was going to have no better luck there. There were no letters; no private papers of any kind. Then just at the last I had a bit of luck. Right down at the bottom of the drawer in Miss Hoyle's desk I found a time-table. I ran through it, not expecting to discover anything there when I noticed that one leaf was turned down. It was a London and South Western Railway Guide, I may mention, and it was one of the "B" pages that was turned down. I ran down it and saw in a minute that some one had been doing so with a lead pencil—there were several marks down the page—and one name, that of Burford in the New Forest, was underlined."

"Burford, Burford!" John Steadman repeated reflectively. "Why, of course I have been there for golf. There are some very decent links. My friend, Captain Horbsham, rented a house in the neighbourhood, and I have been over the course with him."

"Many burglaries down there?" the inspector said abruptly.

The barrister emitted a short laugh. "None that I ever heard of. Why, do you suspect Miss Hoyle—?"

"I don't suspect anybody," the inspector returned. "It isn't my place to, you know, sir. But I am going down to Burford to-morrow morning. Do you feel inclined to come with me?"

"I don't mind if I do," said the barrister cheerfully. "I can always do with a day in the country. We will drive down in the car, and I might take my clubs."

CHAPTER X

"ONE O'CLOCK. We have come down in very decent time. Tidy old bus, isn't it?" John Steadman replaced his watch and looked round with interest as his car slowed down before the "Royal Arms" at Burford. Rather a dilapidated "Royal Arms" to judge by the signboard swaying in the breeze, but quite a picturesque-looking village inn for all that. There was no station within five miles of Burford, which so far had preserved it from trippers. Of late, however, two or three of the ubiquitous char-à-bancs had strayed through the village and there appeared every prospect of its being eventually opened up. This, with other scraps of information, was imparted by the garrulous landlord to Mr. Steadman and his companion, Inspector Furnival. But, though he talked much of the village and its inhabitants, the inspector did not catch the name for which he was listening. At last he spoke."

"I used to know a man named Hoyle who lived somewhere in this part, I wonder if he is still here?"

"Oh, I should think that would be Mr. Hoyle of Rose Cottage," the landlord said at once. "A very nice gentleman. He has been here some years. He is an artist, as no doubt you know, sir. And I have heard that some of his paintings have been exhibited in London in the Royal Academy. Oh, we are very proud of Mr. Hoyle down here."

"He is a good deal away on his sketching expeditions, though, isn't he?" the inspector ventured.

"Well, naturally he is," the landlord agreed. "Sometimes he's away weeks at a time. But he is generally here on a Sunday to take the collection in church. He is a sidesman and takes a great interest in parish matters. I did hear that he was far away the biggest subscriber to the new parish hall that our vicar is having built. Oh, a very nice gentleman is Mr. Hoyle. Mrs. Wye, his housekeeper, can't say so often enough."

"I think that must be the man I used to know," said the inspector mendaciously. "I think we must drive up and pay him a visit, Mr. Steadman. It isn't far, you said, I think, landlord?"

"Get there in ten minutes in the car, sir. Rose Cottage, straight up by the church. You can't miss it. But, there, I doubt if you will find Mr. Hoyle at home. I was at church on Sunday morning and I noticed he wasn't. He usually is when he is at home. I can't always say the same myself!" And the landlord shook his fat sides at his own pleasantry.

"Well, I think we will try anyway," the inspector concluded. "Perhaps Miss Hoyle may be at home if he isn't."

"Miss Hoyle?" The landlord looked puzzled for a moment then his face cleared. "Oh Mr. Hoyle's daughter you mean, sir. No. She is away at school, though Mr. Hoyle did say she would be coming home 'for keeps' this year."

"Anyhow I shall leave a message and Mr. Hoyle will know I have looked him up," said the inspector pleasantly. "I expect he would think me a good deal altered, for we haven't met for something like twelve years, and we none of us grow younger, you know, landlord."

"We don't, sir, that's a fact. Not but what Mr. Hoyle is as little changed as anybody I know. Just the same pleasant-looking gentleman he is as he was the first time I saw him. A nice cheerful gentleman is Mr. Hoyle—always ready with his joke."

The inspector nodded.

"Oh, ay. Just the same, I see. Well, well, we will be off. As likely as not we shall come in here on our way back. Anyhow, I shall not forget your Stilton in a hurry, landlord. I haven't had a cut from a cheese like that since I was a boy in Leicestershire. By the way, what was that I heard of a burglary down this way last week?"

The landlord scratched his head.

"It is funny you should ask that, sir. I haven't heard of anything lately. I was talking to a couple of gents this morning about a robbery there was about this time a year ago—a couple of robberies I might say. Squire Morpeth over at the Park, and Sir John Lington at Lillinghurst were both broken into and hundreds of pounds' worth of goods—silver and what not—taken. Nobody was ever brought to account for it either, though there were big rewards offered."

"Dear, dear! One doesn't expect to hear of such things in a quiet little place like Burford," the inspector observed contradictorily. "Well, so long, landlord. See you again later."

It did not take long, following the landlord's instructions, to run the car up to Rose Cottage, but just as they were nearing it John Steadman looked at his companion.

"I think you're running off on a side track, you know, inspector."

"I'm sure I am!" the other returned cheerfully. "But, when the straight track takes you nowhere, one is inclined to make a little excursion down a side path, right or wrong."

Rose Cottage looked quite an ideal dwelling for an artist. It was a black and white timbered cottage standing back from the road, its garden for the most part surrounded by a high hedge. Over the walls creepers were running riot. Later on there would be a wealth of colour, but to-day only the *pyrus japonica* was putting forth adventurous rosy blossoms. A wicket gate gave access to the gravelled path running up to the rustic porch between borders gay with crocuses—purple and white and gold.

"Evidently cars are not expected here," John Steadman remarked as he and the inspector alighted and walked up to the front door.

There was apparently no bell, but there was a shining brass knocker. Inspector Furnival applied himself to it with great energy.

The door was opened by a pleasant-looking woman, who was hastily donning a white apron.

"Mr. Hoyle?" the inspector queried.

"Not at home," the woman said at once.

The inspector hesitated. "Can you tell me when he will be at home?"

The woman shook her head. "I cannot indeed. He is away on a sketching expedition, and one never knows when he will be back. It may be a week or a month or longer."

"Oh, dear!" The inspector looked at Mr. Steadman. "This is most unfortunate! I was particularly anxious to see him to-day. However, I suppose I must write. I wonder if you would let me just scribble a line here? I should esteem it a great favour if you would."

For a moment the woman looked doubtful, then after a keen glance at the two men she led the way to a sitting-room that apparently ran from back to front of the house. She indicated a writing-table.

"You will find pens and ink there, sir."

The inspector sat down. "A very pretty room this," he began conversationally. "I wonder if I am right in thinking that you are Mrs. Hoyle?"

"Oh, dear, no, sir." The woman laughed. "I am only Mr. Hoyle's housekeeper. I have lived with him ever since he came to Burford."

"And that must be a dozen years or more ago now. And I haven't seen him a dozen times, I should say, the inspector went on. "Dear, dear, how time flies! His daughter must be grown up, I suppose, he went on, examining the pens before him with meticulous care."

"Miss Cecily? Oh, yes; a fine-looking young lady too. She will be here for good very soon."

Meanwhile John Steadman, standing near the door, was glancing appraisingly round the room. It was essentially a man's room. The chairs, square solid table, sideboard and writing-table were all of oak, very strong, the few easy chairs were leather covered and capacious, there was nothing unnecessary in the room. Near the French window looking on to the garden at the back of the house there stood an easel with an untidy pile of sketches piled one on top of the other upon it. A table close at hand held more sketches, tubes of paint, a palette and various paint brushes. Steadman walked across and took one of the water-colours from the easel.

"I like this," he said, holding it from him at arm's length. "It is a charming little view of one of the forest glades near here, taken at sunset. Is there any possibility of this being for sale?"

"Well, I don't rightly know, sir," the housekeeper said, coming over to him. "Mr. Hoyle do sell some of his pictures, I know. But it is always in London. I have never known him do it down here."

John Steadman smiled.

"Well, I shouldn't think there would be many customers down here. But I could do with a couple. This one—and another to make a pair with it."

"Well, sir, perhaps you will write to Mr. Hoyle about it," the housekeeper suggested. "I couldn't say anything about it."

"Of course not," the barrister assented. He looked very closely at the picture for a minute, and then put it back on the easel. "Well, I must leave it at that, and hope to persuade Mr. Hoyle to part with it when he comes back."

As he spoke there came a loud knock at the door. He looked at the housekeeper.

"It's all right, sir," she said composedly. "It is only the baker's man for orders, and my niece will go to the door. She always comes up twice a week to give me a hand with the work. Me not being so young as I might be."

"We none of us are, ma'am," the inspector said with a chuckle as he sealed his letter and placed it in a conspicuous place on the writing-table. "Not that you have much to complain about," he added gallantly as he rose.

The housekeeper smiled complacently as she saw them off to the little garden. The inspector was in an expansive mood and stopped to admire the crocuses as they passed.

"Well?" Mr. Steadman said as they seated themselves in the car before starting.

The inspector waited until they had started before he replied, then he said quietly:

"Well, Mr. Steadman, sir?"

"Well?" the barrister echoed. "I hope you have found what you expected, inspector."

"I hardly know what I did expect," the inspector said candidly. "Except that, if matters are as I suspect, Hoyle is certainly not the man to give himself away."

The barrister coughed.

"And yet I noticed one small thing that may help you, inspector. You saw that water-colour sketch?"

"The one you are going to buy," the inspector assented with a grin. "Ay. I should like to have had a good look round at those drawings. But that blessed housekeeper wasn't giving us any chances."

"Not that she knew of," John Steadman said quietly. "Did you notice the big 'Christopher Hoyle' in the left-hand corner of the painting, inspector?"

"I saw it," said the inspector, "but it didn't tell me much."

"No. That alone did not," John Steadman went on. "But I looked at that and I looked at several of the others. And I am as sure as I can be without subjecting them to a test that in each case that big flourishing Christopher Hoyle has been scrawled with a paint brush on the top of another signature. One, moreover, that from the little I could see of it bore no sort of resemblance to Christopher Hoyle. What do you make of that, inspector?"

"Is Mr. Christopher Hoyle a man with two names?" the inspector questioned. "Or has he some reason to wish to appear to be an artist in simple Burford society when in reality he is nothing of the kind?"

"The latter, I imagine," John Steadman said after a pause. "Because—I don't know whether you know anything of painting, inspector?"

"Bless you, not a thing!" the inspector said energetically. "If I have to do with a picture case, I have to call in experts! But you mean—"

"Judging from the three or four sketches I was able to examine I should say that none of them—no two of them were done by the same hand. There is as much difference in painting as in handwriting, you know, inspector."

"I see!" The detective sat silent for a minute, his eyes scanning the flying landscape. "Well, it is pretty much what I expected to hear," he said at last. "It strengthens my suspicions so far—"

"I can't understand your suspicions," John Steadman said impatiently. "This man Hoyle is a bit of a humbug, evidently, but what connection can there be between him and Luke Be-chcombe's murder?"

"His daughter?" the inspector suggested without looking round.

The barrister shrugged his shoulders. "That girl is no murderess."

"No," agreed the inspector. "But she is helping the guilty to escape."

John Steadman raised his eyebrows. "Who is the guilty?"

For answer Inspector Furnival's keen, ferret eyes looked back at him, focused themselves on the barrister's face as though they would wring some truth from it.

But John Steadman's face would never give him away. In his day he had been one of the keenest cross examiners at the bar. His eyes had never been more blandly expressionless than now as they met the inspector's inquiringly.

Defeated, the detective sank back in his corner of the car with a deep breath, whether of relief or disappointment John Steadman could not tell.

They were just entering Burford again. Before the car stopped the inspector said quietly:

"Don't you know, sir?"

"I do not!" said John Steadman, looking him squarely in the face.

"Don't you guess?"

"Guessing," said the barrister sententiously, "is a most unprofitable employment. One I never indulge in."

"Ah well!" said the inspector as the car stopped before the door of the inn. "I don't know, sir. And you don't guess. We will leave it at that. Well, landlord"—as that worthy came to the door rubbing his hands—"we are back upon your hands for tea. Mr. Hoyle was out."

CHAPTER XI

ANTHONY COLLYER got out of his bus at Lancaster Gate Tube. He looked round, but there was no sign of the figure he was hoping to see. He crossed the road and entered Kensington

Gardens, stopping at the gate to buy some chocolates of the kind that Cecily particularly affected.

Near the little sweet-stall a small ragged figure was skulking. In his preoccupation Anthony did not even see him. Inside the Gardens he turned into a sheltered walk on the right flanked on either side by clumps of evergreens. There was a touch of chill in the wind, but the sun was shining brightly and through the short grass the daffodils were already adventurously poking their gay yellow heads. The urchin who had been lurking by the palings followed slowly. He got over on the grass in a leisurely fashion and ensconced himself out of sight in the shadow of the evergreens.

Anthony had time to glance at his watch more than once and even to grow a little impatient before Cecily appeared.

Then one glance was enough to show him that there was something amiss with the girl. There were big blue half-circles beneath her eyes, and the eyes themselves were dim and sunken. All her pretty colouring looked blurred as she gave her hand to Anthony, and he saw that it was trembling and felt that it was cold even through her glove. He held it in both of his and chafed it.

"You are cold, dear," he said solicitously. "Are your furs warm enough? The wind is treacherous to-day."

"Oh, I don't know. Yes, of course I am warm enough—I mean it does not matter," Cecily said incoherently. "I—I wrote to you—you know—because I wanted to see you."

Tony looked round. No one was in sight. He drew her to a seat beside the path, knowing nothing of the unseen watcher hidden in the rhododendrons.

"I hoped you did. I always want to see you, Cecily," he said simply.

Cecily shivered away from him. "You—you must not."

Anthony stared at her.

"Must not—what?" he said blankly. "Want to see you, do you mean?"

Cecily nodded.

"Oh, but it is no use telling me not to do that," Anthony said quaintly, "I shall want to see you every day as long as I live."

"You will not be able to," Cecily said desperately. "Because now—to-day—I am going right out of your life—you will never see me again."

"Oh!" For a time Anthony said no more. His clasp of her hand relaxed. Very quietly he returned to her the possession of it. "I see," he said at last. "You are giving me the chuck, are you not?"

The girl looked at him with frightened, miserable eyes. "Tony, I can't help it."

"Naturally you can't," Tony assented moodily. "You couldn't be expected to. I never was anything but a wretched match at the best of times—even with the money Uncle Luke left me—but now, now that every damned rag of a paper in the country is saying out as plainly as they dare that I am a murderer, it settles the matter, of course."

Cecily interrupted him with a little cry.

"Tony! You know it isn't that!"

A gleam of hope brightened Anthony Collyer's eyes.

"Not that? Is it just that you are sick of me then? Heaven knows I wouldn't blame you for that. I was always a dull sort of chap. But I love you, Cecily."

The girl's big tragic eyes looked at his bent head with a sudden wave of tenderness in their brown depths. "And I love you, Tony," she said beneath her breath. "But that does not matter."

"Doesn't it?" A sudden fire leaped into Anthony's deep-set eyes. "Why, that is just the one thing that matters—the only thing that does matter. If you love me, I shall never go out of your life, Cecily."

"Oh, yes, you will," the girl said, putting his warm outstretched hand back determinedly. "And it doesn't matter that we love one another, not one bit. Because I am not going to marry anyone."

"Of course you are!" said Anthony, staring at her. "You are going to marry me. Do you really think I am going to let you back out of it now?"

"You can't help yourself," Cecily said, still with that miserable note of finality in her voice. "It is no use, Tony. You have just got to forget me."

"Forget you!" Anthony said scornfully. "That is so likely, isn't it? Now, dear, what is this bogy that you have conjured up that is going to separate us? You say it has nothing to do with me?"

"No, no! Of course it hasn't!"

"And you haven't fallen in love with anyone else?"

"Don't be silly, Tony!" There was a momentary irritation in the clear tones. But something in the accent, even in the homely words themselves roused fresh hopes in Anthony's heart.

"Then it is something some one else has said," he hazarded, "or done."

For a moment Cecily did not answer. She pressed her lips very closely together. At last she said slowly:

"That is all that I can tell you, Tony. I just wanted to say that and—good-bye."

"Good-bye!" Tony repeated scoffingly. "Nonsense, dear! You say that this mysterious something has nothing to do with you or with me personally. And for the rest of the world what does it matter? Nothing counts but just you and me, sweetheart."

"Oh, but it does!" Cecily contradicted firmly. "We—we can't think only of ourselves. It—it is no use, Tony. My mind is made up."

"Then I am going to unmake it," Tony said with equal decision. "And, if you won't tell me what you fancy is going to separate us, I am going to find out for myself."

Then for the first time Cecily's self-possession really deserted her.

"No, no! You must not!" she cried feverishly. "Tony, you must not—you do not know what harm—what terrible harm you might do if you did. Promise me—promise me you will not!" She caught at his arm with trembling hands, as though to stop his threatened action by actual physical force. If ever fear had looked out of human eyes, stark, tragic fear, Anthony saw it then as he met her terrified gaze.

Some shadow of it communicated itself to him. He felt suddenly cold, his face turned a sickly grey beneath its tan. In that moment he realized fully that he was up against some very real and tangible obstacle that stood definitely between Cecily and himself.

"Cecily!" he said hoarsely. "Cecily!"

The girl looked at him a moment, her lips twitching; then, as if coming to some sudden resolution, she bent forward and whispered a few words in his ear.

As he heard them he started back.

"What do you say, Cecily? That you—that you know— But you are mad—mad!"

"Hush!" the girl looked round fearfully. "No, I am not mad, Anthony," she said beneath her breath. "God knows I often wish I were."

Then Anthony looked at her.

"Cecily! I can't believe it. You didn't—" she questioned beneath her breath.

"Did you never suspect—that?"

"Never! Before Heaven, never! How should I? It is inconceivable! But the horrible danger—" His eyes voiced the dread he dared not put into words, and with a stifled cry the girl turned from him.

Tony took off his hat and wiped away the sweat that was standing in great drops on his forehead.

"It—it isn't possible! Cecily!" he murmured hoarsely. "It—it is a lie!"

"I—I wish it was!" the girl said beneath her breath. "Oh, Tony, Tony, I wish it was all a dream—a dreadful horrible dream. Last night I woke and thought it was, and then I remembered. Oh, Tony, Tony!" She shivered from head to foot. "I wish I were dead—oh, I wish I were dead!"

Anthony mopped his forehead again. "In God's name what are we to do?"

Cecily's mouth twisted in something like a wry smile.

"It is not 'we' Tony. It never will be 'we' again. And I—I cannot tell what I shall do yet. I must stay at the Residence of course until the police—" She stopped, her throat working. "Until I am free to go away," she finished forlornly. "Then— then God knows what will become of me! I—I expect I shall live out of England if—if I can."

"Yes," said Anthony slowly. "Yes. But that will not be for ever. We are both young, and we can wait. And some day I will come and fetch you home again."

"No, no!" The horror in the girl's eyes deepened. "Won't you understand, Tony? I shall never come back. I shall never be safe. From to-day I shall be dead to you! But—but wait, Tony. Sometimes I do not think that I shall get away—that I shall escape. For everywhere they follow me. Always I know that I am being watched. They will never let me go away. It is like a cat playing with a mouse. Just when the poor little mouse thinks at last it is safe, the blow falls. Even to-day—to-day— Oh, Tony, look!" As she spoke, she sprang to her feet.

Anthony turned. At first sight there seemed nothing to account for her agitation—just a very ordinary-looking man coming towards them from the direction of the Broad Walk.

But as Tony looked he caught his breath sharply.

Cecily did not wait for him to speak.

"Stop him! Stop him!" she cried feverishly. "Don't let him come after me. Keep him here until I have got away!"

She sped down the path towards Lancaster Gate.

Anthony went forward to meet the new-comer.

"Good morning, Mr. Steadman," he said, endeavouring to make his voice sound as natural as possible.

"Good morning, Tony." John Steadman shook hands with him warmly, his keen eyes taking in all the tokens of disturbance on the young man's face. "I am afraid my appearance is rather inopportune," he went on. "Isn't that your young woman beating a hasty retreat down there?" In the distance Cecily's scurrying figure could plainly be seen.

"Yes, she is in a hurry," Anthony said lamely.

"Obviously!" The barrister smiled. "But I am glad to have this opportunity of seeing you, Tony. I have been hoping to meet you."

Mindful of Cecily's parting injunction Tony turned to the seat behind.

"Have a cigarette, sir?"

The barrister shook his head as he glanced at the open cigarette case.

"De Reszke! No, thanks! You are a bit too extravagant for me, young man! I always smoke gaspers myself." He sat down and took out his own case. "You of course don't condescend to Gold Flake," he went on. "I am rather glad of this opportunity of having a chat with you, Tony."

Tony lighted his cigarette and threw the match away before he spoke, then he turned and looked John Steadman squarely in the face.

"I dare say you are, Mr. Steadman. So is your friend, Inspector Furnival, whenever I meet him, I notice."

The barrister paused in the act of lighting his match.

"You mean—?"

"I mean that, if folks think I murdered my uncle, I would just as soon they said so straight out, as come poking around asking questions and trying to trap me," Anthony retorted bitterly.

John Steadman finished lighting his cigarette and blew a couple of spirals in the clear air before he spoke, then he said slowly:

"The thought that you murdered your Uncle Luke is about the last that would enter my head, Tony. No. What I wanted to ask you was, does that job of yours stand—bear-leader to the young brother of a friend of yours, I mean. The last time I saw you, you spoke as if it were off."

"So it is!" Anthony returned moodily. "People don't want a man who is as good as accused of murdering his own uncle to look after their children. I might strangle the kid if he got tiresome."

The barrister paid no attention to this outburst.

"Then I think I heard of something yesterday that may suit you. A friend of mine has a son who was frightfully injured in the War. Both his legs have been amputated and one wrist is practically helpless. Now he wants some one to act as his secretary, for he has taken to writing novels; passes the time for him, you know, and folks need not read them if they don't want to."

"It is very good of you to think of me," Anthony said gratefully. "But I don't know that I should make much hand at secretarial work. And probably he wouldn't look at me if he knew."

"He does know," contradicted John Steadman. "And he is quite anxious to have you. It won't be all secretarial work, though you will be called a secretary. But you will be wanted to motor with him, to go with him to race meetings; he is a great motoring enthusiast—keeps two touring cars. Before the War he was one of our finest amateur jockeys, and they say he never misses a meeting under N.H. rules now. I believe he even has a couple of hurdlers at one of the big trainers. You will have to go with him wherever he wants you. How does it strike you?"

"The question is, how shall I strike him?" Tony countered. "Will he think he is safe with me?"

"Tony, my lad, you must not get morbid," reproved the barrister. "My friends know all about your connection with the Bechcombes, and are quite prepared to take you on my recommendation. You would not be required to live in, and there is a nice little cottage on the estate near the house that will be placed at your disposal. Your salary will be good, and with what your uncle left you will make matrimony quite possible. Now what do you say?"

"Say? What can I say but take it and be thankful," Tony responded, trying to make his tones sound as grateful as he could. "Would it be far from town—this cottage?"

"Oh, not far!" the barrister said at once. "At Bramley Hall, near Burford, in the New Forest. It is young Bramley, Sir John's eldest son, you are wanted for."

"Bramley Hall," Tony repeated musingly. "I seem to know the name. Wasn't there a burglary there a little while ago?"

"About eighteen months ago," the barrister assented. "The house was practically cleared of valuables in one night. Even Sir John's safe, which he had deemed impregnable, was rifled. Oh, yes, it made quite a stir. It was said to be the work of this Yellow Gang that folks are always talking about, you know."

CHAPTER XII

"I GUESS YOU are Inspector Furnival, sir."

The inspector, with Mr. Steadman, was just about to enter New Scotland Yard. He glanced keenly at his interlocutor. He saw a tall, lantern-jawed, lean-shanked man who seemed in some indescribable way to carry Yankee writ large all over him.

The detective's face cleared.

"Why, certainly, I am William Furnival, sir."

"And you are in charge of the Bechcombe case?"

"Well, I may say I am," the inspector agreed. "And I think you are Mr. Cyril B. Carnthwacke."

"Sure thing. And no reason to be ashamed of my name either," the other said truculently, rather as if he expected the inspector to challenge his statement.

The inspector, however, was looking his blandest.

"The name of Cyril B. Carnthwacke is one to conjure with not only in your own country but in ours," he said politely. "Did you wish to speak to me, sir?"

"I did, very particularly," responded Mr. Carnthwacke. "But"—with a glance at Mr. Steadman—"this gentleman?"

"Mr. Steadman, sir, the late Mr. Bechcombe's cousin, and at one time one of the best-known criminal lawyers practising at the bar. He has been kind enough to place his experience at our disposal in this most perplexing case. Will you come into my office, Mr. Carnthwacke?"

"Sure thing, we can't stand out in the street," responded the millionaire.

The inspector led the way to his private room and then clearing a lot of papers from the nearest chair set it forward.

Mr. Carnthwacke sat down with a word of thanks. John Steadman took up his position with his back to the fireplace, the inspector dropped into his revolving chair and looked at his visitor.

"I am at your service, sir."

Cyril B. Carnthwacke settled himself in his chair and looked back.

"I guess you two gentlemen know pretty well what has brought me here. Mrs. Cyril B. Carnthwacke is at home laid up in bed with the worry of the past few days. I calculate she isn't exactly the stuff criminals are made of. So here I have come in her place for a straight talk face to face. She has told me all about her doings on the day Luke F. Bechcombe was murdered. And she told me that she had been to you on the same subject. So I guess you fairly well know what I have come to talk about."

"Yes, Mrs. Carnthwacke did come to us," the inspector assented. "It would have been wiser to have come earlier."

"Sure thing it would," agreed Mr. Carnthwacke. "But women an't the wisest of creatures, even if they are not scared out of their wits as Mrs. Carnthwacke was when she realized that she was the 'lady of the glove,' that every news sheet in the kingdom was making such a clamour about."

"Perhaps it was a good thing for her that she was," remarked the inspector enigmatically.

Cyril Carnthwacke stared at him.

"I don't comprehend. I wasn't aware you dealt in conundrums, inspector."

"No," the inspector said as he opened a drawer and began to rummage in it. "Ah, here we are! This is the report of the expert in finger-prints and it shows that it was impossible for the fingers that fitted into this glove to have made the prints on Mr. Bechcombe's throat. They were much too small."

"I grasp your meaning." Mr. Carnthwacke sat back in his chair and put his elbows on the arms, joining the tips of his fingers together and surveying them with much interest. "But I reckon I didn't need this corroboration. My wife's word is the goods for me. I guess you gentlemen have tumbled to it that it is to make some inquiries about the diamonds that I have come butting in this morning."

The inspector bowed. "I thought it quite likely."

"Now, I have made certain that by your laws as well as ours the late Mr. Bechcombe's estate is liable for the value of Mrs. Carnthwacke's jewels since he gave my wife a receipt for them, which I believe is held by you gentlemen now," the American said speaking with a strong nasal accent.

Again the inspector nodded his assent.

"Certainly it is. What do you suppose to be the value of the diamonds, Mr. Carnthwacke?"

"Wal, I couldn't figure it off in a minute," the millionaire said in a considering tone. "But a good many thousands of dollars anyway. I did not buy them all at once, but picked up a few good ones when I got a chance. Thought to myself diamonds were always an investment. The gem of the whole lot was the necklace; it was part of the Russian crown jewels and had been worn by the ill-fated Czarina herself. But anyhow I guess my wife's diamonds were pretty well known in London and they were valuable enough to excite the cupidity of this gang of criminals that have been so busy about London of late. You see, I suppose, that it was in order to get them that they broke in to Mr. Bechcombe's office and strangled him."

John Steadman raised his eyebrows as he looked across at the inspector. That worthy coughed.

"You are rather jumping to conclusions, it seems to me, Mr. Carnthwacke. In the first place Mr. Bechcombe's office was not broken into. The murderer, whoever he might have been, entered in the usual fashion and apparently in no way alarmed Mr. Bechcombe. In fact all the indications go to prove that the assassin was some one known to Mr. Bechcombe."

"I don't figure that out." Cyril B. Carnthwacke hunched his shoulders and looked obstinate. "I will take what odds you like that my wife was followed and that, unable to get what he wanted without, the thief strangled Mr. Bechcombe and walked off with the diamonds."

"The diamonds certainly provide a very adequate motive," John Steadman said slowly, taking part in the conversation for the first time. "But there are some very weak points in your story, Mr. Carnthwacke. You must remember that the rubber gloves worn by the assassin as well as the chloroform used seem to prove conclusively that the murder was planned beforehand."

There was a pause.

"That may be, but I don't see that it precludes the motive being the theft of my wife's diamonds," said Mr. Cyril B. Carnthwacke truculently.

"You spoke of Mrs. Carnthwacke's being followed, and of the 'follower' assaulting Mr. Bechcombe and strangling him in the struggle. That rather suggests an accidental discovery of Mrs. Carnthwacke's errand to me," John Steadman hazarded mildly.

"It doesn't suggest anything of the kind to me," the American contradicted obstinately. "Of course somebody had discovered my wife's errand, what it was and what time she was to be there, and followed her there for the express purpose of getting them."

"I should have thought it would have been easier to snatch them from Mrs. Carnthwacke than to get them from Mr. Bechcombe," John Steadman went on, his eyes watching every change of expression in the other's face.

"You wouldn't have if you had heard the strength of Mrs. Carnthwacke's lungs," Mr. Carnthwacke contradicted. "It would have been devilish difficult to get the diamonds from her. She only left the car at the archway, too, and she carried the jewels concealed beneath her coat. It would have been a bold thief who would have attacked her, crossing that bit of a square in front or coming up the steps to the office. No. It was a wiser plan to wait and take them from Mr. Bechcombe."

"I don't think so, and I think you are wrong," John Steadman dissented. "The most probable thing would have been for Mr. Bechcombe to have deposited the diamonds in the safe while Mrs. Carnthwacke was there. That he did not do so is one of the minor puzzles of the case. I cannot understand why he should put them in the cupboard pointed out by Mrs. Carnthwacke, and why he should call it his safe I cannot imagine. He might almost have intended to make things easy for the thief."

"I wonder whether he did," Cyril B. Carnthwacke said very deliberately.

His words had all the force of a bombshell. The other two men stared at him in amazement.

"I do not understand you," John Steadman said at last, his tone haughty in its repressive surprise.

But Cyril B. Carnthwacke was not to be easily repressed.

"Wal, I reckoned I might as well mention the idea—which is an idea that has occurred to more than me. But then I didn't want to put up the dander of you two gentlemen, and you in particular"—with a polite inclination in the direction of Mr. Steadman—"being a cousin of the late Mr. Bechcombe. But I was at a man's dinner last night, and it was pretty freely canvassed. It is hinted that Mr. Bechcombe might have been in difficulties in his accounts—I understand that there are pretty considerable deficiencies in his balance. And though they are all put down by the police to that clerk that can't be found— well, doesn't it pretty well jump to your eye that the late Mr. Bechcombe himself knew all about them, and that it might have suited his book to have my wife's jewels stolen, perhaps by a confederate—the clerk Thompson or another—"

"And arranged to get himself murdered to get suspicion thrown off himself?" Mr. Steadman inquired satirically as the other paused for breath.

"No, not that exactly, though I guess he was pretty slick," returned Mr. Cyril B. Carnthwacke equably. "But I am inclined to size it up that the two had a quarrel and that the other one killed Mr. Bechcombe."

"Are you indeed?" questioned John Steadman, a glitter in his eye that would have warned his juniors that the old man was going to be nasty. But the K.C. had rarely lost his temper so completely as to-day. "I can tell you at once that your idea is nothing but a lie—a lie, moreover, that has its foundation in your own foul imagination!" he said very deliberately. "Luke Bechcombe was the soul of honour. I would answer for him as I would for myself."

"That is vurry satisfactory," drawled Cyril B. Carnthwacke. "Most satisfactory, I am sure. Weel, since that question is settled I will ask another. Was Mr. Bechcombe's face injured at all?"

The other two looked surprised at this question.

"Why, no," the inspector answered. "There was not even a scratch upon it. Why do you ask?"

"Another idea!" responded Mr. Carnthwacke cheerfully. "Another idea. But my last wasn't a success. I guess I will keep this to myself for a time."

"One cannot help seeing that the rubber gloves and the chloroform pretty well dispose of your idea, as they have disposed of a good many others," the inspector remarked. "No, I believe the murder to have been deliberately planned, but I don't think it was the work of one man alone. There have been more jewel robberies in London in the past year than I ever remember and I am inclined to believe that most of them may be set down to the same gang."

"The Yellow Gang!" interjected the millionaire. "I have heard of it."

"The Yellow Gang, if you like to call it so," acquiesced the inspector. "But then there comes up the question, how should they know that Mrs. Carnthwacke was taking her jewels to Mr. Bechcombe that morning?"

"And why does that puzzle you?" Mr. Carnthwacke inquired blandly.

The inspector glanced at him keenly.

"Mrs. Carnthwacke informed me that no one at all knew that she was thinking of parting with her jewels, and that her visit to Mr. Bechcombe that morning had been kept a profound secret."

Mr. Carnthwacke threw himself back in his chair and gave vent to a short, sharp laugh.

"I guess you are not a married man, inspector, or you would talk in a different fashion to that! Is there a woman alive who could keep a secret? If there is, it isn't Mrs. Cyril B. Carnthwacke. Nobody knew! Bless your life, I knew well enough she was in debt and had made up her mind to sell her jewels to Bechcombe. I didn't know the exact time certainly. But that was because I didn't take the trouble to find out. Bless your life, there are no flies on Cyril B. Carnthwacke. When she brought the empty cases to me to put away in the safe after she'd worn her diamonds the other day, she saw me lock them up in the safe and was quite contented, bless her heart. But I guess I was slick enough to look in the cases afterwards, and when I found them empty I pretty well guessed what was up. Then I took the liberty of listening one day when she was talking down the telephone and after that she hadn't many secrets from me. As for nobody else knowing"—with another of those dry laughs—"it would take a cleverer woman than Mrs. Cyril B. Carnthwacke to keep it from her maid."

"That may be," the inspector said, smiling in his turn. "But to be as frank with you as you have been with us, Mr. Carnthwacke, we have taken steps to find out what the maid knows, with the result that we are inclined to think Mrs. Carnthwacke's statement practically correct."

"Is that so?" Mr. Carnthwacke inquired with a satiric emphasis that made John Steadman look at him more closely. "Wal, I came out on the open and tackled Mrs. Cyril B. Carnthwacke myself this morning; we had a lot of trouble, but the upshot of it all was that I got it out of her at last that she had told nobody but that she had just mentioned it to Fédora."

"Fédora, the fortune teller!" Steadman exclaimed.

"The Soothsayer—the Modern Witch," Mr. Carnthwacke explained. "All these Society women are just crazed about her of late. They consult her about everything. And I feel real ashamed to say Mrs. Cyril B. Carnthwacke is as silly as anyone, I taxed her with it and made her own up. 'You'd ask that fortune-telling woman's advice I know,' I said. And at last she burst out crying and the game was up. She swore she didn't mention names. But there, it is my opinion she don't know whether she did or not. Anyhow, gentlemen, I have given you something to go upon. You look up Madame Fédora and her clients. It's there you will find the clue to Luke Bechcombe's death if it took place as you think." He got up leisurely. "If there is nothing more I can do for you gentlemen—"

The inspector rose too.

"I am much obliged for your frankness. If all the witnesses in this most unhappy tangle were Mr. Cyril B. Carnthwackes, we should soon find ourselves out in the open, I fancy."

The millionaire looked pleased at this compliment.

"I know one can't do better than lay all one's cards on the table when one is dealing with the English police," he remarked. "Well, so long, gentlemen. Later on I want to take Mrs. Cyril B. Carnthwacke for a cruise to get over all this worry and trouble. But I guess we will have to stop here awhile in case you want her witness. And so if you want either of us any time—I reckon you know my number—you can ring us up or come round."

With a curiously ungraceful bow he turned to the door. A minute or two later they saw him drive off in his limousine.

John Steadman drew a long breath.

"Well, inspector?"

For answer the inspector handed him his notebook. The last entry was: "Inquire into C.B.C.'s movements on the day."

John Steadman glanced curiously at the inspector as he handed it back.

"Do you think he did not realize? Or is he trying to screen some one?"

"I don't know," the inspector said slowly. "With regard to your second question, that is to say. With regard to your first, to use his own phraseology, I don't think there are any flies on Cyril B. Carnthwacke."

CHAPTER XIII

"Twelve minutes to one." Anthony Collyer turned into the Tube station. He was lunching with Mrs. Luke Bechcombe and the Tube would get him there in time and be cheaper than a taxi. Anthony was inclined to be economical these days. He paused at the bookstall to buy a paper.

The tragic death of a London solicitor was beginning to be crowded out. A foreign potentate was ill. There were daily bulletins in the paper. There were rumours of a royal engagement. A great race meeting was impending, the man in the street was much occupied in trying to spot the winners. Altogether the general public was a great deal too busy to have time to spare for speculations as to the identity of Luke Bechcombe's assassin. Still, every few days there would be a paragraph stating that the police were in possession of fresh evidence, and that an arrest was hourly expected; so far, however, there had been no result. Still, the very mention of the Crow's Inn Tragedy held a morbid fascination for Anthony Collyer. The heading caught his eye now and he paused to turn the paper over.

Standing thus by the bookstall he was hidden from the sight of the passers-by. For his part he was thinking of nothing but his paper, when two sentences caught his ear.

"I tell you, you will have to go to Burford."

"Suppose I am followed?"

Both voices—a man's and a woman's—sounded familiar to Anthony Collyer. The former he could not place at the moment, the latter—the blood ran rapidly to his head, as he gazed after the retreating couple who were now walking quickly in the direction of the ticket office—surely, he said to himself, it was Cecily Hoyle's voice!

Cecily Hoyle it undoubtedly was. He recognized her tall, slim figure and her big grey coat with its square squirrel collar. Her companion was a man at whom Tony could only get a glance; of medium height wearing rather shabby-looking clothes, and with grey, hair worn much longer than usual, his face, as he turned it to his companion, was clean-shaven and rosy as of a man who lived out of doors.

Anthony had not seen Cecily since their meeting in Kensington Gardens now more than a week ago. It was evident that she intended to abide by her words; she had not answered any of Tony's impassioned letters, she had refused to see him when he had called at Hobart Residence, he had asked for her when visiting Mrs. Bechcombe. Now it seemed to him that Fate had put in his hands the clue to the tangled mass of contradictions that Cecily had become.

Hastily thrusting his paper in his pocket he hurried after the couple. But, short as the time was since they passed him, already a queue had formed before the ticket office. As he reached it Cecily and her companion turned away and walked through the barrier. It was hopeless to think of going after them without a ticket. Anthony chafed impatiently as he waited. When at last he was free to follow them they were out of sight and he ran up to the lift just in time to hear the door close and to see the lift itself vanish slowly out of sight. For a moment he felt inclined to run down the steps and then he realized that there was nothing to be gained by such a proceeding and nothing for him to do but wait for the next lift with what patience he could. It seemed to him that he had never had to wait so long before; when at last it did come and he had raced along the passage and down the few remaining steps to the platform, it was only to find the gate slammed before him. Standing there, he had the satisfaction of seeing Cecily's face at the window of the train gliding out of the station while beside her he caught a vision of the silvery locks of her companion.

As he stood there realizing the utter futility of endeavouring to overtake Cecily now, a voice only too well known of late sounded in his ear.

"Good morning, Mr. Collyer. Too late, like myself."

He turned to find Inspector Furnival beside him. A spasm of fear shot through Tony. Was this man ubiquitous? And what was he doing here?

"Going to Mrs. Luke Bechcombe's, sir?" the inspector went on. "Mr. Steadman has just left me to go on there in his car. A family party to celebrate Mr. Aubrey Todmarsh's engagement."

"Yes, to Mrs. Phillimore," Tony assented.

The gate was thrust aside now, the inspector and Tony found themselves pushed along by the people behind. They went on the platform together, the inspector keeping closely by Tony's side.

"Wonderful man, Mr. Todmarsh," he began conversationally. "We in the police see a lot of his work. Mrs. Phillimore too, supports practically every philanthropic work in the East End. Yes, this engagement will be good news to many a poor outcast, Mr. Anthony."

Tony mechanically acquiesced. As a matter of fact mention of Aubrey Todmarsh's good works left him cold. He had no great liking for Mrs. Phillimore either, though the rich American had rather gone out of her way to be amiable to him. This morning, however, he was too much occupied in wondering what was the ulterior motive for the inspector's friendliness to have any thought to spare for his cousin's engagement. He was anxious to ascertain whether the inspector, like himself, had caught sight of Cecily Hoyle and followed her, though he could not form any idea as to the inspector's object in doing so. Still one never knew where the clues spoken of by the papers might lead the police. Thinking of Cecily as the inspector's possible objective a cold sweat broke out on Anthony's brow.

When the train came in the inspector stood aside for Anthony to enter and followed him in. The carriage was full. Anthony had an uncomfortable feeling that people were looking at him. Possibly, he thought, they were pointing him out to one another as Luke Bechcombe's nephew, the one who stood to benefit largely by the murdered man's death, still more largely at the death of the widow, were wondering possibly what he was doing in that half-hour of the day of the murder which he could only account for by saying he was wandering about looking for the Field of Rest. That the general public had at first looked upon him as suspect on this account Anthony knew, but he knew also that the discovery of the clerk Thompson's dishonesty and later on of the loss of Mrs. Carnthwacke's diamonds had been taken as clearing him to a great extent. Until the mystery surrounding the death of Luke Bechcombe had been solved, however, he recognized that he would remain a potential murderer in the eyes of at least a section of the public. Possibly, he reflected grimly, seeing him with the inspector this morning they thought he was in custody.

"Going far, inspector?" he asked at the first stopping-place.

"Same station as yourself, sir," the inspector returned affably. "Matter of fact I am going to the same house too. A message came along for Mr. Steadman just after he had started, and as it seemed to be of some importance I thought I would come after him with it myself. I am hoping to be in time to have a word with him before luncheon. Perhaps you could help me, sir."

"Well, if I can," Anthony said doubtfully. "There won't be much time to spare, though."

"Well, if I am too late I am too late," the inspector remarked philosophically. "It was just a chance. We don't seem to hear of Thompson, sir."

"We don't," Anthony assented. "And I expect he is taking care we shouldn't. You'll forgive me, inspector, but the way Thompson has managed to disappear doesn't seem to me to reflect much credit on the police."

"Ah, I know that is the sort of thing folks are saying," the inspector commented with apparent placidity. "And it is a great deal easier to say it about the police methods than to improve upon them. However, like some others, Thompson may find himself caught in time. One of our great difficulties is that so little is known about him, his friends, habits, etc. Even you don't seem able to help us there, Mr. Anthony." The inspector shot a lightning glance at the young man's unconscious face.

Anthony shook his head.

"Always was a decent sort of chap, old Thompson, or he seemed so—I always had a bit of a rag with him when I went to the office. Known him there years, of course. But, if you come to ask me about his friends, I never saw the old chap in mufti, as you might say, in my life. Still, I don't think Thompson had any hand in murdering Uncle Luke."

"I know. You have said so all along," the inspector remarked. "But, if you don't think he had anything to do with the murder, what do you think of his disappearance?"

"Suppose the old chap had been helping himself to what wasn't his, and got frightened and bolted."

"Um, yes!" The inspector stroked his chin thoughtfully. "Do you think you would recognize Thompson in the street, Mr. Anthony?"

"Should think I was a blithering idiot if I didn't," Anthony responded. "Never saw him with a hat on certainly, but a hat don't matter—it can't alter a man beyond recognition."

"Not much of a disguise, certainly," the inspector admitted, looking round him consideringly as they entered Carlsford Square. "Still, I wonder—"

Anthony came to a standstill.

"Now *I* wonder what you are getting at. Do you think I have seen Thompson anywhere?"

The inspector did not answer for a minute, then he said slowly:

"I shouldn't be surprised if a good many of us had seen him, Mr. Anthony."

Anthony stared. "Then we must be a set of fools."

"A good many of us are fools," Inspector Furnival acquiesced as they came to a standstill.

Anthony applied himself to the knocker on the door of the Bechcombes' house. There were a couple of cars in the street, one John Steadman's, the other a luxurious Daimler evidently fitted with the latest improvements.

"You will have time for your talk, old chap," said Anthony, looking at his watch as the door opened.

Somewhat to his surprise Steadman came out. The barrister for once was not looking as immaculately neat as usual. His coat was dusty and he was carrying his right arm stiffly. He held out a note to his chauffeur.

"There. It's quite close to Stepney Causeway. Get the woman to the hospital as soon as possible. Hello, inspector—a word with you."

"Have you had an accident?"

"No," responded the barrister curtly. Then with a jerk of his head in the direction of the other car, "That fellow, Mrs. Phillimore's man, isn't fit to drive a donkey cart. Nearly ran over a child just now. All we could do to get her out alive save with a broken arm, I took her to the Middlesex Hospital and now I'm sending for her mother. Mrs. Phillimore doesn't seem very helpful except in the matter of weeping. Well, so long, my boy—see you again in a minute or two."

He turned off with the inspector. Anthony went through the hall to the drawing-room where he found his father talking to Mrs. Bechcombe and a small, fair, handsomely dressed woman with brilliant blue eyes—his cousin's American fiancée, Mrs. Phillimore.

Anthony was no stranger to her. He had met her on several occasions and while admitting her undoubted charm he was conscious that somehow or other he did not quite like Mrs. Phillimore, the Butterfly, as he had named her. Apparently the feeling was not mutual, for Mrs. Phillimore always seemed to go out of the way to be gracious to her fiancé's cousin.

To-day, however, he did not receive his usual smile, and he saw that in spite of her make up she was looking pale and worried.

"Where is Aubrey?" he inquired, as he shook hands. "Got a holiday from his blessed Community to-day, I suppose?"

"Oh, yes," she returned, "He was to have brought me here, but he was sent for, I couldn't quite understand by whom. But he said he should not be long after me."

"Nor has he," interposed Mrs. Bechcombe at this juncture. "He is coming up the steps now with John Steadman."

Mrs. Phillimore's relief was apparent in her countenance. Anthony felt a touch of momentary wonder as to why his cousin's temporary absence should cause her so much apparent anxiety.

Aubrey was talking to Mr. Steadman in a quick, nervous fashion as they entered the room together.

The first glance was enough to show every one that something had seriously disturbed Aubrey Todmarsh. His face was white, his eyes were bloodshot, he was biting his lips nervously. Altogether he looked strangely unlike the enthusiastic young head of the Community of St. Philip.

Mr. Collyer was the first to speak.

"Aubrey, my dear boy, is anything the matter?"

Apparently Todmarsh only brought himself to speak with difficulty. Twice he opened his lips, but no words came. At last he said hoarsely:

"Hopkins!"

The name conveyed nothing to the majority of his hearers, only the rector of Wexbridge twisted up his face into a curious resemblance to a note of interrogation, and Mrs. Phillimore uttered a sharp little cry.

"Hopkins! Oh, Aubrey!"

"Hopkins!" he repeated. "He—he is my right hand, you know, Uncle James. I—I would have staked my life on Hopkins."

The clergyman pushed a chair up to his nephew.

"Sit down, my dear boy. What is this about Hopkins? I remember him well. Has he—?"

"He has been away for a few days' holiday. He said his sister was ill and he must go to see her. In the early hours of this morning"—Todmarsh's voice grew increasingly husky—"he was arrested with two other men breaking into Sir Thomas Wreford's house, Whistone Hall in the New Forest. I—I can't believe it!" His head fell forward on his hands.

Mrs. Phillimore drew a long breath, and for a moment nobody spoke. Then the rector said slowly:

"My dear boy, I can hardly believe this is true. Is there no possibility of a mistake? A false report or something of that kind?"

Aubrey shook his head.

"No. The telegram came from Wreford Hall Post Office—Hopkins sent it himself to me at the Community House and it was brought to me here."

"Dear, dear! I wish I could help. But you must remember, my dear Aubrey, that we workers for others must be prepared to meet trouble and disappointment, ay, even in those of whom we have felt most sure." The rector laid his hand on the young man's shoulder. "Pull yourself together, my dear Aubrey. Remember the many signal causes of thankfulness that have been granted to you. The many other lives that you have brightened and saved from shame."

"How can I tell who will be the next?" Todmarsh groaned. "I tell you, I would have staked my life on Hopkins."

"We cannot answer for our brothers, any of us," Mr. Collyer went on. "But now, my boy, you must make an effort. You must think of your Aunt Madeleine, of Mrs. Phillimore."

There was a moment's silence, then Todmarsh raised his head.

"You are right. You always do me more good than anyone else, Uncle James. But here I am keeping you all waiting. I beg your pardon, Aunt Madeleine. And after lunch there is much to be done. I must see about getting Hopkins bailed out."

"Where is Hopkins?" questioned Anthony, taking part in the conversation for the first time.

"At a place called Burchester," Aubrey answered. "I fancy it is quite a small place. Probably it is the nearest police court to Whistone Hall."

"Whistone Hall, in the New Forest, you said, didn't you?" Anthony went on. "Is it near Burford, do you know?"

He hardly knew what made him ask the question. John Steadman glanced at him sharply.

Aubrey Todmarsh turned a surprised face towards him.

"I don't know. I don't know anything about the place. And I never heard of Burford."

CHAPTER XIV

LUNCHEON, not a particularly cheerful meal, was over. Mrs. Phillimore's jewelled cigarette case lay on the table beside her, but her cigarette had gone out in its amber holder, and her eyes were furtively watching her fiancé as she chatted with Mr. Collyer, who sat opposite.

Aubrey Todmarsh had taken his uncle's advice and pulled himself together. He was talking much as usual now, but John Steadman watching him from his seat opposite thought that his face looked queer and strained. His eyes no longer seemed to see visions, but were bloodshot and weary. His high cheek-bones had the skin drawn tightly across them to-day and gave him almost a Mongolian look, his usually sleek, dark hair was ruffled across his forehead.

John Steadman had not hitherto felt particularly attracted by the young head of the Community of St. Philip. Apart from the natural contempt of the ordinary man for a conscientious objector, there always to Steadman appeared something wild and ridiculous about Todmarsh's visionary speeches and ideas. To-day, however, his sympathies were aroused by the young man's obviously very great disappointment over Hopkins's defection. He felt sorry for Mrs. Phillimore too. The poor little widow was evidently sharing her lover's depression, and, though she did her best to appear bright and cheerful, was watching him anxiously while she talked to her hostess or to Steadman himself.

It seemed to Steadman that he had never realized how protracted a meal luncheon could be until to-day, and he was on the point of making some excuse to Mrs. Bechcombe for effecting an early retreat when the parlourmaid entered the room with two cards—on one of which a few words were written—upon her silver salver.

Mrs. Bechcombe took them up with a murmured excuse. She glanced at them carelessly, then her expression changed. She looked round in indecision then turned to Steadman.

"I—I don't know what to do. That woman—"

The momentary lull in the conversation had passed; every one was talking busily. Under cover of the hum, Steadman edged himself a little nearer his hostess.

"What woman?"

For answer she handed him the larger of the two cards.

"Mrs. Cyril B. Carnthwacke," he read. He glanced at Mrs. Bechcombe. "What does this mean?"

"That woman—I have always felt certain she was responsible for Luke's death," Mrs. Bechcombe returned incoherently. "Oh, yes"—as Steadman made a movement of dissent—"if she did not actually kill him herself she took her horrid diamonds to him and let the murderer know and follow her. Oh, yes, I shall always hold her responsible. But to-day you see she—I mean he—the man says their business is important. Perhaps he has found out—something."

"What am I to do?"

"Why not ask them to come in here?" John Steadman suggested. "We are all members of the family," glancing round the room.

Mrs. Bechcombe hesitated. Aubrey Todmarsh sprang to his feet.

"I must go, Aunt Madeleine. I have to see about bail for Hopkins, and that he is legally represented. And, besides, I don't really feel that I can stand any more to-day."

His face was working as he spoke, and they all looked at him sympathetically as he hurriedly shook hands with Mrs. Bechcombe. His absorption in Hopkins's backsliding was so evidently of first consideration, rendering him oblivious even of his fiancée. As for the poor little Butterfly, her spirits, which had been gradually rising, seemed to be finally damped by this last contretemps. She raised no objection to her lover's abrupt departure, but sat silent and depressed until the Carnthwackes were ushered into the room.

One glance was enough to show John Steadman that both the American and his wife were looking strangely disturbed. They went straight up to Mrs. Bechcombe.

"I am obliged to you, ma'am, for receiving us," Mr. Cyril B. Carnthwacke began, while his wife laid her hand on Aubrey Todmarsh's vacant chair as though to steady herself.

"You said it was important," Mrs. Bechcombe's manner was distant. She did not glance at Mrs. Carnthwacke.

"So it is, ma'am, very important!" the American assented. "Sure thing that, else I wouldn't have ventured to butt in this morning. Though if I had gathered your guests were so numerous"—looking round comprehensively and making a slight courteous bow to Steadman and Collyer—"but I don't know. It is best that a thing of this importance should be settled at once."

As he spoke he was slowly removing the brown paper covering from a small parcel he had taken from his breast pocket. Watching him curiously Steadman saw to his amazement that when the contents were finally extracted they appeared to be nothing more important than the day's issue of an illustrated paper.

Cyril B. Carnthwacke spread it out. Then he looked back at Mrs. Bechcombe.

"Sure I don't want to hurt your feelings, ma'am. And it may be that some one else belonging to the house, perhaps that gent I saw down at the Yard"—with a gesture in Steadman's direction—"would just look in this picture."

Steadman stepped forward. But Mrs. Bechcombe's curiosity had been aroused. She leaned across.

"I will see it myself, please."

Cyril B. Carnthwacke laid it on the table before the astonished eyes of the company. A glance showed John Steadman that the centre print was a quite recognizable portrait of Luke Bechcombe. There were also pictures of the offices in Crow's Inn, both inside and out, an obviously fancy likeness of Thompson "the absconding manager," and of Miss Cecily Hoyle, the dead man's secretary.

Steadman half expected to find Mrs. Cyril B. Carnthwacke figuring largely, but so far as he could see there was nothing to account for that lady's excessive agitation.

She passed her handkerchief over her lips now as she sat down sideways on the chair that Tony Collyer placed for her, and he noticed that she was trembling all over and that every drop of colour seemed to have receded from her cheeks and lips. Her admirers on the variety stage would not have recognized their idol now.

Cyril B. Carnthwacke cleared a space on the table and spread out his paper carefully, smoothing out the creases with meticulous attention. Then he pointed his carefully manicured forefinger at the portrait of Luke Bechcombe in the middle.

"Would you call that a reasonably good picture of your late husband, ma'am?"

Mrs. Bechcombe drew her eyebrows together as she bent over it.

"Yes, it is—very," she said decidedly. "I should say unusually good for this class of paper. It is copied from one of the last photographs he had taken, one he sat for when we were staying with his sister in the country. You remember, James?" appealing to the rector.

Mr. Collyer smiled sadly.

"Indeed I do. We were all sitting on the lawn and that friend of Tony's, Leonard Barnes, insisted on taking us all. Poor Luke's was particularly good. Why are you asking, Mr. Carnthwacke?"

Cyril B. Carnthwacke wagged his yellow forefinger reprovingly in the direction of the rector.

"One moment, reverend sir. It may be, ma'am, that you have another portrait of your lamented husband that you could let us glimpse?"

Mrs. Bechcombe hesitated a moment and glanced nervously at John Steadman. In spite of all her preconceived notions, the American was beginning to impress her. There was something in his manner, restrained yet with a sinister undercurrent, that filled her with a sense of some hitherto unguessed at unnamable dread. At last, moving like a woman in a dream, she went across to the writing-table that stood between the two tall windows overlooking the square, and unlocking a drawer took out a cabinet photograph.

"There, that is the most recent, and I think the best we have. It was taken at Frank and Burrows, the big photographers in Baker Street."

"Allow me, ma'am." Cyril B. Carnthwacke held out his hand. He studied the photograph silently for a minute or two, laying it beside the paper and apparently comparing the two. Everybody in the room watched him with curious, interested eyes. His wife sat crouching against the table, leaning over it, her handkerchief, crushed into a hard little ball, pressed against her lips.

At last Mr. Carnthwacke laid both the portraits down together and stood up with an air of finality.

"Mrs. Cyril B. Carnthwacke, I rather fancy the moment to speak has come. Now, don't fuss yourself, but just tell these ladies and gentlemen what you have to say simply, same way as you did to me."

It seemed at first, as Mrs. Carnthwacke appeared to struggle for breath and caught convulsively at her husband's hand, that she would not be able to speak at all. But his firm clasp drew her up. The magnetism of his gaze compelled her words.

"If that is Mr. Bechcombe," she said very slowly, "that portrait, I mean, and if it is a really good likeness of him, I can only say"—she paused again and gulped something down in her throat—"that that is not the man I saw at the office, not the man to whom I gave my diamonds."

A tense silence followed this avowal—a silence that was broken at last by a moan from Mrs. Bechcombe.

"What do you mean? What does she mean?"

There was another momentary silence, broken this time by John Steadman. He had remained standing since the Carnthwackes came in, on the other side of the table. He came round towards them now.

"I think you must give us a little further explanation, Mrs. Carnthwacke," he said courteously.

Mrs. Carnthwacke was pressing the little ball that had been her handkerchief to her lips again. She turned from him with a quick gesture as though to shut him, the other guests, the whole room, out of her sight.

Cyril B. Carnthwacke laid his hand on her shoulder, heavily yet with a certain comfort in its very contact.

"That is all right, old girl. You just keep quiet and leave it to me. She can't give you any explanation. That is just all she can say," he went on in a determined, almost a hostile voice. "As soon as she saw that portrait, she knew, if that was Luke Bechcombe, that she never saw him at all on the day of his death—that she gave the diamonds to some one else, some one impersonating him."

"And who," inquired John Steadman in that quiet, lazy voice of his, "do you imagine could have impersonated Luke Bechcombe?"

The American looked him squarely in the eyes.

"Sure, that's for you legal gentlemen to decide. It is not for me to come butting in. But I can put you wise on one thing that stares one right in the face, so to speak, that I can say before I quit. I don't guess who it was who impersonated Luke Bechcombe, or where he came from or how he got right there. But there is only one man it could have been, and that is the murderer!"

CHAPTER XV

HE LOOKED from one to another as he spoke and as he met John Steadman's glance his grey eyes were as hard as steel and his thin lips were drawn and pinched together like a trap.

The horror in his hearers' faces grew and strengthened. Mrs. Bechcombe alone tried to speak; she leaned forward; in some inscrutable fashion her figure seemed to have shrunk in the last few minutes. She looked bent and worn and old, ten years older than Luke Bechcombe's handsome wife had done. Her face was white and rigid and set like a death-mask. Only her eyes, vivid, burning, looked alive. No sound came from her parted lips for a moment, then with a hoarse croak she threw up her hands to her throat as though she would tear the very words out:

"What was he like?"

Mrs. Carnthwacke cast one glance at her and began to tremble all over, then she clutched violently at her husband's hand.

"It—it is easier to say that he wasn't like that portrait," she confessed, "than to tell you what he really was like. He gave me the impression that he was a bigger man; his beard too was not neat and trimmed like that—short, stubbly and untidy-looking. His hair grew low down on his forehead. That— that man's hair," pointing with shaking fingers to the paper portrait, "grows far back. He is even a little bald. I don't know that I can point out any other differences, but the two faces are not a bit alike really. Oh, if I had only known Mr. Bechcombe by sight this dreadful thing might never have happened! She leaned back in her chair trembling violently."

Cyril B. Carnthwacke placed himself very deliberately between her and the rest of the room. His clasp of her cold hands tightened.

"Now, now, be a sensible girl!" he admonished, giving her a little shake as he spoke, yet with a very real tenderness in his gruff tones. "Quit crying and shaking and just say what you have to say as quietly as possible. Nobody can hurt you for that. And if they do try to, they will have to reckon with Cyril

B. Carnthwacke. Now, sir." He looked at John Steadman. "I guess there will be other questions you will have to ask, and it may be as well to get as much as we can over at once."

The barrister cleared his throat.

"I am afraid it will be impossible to do that here. The very first thing to be done is to inform Scotland Yard of Mrs. Carnthwacke's tragic discovery."

The American bent over his wife for a minute then drew aside.

"I guess it will have to be as the gentleman says, Mrs. Carnthwacke. Now just as plain as you can put it, and remember that Cyril B. Carnthwacke is standing beside you."

Mrs. Carnthwacke drew one of her hands from his and passed her handkerchief over her parched lips. Then she looked at Steadman.

It seemed to him that it was only by a supreme effort that she became articulate at all.

"I knocked at the door—I knew how to find it, Mr. Bechcombe had told me how on the phone. Down the passage to the right, past the clerks' office. It—it wasn't opened at once—I heard some one moving about rather stumblingly, and I was just going to knock again when the door was opened, and—" She stopped, shivering violently.

"Now then, now then!" admonished her husband. "You just quit thinking of what you are wise about now, and tell us just what took place as quickly as you can."

Mrs. Carnthwacke appeared anxious to obey him.

"He—he opened the door, the man I—I told you about. 'Come in, Mrs. Carnthwacke,' he said. I never doubted its being Mr. Bechcombe—why should I? He knew my name and my errand. Certainly I thought he had an unpleasant voice, husky—not like what I had heard when I rang him up. But he said he had a cold." She stopped again.

This time John Steadman interposed.

"Now the details of your interview you have told us before—"

"Ever so many times," she sobbed. "I can't say anything but what I told you at the inquest."

"But, now that this extraordinary new light has been thrown upon everything, do you recollect anything—anything that may help us? You know the veriest trifles sometimes provide the most successful clues—a mark on hands or face, for example."

"There wasn't any," Mrs. Cyril B. Carnthwacke answered, shaking visibly. "Or if there was, I didn't see it. But my eyesight isn't what it was, and the room was very dark, so I couldn't see very well."

"Dark! I shouldn't call it a dark room," contradicted John Steadman. "And the day was a clear one, I know."

"The room itself mightn't be dark," Mrs. Carnthwacke said obstinately. "But the blinds were drawn partly down and that heavy screen before the window nearest the desk would darken any room."

"Screen!" John Steadman repeated in a puzzled tone. "I have seen no screen near the window."

"Oh, but there is one," Mrs. Carnthwacke affirmed positively. "A big heavy screen, stamped leather it looked like. It was opened out, and stood right in front of the window nearest the desk, I remember wondering he should have it there. It blocked out so much of the light."

"What a very curious thing!" The rector interjected. "Often as I have been in to see my lamented brother-in-law, I have seen no screen. Nor have I found him with drawn blinds."

"It was not Mr. Bechcombe who was so found by Mrs. Carnthwacke," John Steadman corrected. "Of course the semi-darkness of the room was purposely contrived for one of two reasons, either that the murderer should not be recognized or that his disguise should not be suspected."

"Your two reasons seem to me to mean the same thing, my dear sir," Mr. Cyril B. Carnthwacke drawled. "But there, if that is all—"

"They do not mean the same thing at all," John Steadman retorted. "Anybody might suspect a person of being disguised. But only some one who was personally acquainted with the murderer could recognize him. Now what we have to discover is which of these reasons was operating in this case. Or whether, as is possible, we have to reckon with both."

Cyril B. Carnthwacke's sleepy-looking eyes were opened sharply for once.

"I don't understand you," he drawled. "But I can put you wise on one of your points. Mrs. Cyril B. Carnthwacke ain't acquaint with any murderers. So she could not have recognized the man."

The barrister did not appear to be impressed.

"Nobody is aware that he is acquainted with murderers until the murderer is found out," he remarked with a certain air of stubbornness. "Besides, it might not have been from Mrs. Carnthwacke that this murderer had to fear recognition. He may have been known by sight to lots of people who might possibly have encountered him on his way to and from the room. All the clerks for example, the messengers, office boys, tenants of the neighbouring offices. Other people might have come to Mr. Bechcombe's private room too. Mrs. Carnthwacke may not have been the only expected client. But one thing is certain; this new evidence of Mrs. Carnthwacke's does throw a good deal of light on the much vexed question of the time at which the murder took place."

"As how?" Cyril B. Carnthwacke's voice did not sound as though he would be easily placated.

Steadman shrugged his shoulders.

"Don't you realize that the medical testimony that Luke Bechcombe met his death soon after twelve o'clock has always been at variance with Mrs. Carnthwacke's statement that she saw him alive and well at one o'clock, and afterwards Miss Hoyle too heard some one moving about in Mr. Bechcombe's room when she returned from lunch? Now we realize that the doctors were right and that Mrs. Carnthwacke's interview took place with the murderer and that Miss Hoyle—"

The last word was interrupted by a hoarse, muffled shriek from Mrs. Carnthwacke. "I can't bear it, Cyril B. Carnthwacke. If you don't take me away I shall die."

The American looked round doubtfully, then he drew her to her feet and supported her with one arm.

"Guess there is nothing to be gained by staying any longer," he said, a certain note of truculence in his voice as he met Steadman's eyes. "Sure thing you know where to find us if you want us. Come then, little woman, we will just say good morning."

No one made any effort to detain them as they went towards the door. John Steadman followed them into the hall.

Cyril B. Carnthwacke was bending over his wife and saying something to her in a low, earnest voice. As John Steadman came up to them he turned.

"Guess that little fair lady on your side the table is some one you know well, sir?"

Steadman looked at him curiously.

"Well, fairly well. She is engaged to Luke Bechcombe's nephew. She is a compatriot of yours too—a Mrs. Phillimore."

"Gee whiz!" ejaculated the American. "And is that Mrs. Phillimore?"

"You have heard of her?" Steadman questioned.

"Reckon I have," Cyril B. Carnthwacke assented, "and seen her too. Though it don't seem to me she was called Phillimore then."

"Before she was married perhaps," suggested Steadman.

"Perhaps," drawled the American. "Anyway I have glimpsed the lady somewhere. Americans mostly know one another by sight you know," a faint twinkle in his eye as he glanced over his wife's head at the barrister.

When Steadman went back to the dining-room Mrs. Bechcombe was lying back in her chair apparently in a state of collapse. Mrs. Phillimore was bending over her, looking very little better herself. All her little butterfly airs and graces had fallen from her. Her make-up could not disguise the extreme pallor of her cheeks, the great blue eyes were full of horror and of dread. She appeared to be trying to persuade Mrs. Bechcombe to drink a glass of wine which Mr. Collyer had poured out for her.

But as Steadman re-entered the room Mrs. Bechcombe sprang up, pushing Mrs. Phillimore aside and throwing the wine over the table cloth.

"Have you let her go?"

Steadman looked at her.

"Control yourself, my dear Madeleine. Let who go?"

"That—that woman. That Mrs. Carnthwacke," Mrs. Bech-combe stormed hysterically. "I thought at least that you could see through her, that you had gone with her to make sure that she was arrested, that—"

A gleam of pity shone in Steadman's eyes as he watched her—pity that was oddly mingled with some other feeling.

"There is not the slightest ground for arresting Mrs. Car-nthwacke, Madeleine. I have told you so before. Less than ever now."

"Why do you say less than ever now?" demanded Mrs. Bechcombe. "Are you blind, John Steadman? Or are you wil-fully deceiving yourself? Do you not know that that woman was telling lies? I can see—I should think anyone with sense could see—what happened that dreadful day in Luke's office. She took her jewels there, her husband followed her—I believe he is in it too. Probably he has lost his money—Americans are like that, up one day and down the next. He didn't want it to be known that his wife was selling her jewels. Yes. Yes. That is how it must have been. He sent her with the diamonds to Luke and followed her to get them back and make it look as if Luke had been robbed. Luke resisted and he was killed in the struggle. Oh, yes, That was how it was! And this cock and bull story of theirs—" She paused, literally for breath.

Steadman looked pityingly at her wide, staring eyes, at her twitching mouth and the thin, nervous hands that never ceased clasping and unclasping themselves, working up and down.

"Madeleine, this suspicion of Mrs. Carnthwacke is becom-ing a monomania with you. It is making you unjust and cruel," he said, then waited a minute while she apparently tried to gather strength to answer him. Then he went on, "There is not the slightest ground for this new idea. Cyril B. Carnthwacke's name is one to conjure with in Wall Street as well as on the Stock Exchange here. Do you imagine that the police have ne-glected so very ordinary a precaution as an inquiry into his circumstances?"

With a desperate struggle Mrs. Bechcombe regained her power of speech.

"The police—the police are fools!" she cried passionately. "If a crime of this kind had been committed in Paris or New York, the murderer would have been discovered long ago, but in London—Scotland Yard cannot see what the merest tyro in such matters would recognize at once."

"Do you think so?" John Steadman's clean-cut, humorous mouth relaxed into a faint half-smile. "I can tell you, Madeleine, that both in New York and Paris it is recognized that our Criminal Investigation Department is the finest in the world. But your feeling towards Mrs. Carnthwacke is becoming an obsession. When the mystery surrounding Luke's death is cleared up, and somehow I do not think it will be long now before it is, I prophesy that you will repent your injustice."

"I prophesy that you will repent your folly in not listening to me," retorted Madeleine Bechcombe obstinately. "That woman was lying. Ah, you may not have thought so. It takes a woman to find a woman out. If I had my way I would have women detectives—"

"Do you suppose we haven't?" John Steadman interposed gently. "Dear Madeleine, no stone is being left unturned in our endeavours to bring Luke's murderer to justice. Have patience a little longer!"

"Patience, patience! I have no patience!" Mrs. Bechcombe pushed Steadman's outstretched hand away wrathfully and turned to Mrs. Phillimore. "Sadie, you thought the same—you said you did just now!"

In spite of her pallor Steadman fancied that the Butterfly looked considerably taken aback.

"I don't think I said quite that," she hesitated, "I don't know what to think. I feel that I can't—daren't think—anything."

"What?" Mrs. Bechcombe raised her hand.

For one moment Steadman thought she was about to strike her guest, and with some instinct of protection he stepped to the Butterfly's side.

The Butterfly visibly flinched. "I—I think I said more than I ought," she acknowledged frankly. "When you said she was telling lies, I—I didn't know what to say."

"What did you say?" Steadman inquired quietly. "Did you say anything that could be misinterpreted?"

The Butterfly raised a fragment of cambric, widely edged with real lace. Apparently it did duty as a pocket-handkerchief. She pressed it to her eyes, taking care, as Steadman noticed, not to touch her carefully pencilled eyebrows.

"I said I didn't think Mrs. Carnthwacke was telling us all she knew," she confessed. "I cannot tell what made me feel that, but I did. She—she was keeping something back, I am sure, and her husband knew that she was."

"I wonder whether you are right," said John Steadman slowly.

CHAPTER XVI

"I HEAR YOU are very busy, Aubrey, and I am very sorry to interrupt you. But I thought perhaps you would spare me a few minutes."

The head of the Confraternity of St. Philip was sitting at his writing-table apparently absorbed in some abstruse calculations. He looked up with a furrowed brow and without his usual smile as the rector of Wexbridge advanced into the room.

"I can't spare very long, Uncle James. This enforced absence of Hopkins is throwing double work on my shoulders."

"I know, I know!" assented Mr. Collyer. "You must realize how sincerely I sympathize with you, my dear Aubrey. But I bring some news that I feel sure will interest you. The police have found some of the emeralds."

"Is that so?" There was no doubting the interest in Todmarsh's voice now. "Where? And why only some? Why not all?" He sprang up as he spoke and took up a position with his back to the fire, one elbow resting on the high wooden mantelpiece. "My dear Uncle James, this is good news indeed! And I am sure we all need some!"

"We do!" assented Mr. Collyer. "As to your questions, my dear Aubrey, the police preserve a reticence that I find extremely trying. They have just told me that they have found them, not when or where. The only thing they will say is that they believe they were stolen by the Yellow Gang. It may retard developments to say much of their find now, they say.

"But how?" questioned Todmarsh.

The rector shook his head.

"I don't know. I don't know how they can even be sure that the ones they have are my emeralds. They all look alike to me. However, they seem very certain. But what I came in for now, my dear Aubrey, is to ask if you can come to Scotland Yard with me. I don't seem much good alone and Anthony went away for the week-end last night. And I do know you would be more useful in identifying the jewels than he would."

"I wonder whether I could," debated Aubrey. "Perhaps if we took a taxi and I came straight back— Stolen by the Yellow Gang, you say, Uncle James?"

"Well, the police seem to think so," Mr. Collyer assented. "But I doubt it myself. What should the Yellow Gang be doing at quiet little Wexbridge?"

Aubrey smiled in a melancholy fashion that was strangely unlike his old bright look.

"The Yellow Gang infests the whole country. They brought off a big *coup* at a country house in the north of Scotland a week or two ago. That they should be able to do so and escape unpunished shows the absolute inefficiency of the police system. The Yellow Dog, as they call him, sets the whole authority of the country at defiance. Personally I find myself up against him at every turn."

"How?" the rector questioned.

"Why, all this." Todmarsh made a comprehensive gesture with his arm that seemed to include not only the Community House but the men playing squash racquets and cricket outside. "All this is a direct challenge to the Yellow Dog. We get hold not only of those who have already gone astray, but of the potential young criminals who are his raw material, and do our best to turn them into decent members of society."

Mr. Collyer looked at him.

"But do you mean that any of your community men were ever members of the Yellow Gang?"

"Many of them—Hopkins himself and at least two more of my best workers."

"Then I should have thought it would have been a comparatively easy matter to get such information from them as would enable you to have broken up the Yellow Gang," argued Mr. Collyer shrewdly.

Todmarsh shook his head.

"One would think so on the face of it. But, as a matter of fact, not one of them has ever seen the Yellow Dog. His instructions have always reached them in some mysterious fashion and they have known nothing of the headquarters of the gang. We have never been able to get hold of anyone who knows anything of the inner workings."

"Extraordinary!" said the rector. "Still, I can't believe that they took my emeralds. With regard to your Uncle Luke, it is a very different matter. What do you think?"

"I have not had time to think lately," Aubrey Todmarsh said dully. "This terrible affair of Hopkins obsesses me, Uncle James. I cannot help thinking that l am responsible for the whole thing."

The rector looked at him pityingly.

"I know you do, my dear Aubrey. But you have described this idea of yours rightly when you call it an obsession—you are not struggling against it as you ought. No. That is not quite what I mean—you can't struggle against an idea. What I mean is that you should try to realize, as your friends do, how very much you did for Hopkins, and how entirely blameless you are in the matter of his downfall."

This was rather in the rector's best pulpit style, and the young head of the Community House of St. Philip moved his shoulders restlessly.

"You see we don't look at the matter from the same standpoint, Uncle James. I do not acknowledge that Hopkins has fallen."

Mr. Collyer stared.

"I don't understand you, my dear Aubrey."

"No," said Todmarsh, speaking very rapidly. "I don't suppose you do. But I saw Hopkins yesterday and heard his story. It made me feel both thankful and ashamed," pausing to blow his nose vigorously. "Uncle James, when you know it, I am certain you will feel as I do, that it bears the stamp of truth. Hopkins, has been working of late among some of the plague spots of the East End, and has been most marvellously successful. By some means he learned of the intended burglary at Whistone Hall, and also that one of the men engaged was one whom he had regarded as a most promising convert. He came to ask my advice, but I was out with Sadie and he couldn't reach me. I shall never cease to regret that I failed him then. In his anxiety to stop the plot he could think of no better plan than going down to Whistone himself and reasoning with the men. Only in the event of their very obstinate refusal did he intend to give the alarm. However, when he reached the scene of action, he found that operations had been begun sooner than he expected and that they had already effected an entrance. Hopkins went after them. He pleaded, he argued and just as he thought he was on the point of success he found that they were surrounded. Then, it is a moot point what he ought to have done. So conscious was he of his own integrity that the idea of making his escape never occurred to him; and, when he found himself arrested with the others, he thought he only had to explain matters. His amazement when he was disbelieved was pathetic—so pathetic that I lost my own composure when listening to him."

"Um!" The rector raised his eyebrows. "But, my dear Aubrey, in the account in the papers it said that he was evidently the ringleader and that he was caught red-handed with a revolver in his possession."

Aubrey cast a strange glance at his uncle from beneath his lowered eyelids.

"The papers will say anything, Uncle James. Though as a matter of fact Hopkins had a revolver. He had just persuaded one of the more reckless men to give it up to him. Uncle James, in another minute Hopkins believes and I believe he would have got them safely out of the house. He has wonderful powers of persuasion."

Mr. Collyer did not speak. Remembering Hopkins's gloomy countenance and pleasing habit of opening and shutting his mouth silently, he was inclined to think that Hopkins's powers of persuasion if effective must be little short of marvellous. His defence too did not strike him in the same light as it apparently did Aubrey. He was inclined to think it as lame a tale as he had ever heard.

Presently Todmarsh resumed.

"Keith and Swinnerton are taking up the case. They are the keenest solicitors I know and they are briefing Arnold Wynter for the defence. Oh, we shall get Hopkins off all right at the assizes. But it is the thought of what the poor old chap is going through now, locked up there alone and knowing how the world is misjudging him that bowls me over." He stopped and blew his nose again.

"But, my dear boy, you cannot be held responsible for that. And I am certain that nobody could have done more for him than you, if as you say he is to be defended by Arnold Wynter. But I am afraid, my dear Aubrey, that it is likely to prove an expensive matter for you, for it is absurd to suppose that Hopkins—"

"I shall not allow Hopkins to pay a penny if it costs the last one I possess," Todmarsh interrupted, a dull shade of red streaking his sallow face as he spoke. "You can have no idea what Hopkins was to me. To speak to a crowd of all sorts of men, and to have Hopkins sitting in the front with his wonderful responsive face was like an inspiration. You who preach must know what I mean."

"Um! Well, I hope you may soon have him back," the rector said slowly.

Todmarsh smiled for the first time that day.

"Uncle James, I do not believe you appreciate my poor Hopkins any more than those people at Burchester do."

Mr. Collyer twisted himself about impatiently.

"I really did not know Hopkins at all, Aubrey. I did not take to him, I must confess. Burchester? I did not think that was the name of the place where he was taken."

"Oh, of course he was taken at Whistone. I suppose Burchester was the nearest gaol," Aubrey said carelessly. Then with a little more appearance of interest, "Why, do you know Burchester, Uncle James?"

Mr. Collyer shook his head.

"No. My interest has always lain in the North or the Midlands. But Mr. Steadman has got Tony the offer of a post near there. He went down somewhere there the other day with Inspector Furnival. I thought them rather mysterious about it, I must say. I should have enjoyed the ride, for they went down in the car, and it was a lovely day. But I soon found that they did not want a companion."

"Business, perhaps," Todmarsh suggested. His face was dull and uninterested now: the enthusiasm so remarkable when he spoke of Hopkins had died out.

"Oh, I shouldn't think so!" Mr. Collyer dissented. "What connection could there be between your Uncle Luke's death and a quiet little country town such as Burchester? No, Burford was the place they went to—has been described to me to be."

"Oh, well, as we don't know who the murderer was, or where he came from, he may just as well have been connected with Burford as anywhere else. Uncle James, who do you think killed Uncle Luke?"

"My dear boy!" The sudden question seemed to embarrass the rector. He took off his pince-nez and rubbed them, replacing them with fingers that visibly trembled. "How can we tell? How can any of us hazard an opinion? Heaven forbid that I should judge any man! The only idea I have formed on the subject can hardly be called original since I know it is shared by your Aunt Madeleine, who has been voicing it much more vehemently than I should ever do."

"Aunt Madeleine!" Todmarsh looked up quickly. "What does she say! I have not seen her since the interrupted luncheon party. I have called, but she was out. But what can she know?"

"She does not know anything, of course." The rector hesitated, his face looking troubled and disturbed. "But like myself, dear Aubrey, she was listening very intently to Mrs. Carnthwacke. I may say that my attention was fixed entirely on the lady and it may be that my profession makes me particularly critical and observant. I dare say you have noticed that it does?"

"Naturally!" Todmarsh assented. But as he spoke the fingers of his right hand clenched themselves with a quick involuntary movement of impatience. Observant as Mr. Collyer had just proclaimed himself to be he did not notice how his nephew's fingers tightened until the knuckles shone white beneath the skin.

"Yes. We parsons so often have to form our own judgments on men and women quite independently of all external things," the Rev. James Collyer prattled on, while only something in the restrained immobility of his nephew's attitude might have made a close observer guess at impatience resolutely held in check. "Therefore, as I said, I watched Mrs. Carnthwacke very closely, and formed the opinion—the very strong opinion that, though she was undoubtedly speaking the truth as far as she went, she was not telling us the whole truth. So far I agree with your Aunt Madeleine. But I feel sure that she recognized—I will not say the murderer, the man who was impersonating your Uncle Luke, but I think that she saw something that might give us a clue to him, put the police on his track. And in fact I know that this opinion is that of Mr. Steadman if not of the police. It is from Mrs. Carnthwacke that the identification of the murderer will come, I feel sure. Still, I may be wrong. You, my dear boy—"

A sharp cry from Todmarsh interrupted him. The penknife with which he had been sharpening a pencil had slipped, inflicting for so slight a thing quite a deep gash in his wrist. The blood spurted out.

His uncle looked at him aghast.

"My dear Aubrey! You must have cut an artery. What shall we do? A doctor—"

Todmarsh wrapped his handkerchief hurriedly round his wrist and tied it. He held one end out to the clergyman.

"Pull as tight as you can, I must have cut a vein. Excuse me, Uncle James. I will just get Johnson to make a tourniquet. He is as good as a doctor. I must apologize for making such a mess. If you will just have a look at the papers; you will find them over there," jerking his head in the direction of the table at which he had been writing when his uncle came in. "I won't be a minute, and then I shall be quite at your service." He hurried out of the room.

Mr. Collyer walked over to the writing-table and took up a paper. But he was feeling too restless and excited to read. Events were moving too quickly for the rector of Wexbridge. Hitherto, except for his anxiety over Tony, his had been a calmly ordered life. Now, with his journey to London and subsequent discovery of the loss of the emeralds, he had been plunged into a veritable vortex of horror and bewilderment. Two things alone he held to through all: his faith in Heaven and his faith in Tony. Whoever else might distrust Tony Collyer and think that he had had far more opportunities than anyone else in the world of possessing himself of the emeralds, his father had never doubted him. He had seen a gleam of pity in the eyes of the detective who had brought him the news that the emeralds had been traced, which had told him who was suspected of having taken them. He was thinking of it now, and asking himself for the hundredth time who the culprit could have been, as at last he seated himself in Todmarsh's chair and reached out for a paper which lay folded at the back of the inkstand. But he drew back with an exclamation of distaste.

There was blood on the writing-table, on the inkstand, on the cover of the blotting-book. The first spurt from Aubrey's wrist had apparently gone right over them all. The orderly soul of the rector was revolted. He opened the blotting-book and tearing out a sheet proceeded to mop up the blood. He tore up the blotting-paper and took up each spot separately. But when the paper was finished there were still spots of blood scattered over the writing-table. Turning back to the blotting-book he tore out another sheet.

"Wonderful!" he said to himself. "It is wonderful that so slight a thing, a mere slip of the knife, should inflict so much damage. I should not have thought it possible."

And as he voiced his thoughts, his long, lean fingers were pulling out bits of pink blotting-paper and dabbing them down on the drops of scarlet blood, then rolling them up into damp red pellets and dropping them into the waste-paper-basket. Then all at once a strange thing happened. As his fingers moved swiftly, mechanically over their work, his gaze went back to the open blotter.

There on the leaf, as it had lain beneath the paper he had torn out, was a piece of paper. Just a very ordinary piece of paper with a few lines in a woman's clear writing scrawled across it.

The Rev. James Collyer read them over with no particular intention of doing so, then as his brain slowly took in the sense of what he read his fingers stopped working. He never knew how long he stood there, staring at that paper, while his lips moved noiselessly, while every drop of colour drained slowly from his face and the stark horror in his eyes deepened. At last he moved. The bits of paper had dropped from his hands and lay in an untidy heap on the table. With a quick, furtive gesture he caught up the piece of paper, and moving quickly he thrust it between the bars of the grate into the sluggish fire inside. It burst into a flame and the rector stood there and watched it burn. When nothing was left but bits of greyish ash he turned away and put up his hands to his forehead. It was wet—great drops of sweat were rolling into his eyes. A few minutes later a messenger, one of the Confraternity, coming down from the room of the Head, found the Rev. James Collyer letting himself out at the front door.

"Mr. Todmarsh desired me to say, sir, that the cut is much deeper than he thought. We have sent for the doctor, and it may be some time before he is ready to come to you. But, if you will wait, he will be very pleased—"

"No, no! I won't wait," said the rector thickly, in tones that none of his parishioners would have recognized as his. "He—he—my business is not important."

A wild idea that of a certainty the clergyman had been drinking shot through the brain of Todmarsh's messenger, as he stood at the open door watching the tall, lean figure of the clergyman making its way along the pavement and saw it sway more than once from side to side.

CHAPTER XVII

"You IDENTIFY these emeralds as yours?"

"No, I can't. I don't see how anybody could identify unset stones," said the rector wearily.

"H'm!" Inspector Furnival stopped, nonplussed. "But these exactly answer to the description that has been circulated, that you yourself supplied to the police."

Mr. Collyer's face looked drawn and grey as he turned the stones over with the tip of his finger.

"Yes, yes! But emeralds look the same, and these seem to fit in their settings. I—I really can't say anything more definite. I thought mine were larger."

The inspector swept the emeralds in their wadded box into a drawer.

"Well, there is no more to be said. We shall have to rely on expert evidence as to identity. Unless—wouldn't it be possible that young Mr. Anthony might be able to help us?"

"I should think it extremely unlikely," said Tony's father decisively. "In fact I am sure it is impossible. I always took charge of the emeralds. Tony had not seen them for years before their disappearance."

The inspector pushed the drawer to and locked it.

"That is all that can be done this afternoon, then. I quite understood that you were prepared to be definite with regard to the identification or I would not have troubled you."

"I am sorry!" the rector said hesitatingly. "Then—then there is nothing more?"

"Nothing more!" the inspector responded curtly.

He and John Steadman were standing against the writing-table, in one drawer of which the emeralds had been deposited. Mr. Collyer paused a moment near the door and looked at them doubtfully. Once he opened his mouth as if to speak, then apparently changing his mind closed it again dumbly.

When the sound of his footsteps had died away on the stone passage outside, Steadman glanced across at the inspector.

"Unsatisfactory, isn't it?"

"Very," the inspector returned shortly. "Thank you, sir." He took a cigarette from the case Steadman held out to him. "Well, fortunately, the cross was exhibited at the Great Exhibition in '51, so I think we shall be able, with the description then given and the expert evidence of to-day, to reconstruct the cross and make sure about the emeralds. But what can be wrong with the rector?"

"Is anything wrong with him?" Steadman questioned in his turn as he lighted a match.

"He looks like a man who has had some sort of a shock," the inspector pursued. "I wonder if it means that Mr. Tony—"

"Tony had nothing to do with the loss of the emeralds," John Steadman said in his most decided tones. "You can put that out of your mind." The inspector paced the narrow confines of his office in Scotland Yard two or three times before he made any rejoinder. Then as he cast a lightning glance at Steadman he said tentatively:

"I have sometimes wondered what Mrs. Collyer is like."

"Not the sort of woman to substitute paste for her own emeralds," Steadman said ironically. "No use. You will have to look farther afield, inspector."

"I am half inclined to put it down to the Yellow Gang," the inspector said doubtfully. "But it differs in several particulars from the work of the Yellow Dog, notably the substitution of the paste. But—well, there may have been reasons."

Still his brow was puckered in a frown as he turned to his notebook.

"Now, Mr. Steadman, I have some one else for you to interview." He sounded his bell sharply as he spoke. "Show Mr. Brunton in as soon as he comes," he said to the policeman who appeared in answer.

"He is waiting, sir."

"Oh, good! Let him come in. This Brunton, Mr. Steadman, is one of the late Mr. Bechcombe's younger clerks. I do not know whether you knew him."

John Steadman shook his head.

"No, I have no recollection of any of the clerks but Thompson."

"He is with Carrington and Cleaver, who are carrying on Mr. Bechcombe's clients until, if ever, some one takes on the practice," pursued the inspector. "And I should like you to hear a story he brought to me this morning."

Almost as the last word left his lips, the door opened again and a lanky, sandy-haired youth was shown in.

The inspector stepped forward.

"Good afternoon, Mr. Brunton. Now I want you just to repeat to this gentleman, Mr. Steadman, what you told me this morning."

Mr. Brunton coughed nervously.

"I thought I did right in coming to you."

"Certainly you did," the inspector reassured him. "Your evidence is most important. Now, from the beginning, please, Mr. Brunton."

"Well, it was last night. I left the office early because I had an errand to do for Mr. Carrington," the youth began. He kept his eyes fixed on the inspector—not once did he glance in Steadman's direction. His hands twisted themselves nervously together. "It took me some time longer than I expected and it was getting late when I started home. You will remember perhaps, inspector, that there was a bit of a fog here, but on the other side of the river where I had to go it was much worse, and the farther I went the denser it became. I got out of the bus at the Elephant, which is not far from my rooms, you know." He paused.

"I know. Go on, please."

"Well, I had to walk from there—there's no bus goes anywhere near. The fog was getting dangerous by then. You couldn't see your hand before your face, as the saying is. I know the way well enough in the daylight, but in a fog things look so different. It is a regular network of small streets behind there, you know, and one seemed just like the other. I lost my bearings and began to wonder how I was going to get home. There were no passers-by—I seemed to be the only living creature out—and I was just making up my mind to ring the bell at one of the houses and see if anyone could direct me or help me at all, when a strange thing happened; though I hadn't known there was anyone about, a voice spoke out of the fog close beside me as it seemed. 'It is the only thing to be done—you can't make a mistake.' The rejoinder came in a woman's voice. 'But I can't do it. It wouldn't be safe. They might follow me. You must shake them off if you have any affection for me.' The man's voice said again, 'If you have any thought for the future you will get it for me. Would you like to see me in prison and worse? Would you like to be pointed at as—' That was all I heard, sir." Mr. Brunton turned himself from Mr. Steadman to the inspector, then back again to Steadman. "I was listening for all I was worth, trying not to miss a word, when that horrid fog got down my throat and tickled me, and before I could help myself I had given a great sneeze. There was a sharp exclamation, and I thought I caught the sound of footsteps, deadened by the fog. That was all I could hear, sir—every word," looking from one to the other.

"Very good, Mr. Brunton," the inspector said as he stopped. "And now just you tell Mr. Steadman why you listened—why you were anxious to hear."

The youth glanced at Steadman in a scared fashion. "I—I listened, sir, because I recognized the voices, one voice at least for certain—the man's. It was Mr. Amos Thompson's, the late Mr. Bechcombe's managing clerk."

John Steadman raised his eyebrows. "You are sure?"

"Quite certain, as certain as I could be of anything," asseverated Brunton. "I knew Mr. Thompson's voice too well to make any mistake, sir. I had good reason to, for he was for ever nagging at me when I was at Mr. Bechcombe's. There wouldn't be one of us clerks who wouldn't recognize Mr. Thompson's voice."

"Is that so?" Mr. Steadman raised his eyebrows again. "And the other voice—the woman's?"

Mr. Brunton fidgeted. "I wasn't so certain of that, sir. I hadn't had so many opportunities of hearing it, you see. But it sounded like Miss Hoyle's—Mr. Bechcombe's secretary. I heard it at the inquest."

"I understand you saw absolutely nothing to show that you were right in either surmisal," John Steadman said, his face showing none of the surprise he felt at hearing Cecily's name.

"Nothing—nothing at all!" Mr. Brunton confirmed. "But, if I ever heard it on earth, it was Mr. Thompson's voice I heard then. And I don't think—I really don't think I was wrong in taking the other for Miss Hoyle's, as I say I heard it at the inquest, and I took particular notice of it."

"Um!" John Steadman stroked his nose meditatively. "How long had you been in Mr. Bechcombe's office, Mr. Brunton?"

Mr. Brunton hesitated a moment.

"Five years, sir. I began as office boy to—to gain experience, you know. I was fourteen then and I am nineteen now."

"No more?" said Mr. Steadman approvingly.

Mr. Brunton, who had looked distinctly depressed at the mention of his lowly beginning, began to perk up.

"And Mr. Thompson has been managing clerk all the time," the barrister went on. "No, I don't think you could very well mistake his voice. But Miss Hoyle had only been a short time with Mr. Bechcombe, you say—you had not seen much of her? At the office, I mean, not the inquest."

"Not much, sir. Because she never came into our office. She always went into her own by the door next Mr. Bechcombe's room. Most of the clerks really did not know her by sight at all, let alone recognize her voice. But it was part of my job to go into Mr. Bechcombe's room with the midday mail, and more often than not she would be there taking down Mr. Bechcombe's instructions in shorthand. Very often too he would make her repeat the last sentence he had given her before he broke off. It was in that way I got to know her voice a little, for I never spoke to her beyond passing the time of day if we met accidentally, for she was always one that kept herself to herself," Mr. Brunton concluded, quite out of breath with his long speech.

John Steadman nodded.

"Yes, you would have a fair chance of becoming acquainted with her voice that way. Better, I think, than at the inquest. The words that you overheard, I take it you reported as accurately as possible."

"Oh, yes, sir." Mr. Brunton moved restlessly from one leg to the other. "You see, I recognized Mr. Thompson's voice with the first words and, knowing how important it was that the police should find him, I listened for all I was worth."

"I take it from the words you have reported that Thompson had some hold over the girl?" Mr. Steadman pursued. "Had you previously had any idea of any connection between them?"

Mr. Brunton shook his head in emphatic negative.

"Not the least, sir. If you had asked me I shouldn't have thought Mr. Thompson would have known Miss Hoyle if he had met her."

"And yet Miss Hoyle's portrait was found in Thompson's room," Mr. Steadman said very deliberately. "One might say the only thing that was found there in fact."

"Was it, indeed, sir?" Young Brunton looked dumbfounded. "Well, if they were friends, there was none of us in the office suspected it," he finished.

"And that was rather remarkable among such a lot of young men as there were at Luke Bechcombe's, remarked John Steadman. "They generally have their eyes open to everything. Now as to where they were when you overheard them. You do not think you could recognize the place again?"

"I am afraid not, sir. You see, the fog alters everything so. I seemed to have been wandering about for hours when I heard Thompson's voice, and it appeared to me that I walked about for hours afterwards before the fog lifted. When it did I was quite near home, but I haven't the least idea whether it meant that I had been sort of walking round about in a circle, or whether I had been further afield."

"Anyway we shall have all that neighbourhood combed out," interposed Inspector Furnival. "If Mr. Thompson is in hiding anywhere there I think that we may take it his capture is only a matter of time. I am much obliged to you, Mr. Brunton. I will let you know in good time when your evidence is likely to be required."

"Thank you, sir." With an awkward circular bow intended to include both men Mr. Brunton took his departure.

The inspector shut the door behind him.

"What do you think of that?"

"I was surprised," Steadman answered. "Surprised that they were not more careful," he went on. "There is nothing more unsafe than talking of one's private affairs abroad in a fog. Buses and trains are child's play to a fog."

The inspector smiled.

"Oh, well, don't criminals always overlook something? Which reminds me—this came an hour ago."

He handed a piece of paper to Steadman. The latter regarded it doubtfully. It had evidently been torn out of a notebook, and looked as though it had passed through several hands, for it was dirty and thumb-marked and frayed at the edges as though it had been carried about in some one's pocket. Across one corner of it were scrawled some letters in pencil. He put up his pince-nez and looked at it more closely. The few words scrawled across it were very irregularly and illegibly written in printed characters. After scrutinizing it for some time through his glasses Steadman made them out to be: "Wednesday night, 21 Burlase Street, Limehouse. Chink-a-pin."

"What is to take place at 21 Burlase Street on Wednesday night?" he questioned as he laid it down.

"A meeting of the Yellow Gang, and I hope the capture of the Yellow Dog," the inspector answered pithily and optimistically.

"And this comes from—?" Steadman went on, tapping the paper with his eyeglasses.

"One of the Gang. It is pretty safe to assume that sooner or later there will be an informer."

"You will be there?"

The inspector nodded. "But we are taking no risks. The informer may be false to both sides. The house will be surrounded. Whole squads of men are being drafted to the neighbourhood, a few at a time, to-day. I fancy we shall corner the

Yellow Dog at last. With this password I shall certainly get into the house and arrest the Yellow Dog. Then at the sound of the whistle the house will be rushed."

"I will come with you," said John Steadman. "I fancy an interview with the Yellow Dog may be extraordinarily interesting."

CHAPTER XVIII

"I CANNOT LIVE without you, Cecily. This bogy of yours shall not separate us. Surely my love is strong enough to help you to bear whatever the future can hold. Till the last hour of my life I shall be your devoted lover, Tony."

A momentary sensation of warmth and light ran through Cecily's cold frame as she read the impassioned sentences. Very resolutely she had put Anthony Collyer's love from her. She had told herself that she was a moral leper set far apart from all thoughts of love or marriage. It was not in the nature of a mortal girl to read such words and remain unmoved.

She was sitting at her table in Madeleine Bechcombe's private sitting-room. As she finished reading her letter she made a movement as though to tuck it in the breast of her gown, then, changing her mind, she tossed it into the very centre of the bright fire on the hearth.

At this same moment Mrs. Bechcombe came into the room. She glanced curiously at the paper just bursting into momentary flame.

"I wish you would not burn papers here, Miss Hoyle," she said fretfully. "It does litter up the hearth so and there is a waste-paper-basket over there."

"I am very sorry, I quite forgot," Cecily said penitently. "Mrs. Bechcombe, this is a letter from Lady Chard-Greene. She wants you to go to them for a week-end, the 3rd—or the 10th if that would suit you better."

"They will neither of them suit me at all," Mrs. Bechcombe said decisively. "You can tell her so. I wonder whether she would feel inclined to go about week-ending if her husband had been cruelly murdered?"

Cecily shivered as she took up the next letter.

"This is from Colonel Chalmers. He has just returned to England, and—"

"I don't care what he has done," Mrs. Bechcombe interrupted. "I really only came in to tell you that I do not feel well enough to attend to letters or anything else this morning. So you need not stay—it will give you a little more time to yourself."

"Thank you very much." Cecily hesitated. "But can I not do anything for you, Mrs. Bechcombe? Perhaps if your head is bad again, you might let me read to you."

"No, no! I could not stand it. It would drive me mad," Mrs. Bechcombe responded, with the irritability that was becoming habitual with her. "No, when I feel like this, I must be alone. I mean it."

Cecily was nothing loath to leave her work and go out into the air. It was a lovely day. The sky was blue as Londoners seldom see it, tiny fleecy clouds of white just floating across it emphasized the depth of colour. Spring seemed to be calling to the youth in her to come into the country and rejoice with the new life that was springing into being everywhere. And Cecily must go to Burford. She had intended to go when her day's work was over, but now she could start at once. Like a great black thundercloud over the brightness of the day the thought of Burford and of her errand there overhung everything. She made up her mind to take the first train down and get the thing over.

She made her way to the station at once. Trains to Burford ran fairly frequently and she had not long to wait. She occupied the time by getting a cup of tea and a bun in the refreshment room, but though she had had nothing but a piece of dry toast for her breakfast she could not eat. She only crumbled the bun, one of the station variety, while she drank the tea thirstily. She did not notice that a shabbily dressed small boy who had been loitering outside the house in Carlsford Square had dogged her steps to the station and now sat reading a dilapidated copy of "Tit-Bits" outside on the seat nearest the refreshment room.

The station for Burford was soon reached. Cecily, who was fond of walking, made up her mind to walk to Rose Cottage instead of taking the shabby one-horse cab that stood outside the station, but she was out of practice and she was distinctly tired when she reached her destination.

The housekeeper received her with evident amazement.

"Miss Hoyle! Well, I never! And I have been expecting your pa down every day this past week!"

"Well, I have come instead, you see. I hope I am not a dreadful disappointment," Cecily said, calling up a smile with an effort as she shook hands. She did not know much of Mrs. Wye and what little she did know she did not much like, but she knew that the woman had been a long time with her father and felt that it behoved her to make herself pleasant.

The housekeeper held open the sitting-room door and Cecily walked in and sat down with an air of relief.

"My father has been ill, Mrs. Wye. That is why he has not been down here lately. He is much better now and I am hoping to take him to the sea soon to convalesce. In the meantime he wants some papers from the desk in his bedroom and I have come to fetch them."

"I am very sorry to hear Hoyle has been ill, miss," and the woman really did look concerned. "We have had several people here asking after him of late and there is a lot of letters. But I never know where to forward them. I take it Mr. Hoyle will have been in a nursing-home, miss?"

"Er—oh, yes." Cecily began to feel that even this woman might want to know too much. "Perhaps you would get me a cup of tea, Mrs. Wye," she went on. "I hadn't time for lunch before I started and though I had some tea at the station it wasn't up to much. It never is at stations, somehow."

"You are right there, miss," Mrs. Wye agreed. "And is the master out of the nursing-home now, might I ask, miss?"

"Oh, yes. He is with friends," Cecily said vaguely. Her colour deepened as she spoke.

The housekeeper's little eyes watched her curiously.

"Perhaps you would give me an address I could forward the letters to, miss."

"Oh, of course!" Cecily got up. She could not sit here to be badgered by this woman who she began to feel was inimical to her.

"I will get the things my father wants," she went on. "For I must catch an early train back. I do not want to be away longer than necessary."

She went upstairs to the front bedroom which she knew to be her father's. It was spotlessly clean and tidy, but it had the bare look of a room that has been unoccupied for a long time. The desk stood on a small table near the window. Cecily had the key, and the envelope for which she had come down was lying just at the top. A long rather thin envelope inscribed 11260. Doubled up it just fitted into Cecily's handbag. She pushed it in and shut it with a snap. Then she sat down in a basket-work chair near the open window. She really could not start back without some rest, and she was not anxious to encounter Mrs. Wye again. As she sat there her thoughts went back to Tony's letter; and though she told herself that nothing could come of it the recollection of his love seemed to fall like sunshine over her, cheering and enveloping her.

She was feeling more herself when her eyes, mechanically straying past the little garden with its ordered paths and flower-beds fixed themselves on the road that ran beyond. Suddenly they focused themselves upon an object nearly opposite the cottage gate. Slowly the colour ebbed from her cheeks and lips, her eyes grew wide and frightened, the hands lying on her lap began to twitch and twine themselves nervously together.

Yet at first sight there seemed nothing in the road outside to account for her agitation—just a heap of broken stones and sitting by it a worn, tired-looking old tramp. Just a very ordinary-looking old man. Yet Cecily got up, and, craning forward while keeping herself in the shadow as much as possible, tried to view him from every possible angle. Surely, surely, she said to herself, it could not be the very same old man to whom she had seen John Steadman give a penny outside the house in Carlsford Square only that very morning! Yet try to persuade herself that it could not be the same as she might, she knew from the first moment beyond the possibility of a doubt that there was no mistake. And that could mean only one thing, that she was being followed, that they suspected—what? She began to shiver all over. Then one idea seemed to take possession of her. Almost she could have fancied it had been whispered in her ear by some outside unseen agency. She must get back to town without delay, by the very next train, she must take that mysterious envelope to its destination at once. She ran downstairs. Mrs. Wye was laying the table.

"I thought maybe you would relish a dish of ham and eggs. Butcher's meat is a thing we can't come at out here at the end of the week, not unless it is ordered beforehand."

"Oh, no, no! Please don't trouble to cook anything. I will just have a bit of bread and butter. Indeed I would rather," Cecily protested. "I find I must get back again as quickly as possible, I have forgotten something in town."

She sat down and drawing the plate of brown bread and butter towards her managed to eat a piece while she drank a cup of the strong tea Mrs. Wye poured out for her.

"It isn't any use your hurrying," the housekeeper babbled on. "You will have plenty of time to make a good meal and walk slowly to the station and still have time to spare, before eight o'clock."

"Ah, but I want to get the half-past six," Cecily said quickly. "I shall have time if I start at once, I think."

"You might, but then again you might not," Mrs. Wye said in a disappointed tone. The hour's gossip to which she had been looking forward was apparently not coming off. "You would save a few minutes by taking the footpath at the back," she added honestly. "You cut off a good bit beside Burford Parish Church that way."

The back! Cecily's heart gave a great throb. Would she be able to escape that watcher in the front after all?

"Do you mean at the back of this cottage?" she questioned.

"Dear me, yes, miss. It is a favourite walk of the poor master's. If you go out of the front you just go round the house. Or you can get on to the path by our back door and the little gate behind we use for bringing in coal and such-like."

"I will go by the back, please," Cecily said, standing up. "No, thank you, Mrs. Wye, I really can't eat any more. And I will write and let you know how my father is in a day or two."

She made her escape from the loquacious housekeeper with a little more difficulty, and sped quickly on to the path pointed out to her, clutching the precious handbag tightly to her side. She almost ran along the footpath in her anxiety to reach the station and was delighted to find herself there with a quarter of an hour to spare. She got her ticket and then ensconced herself in the waiting-room in a corner so that she could watch the approach to the station and find out whether the old beggar was on her track.

As soon as the train was signalled she went out on to the platform, and managed to get a seat in an empty carriage. It did not remain empty long, however. There were more people waiting for the train than she had expected. Evidently the 6.30, slow though it might be, was popular in Burford. The carriage, a corridor one, was soon full. Cecily took her seat by the window, clutching her handbag closely to her, and winding the cord tightly round her wrist. Opposite to her was a young, smart-looking man, who showed a desire to get the window to her liking which was distinctly flattering. Next to him sat a young woman, very pale and delicate-looking. Beyond her again was an elderly woman apparently of the respectable lodging house keeper type. The other seats were occupied by a couple of working men, one with his bag of tools on his shoulder. Cecily, after one look round, decided that she was certainly safe here. She had brought a pocket edition of Keats's poems with her, and she took it out now and, opening the book at "Isabella and the Pot of Basil," was soon deep in it.

The man opposite was reading, the old lady beside him was sleeping, the two working men were staring at the flying landscape with uninterested, lack-lustre eyes, half open mouths and one hand planted on each knee. Cecily after her unwonted exercise in the open air felt inclined to sleep herself, but she remembered the contents of her bag and resolutely resisted the inclination of her eyelids to droop. Still she was feeling pleasantly drowsy when they ran into the long tunnel between

Rushleigh and Fairford. The man opposite her put down his paper and leaned across her to draw up the window with a murmured "Excuse me."

At the same moment the light went out. There was a chorus of exclamations, a shriek from the old lady beside Cecily, something very like a swear word from the man opposite. In a trice he had lighted a match and held it up. "It is not much of a light," he said apologetically, "but it is better than nothing and I have plenty to last to the end of the tunnel."

Then he uttered a sharp exclamation. Cecily's eyes followed his. She saw that the old lady next her had slipped sideways, the pretty apple colour in her cheeks had faded, that the pendulous cheeks had become a sickly indefinite grey. The man in the corner dropped his match and lighted another. He moved up the seat and struck another.

"She has fainted," he announced. "In itself that is not serious, but I am a doctor and I should say she has heart trouble. She certainly ought not to travel alone."

Already they were getting through the tunnel. Cecily felt the old lady lurch against her and lie like a dead weight against her arm. The girl put out her other hand and held the helpless form tightly. As the light spread the doctor leaned over and felt the woman's pulse.

"She must be laid flat," he said briefly. "Will you help me?" He beckoned to the man at the other end, and between them they raised the woman, and laid her down. Cecily unfastened a scarf that was twisted tightly round the flabby neck. The doctor's quick, capable fingers produced a pair of scissors from a case and cut down the woollen jumper in front, then from a handbag he produced a tiny phial. From this he poured just one drop into the poor woman's mouth, while Cecily by his directions fanned her vigorously with a sheet of newspaper. By and by they were rewarded by signs of returning consciousness, and presently the patient opened her eyes and gazed round questioningly at the strange faces. Then she began to sit up and try to pull her jumper together with shaking fingers.

"Did I faint?" she asked tremulously. "I know it all went dark, and then I don't remember any more."

"Don't try!" advised the doctor, "just rest as long as you can. I think we can manage a pillow for you." He disposed his bag and rug behind her so that she was propped up against the end of the carriage.

As she watched him fix the handbag, Cecily was suddenly reminded of her own bag with its precious contents. With a certain prevision of evil she clapped her free hand on her wrist. The bag was gone! She remembered that it had been in her way when she began to help with the invalid—then she could remember no more. Withdrawing her hand from the sick woman's grasp, she began to search feverishly among the newspapers and various odds and ends that were strewn all over the compartment. The doctor looked at her.

"You have lost something? Your bag? Oh, now where did I see it? Oh, I remember—you put it down here." He produced it from the side of his patient, from between her and the wood of the compartment, and handed it to her.

Cecily almost snatched it from him. How had she come to let it fall, she asked herself passionately. But had she dropped it or had it been taken from her? She fumbled with the clasp with fingers that were numb with fear. Yes, yes! There it was, that mysterious packet, just as she had placed it, and with a sigh of relief she sat down again and leaned back.

There was little more to be done for the woman who was ill. She lay quietly in her seat until they ran into the London terminus. Then Cecily leaned forward.

"Will your friends meet you?" she asked gently. "Or can I help you?"

The sick woman did not open her eyes.

"I shall be met, thank you. Thank you all so much."

Quite a crowd of porters, apparently beckoned by the guard, appeared at the door. The doctor smiled as he stood aside for Cecily.

"You have been a most capable assistant."

"Thank you!" Cecily gave him a cold little smile of farewell as she sprang out.

She hesitated a moment outside the station, then she beckoned to a passing taxi and gave her address at the Hobart Residence. She was taking no further risks, and her hand held the handbag firmly with its precious contents intact inside until it had been safely locked up in her desk.

Meanwhile another taxi had flashed out of the station and bowled off swiftly in the opposite direction to that which she had taken. In it were seated side by side the woman who had been ill in the train, now marvellously recovered, and the smart young doctor, while opposite to them there lounged one of the working men who had been sitting at the other end of the compartment.

Half an hour later, Inspector Furnival, busily writing at his desk in his room at Scotland Yard, looked up sharply as there was a tap at the door.

"Come in!"

The door opened to admit a man who bore a strong resemblance to the young doctor of the train, though in some subtle fashion a curious metamorphosis seemed to have overtaken him. To Cecily he had seemed to be all doctor—now, he looked to even a casual observer all policeman as he saluted his superior.

The inspector glanced at him.

"Any luck, Masterman?"

For answer Masterman held out a piece of paper on which a few words were scrawled.

The inspector drew his brows together over it.

"Samuel Horsingforth," he read. "Sta. Irica. Portugal." Then he looked up at his subordinate. "You have done very well, Masterman. This is really all that is essential."

Masterman, well-pleased, saluted again.

"I thought it would be, sir. And it was really all we had time for. Miss Hoyle is not an easy nut to crack."

CHAPTER XIX

JOHN STEADMAN was hard at work in Luke Bechcombe's study. He was finding his co-executor, the Rev. James Collyer, of very little use. It was rumoured that the rector had had a nervous breakdown, at any rate it appeared impossible to get him up to town and documents requiring his signature had to be sent to Wexbridge Rectory by special messenger.

Steadman was cogitating over this fact in some annoyance and deliberating the advisability of applying for the appointment of another executor, when he heard the sound of a taxi stopping before the door, and looking up he saw Inspector Furnival getting out. He went into the hall to meet him.

The inspector was looking grave and perturbed.

"Have you heard?" he questioned breathlessly.

"Nothing!" Steadman answered laconically.

"Mrs. Carnthwacke was murderously assaulted this morning in her own carriage in one of London's best-known thoroughfares!"

"What!" The barrister stared at him in a species of stupefaction.

Instead of answering the inspector stepped back to the open door of the study.

"One moment, please."

But if to speak to John Steadman in private was his objective he did not obtain it. Mrs. Bechcombe came quickly into the hall with Cecily Hoyle close behind her.

"Inspector," she cried, "what is it? You have discovered my husband's murderer? I heard you say 'Mrs. Carnthwacke.'"

The inspector's face was very grave as he turned. Then he stood back for her to pass into the study. He did not speak again until they were all in the room, then he closed the door and looked at Luke Bechcombe's widow with eyes in which pity was mingled with severity.

"Mrs. Carnthwacke has nearly shared your husband's fate, madam," he said very deliberately. "I think you must be convinced now of the absolute impossibility of the theory you have not hesitated to broadcast all along."

"What do you mean?" Mrs. Bechcombe questioned sharply.

The inspector spread out his hands.

"As I was just telling Mr. Steadman, Mrs. Carnthwacke was murderously assaulted and left for dead in her own carriage this morning, in circumstances which leave small doubt in my mind that the miscreant who attacked her was Mr. Bech-combe's murderer."

"I do not believe it! The Carnthwackes—one of them, mur-dered my husband," Mrs. Bechcombe said uncompromising-ly. "I have the strongest possible—"

She was interrupted by an odd sound, a sort of choking gasp from Cecily. They all turned. The girl was deathly white. She caught her breath sharply in her throat.

"It—it can't be true! I don't believe it! Why should he want to hurt Mrs. Carnthwacke?"

"Why should who want to hurt Mrs. Carnthwacke?" the in-spector counter-questioned.

"Because—oh, I don't know—Oh, I know he didn't!" Cecily accompanied this asseveration with a burst of tears. "Nobody could be so cruel."

"Somebody has!" the inspector said dryly. "Is it any con-solation to you to think that there are two murderers at large instead of one, Miss Hoyle?"

Cecily stared at him, twisting her hands about, apparently in an agony of speechlessness. She made two or three hoarse attempts to answer him. Then, with a wild glance round at the amazed faces of Steadman and Mrs. Bechcombe, she turned and rushed out of the room.

The inspector glanced at John Steadman—a glance inter-cepted by Mrs. Bechcombe.

"Hysteria!" that lady remarked scornfully. "I fancy she thinks that you suspect Anthony, and that naturally— But enough of Cecily Hoyle. What is this wild tale of yours about Mrs. Carnthwacke, inspector?"

"It is no wild tale, madam," the inspector said coldly. "I have just come from the Carnthwackes' house, where Mrs. Carnthwacke lies at death's door. I came here by Mr. Car-nthwacke's express desire to see whether I could induce Mr. Steadman to accompany me to consult with Mr. Carnthwacke as to the best measures to be taken now."

"Of course I will come, inspector," the barrister said readi-ly. "As I should go anywhere where it was in the least probable that I should hear anything at all bearing upon our own case. One never knows from what point elucidation may come."

Mrs. Bechcombe turned her shoulder to him.

"Oh, please don't prose, John! Now what has happened to Mrs. Carnthwacke, inspector?"

"Mrs. Carnthwacke, madam, was just taking a drive as you might yourself. She came up Piccadilly, left an order at a shop in New Bond Street, told her man to drive by way of Regent Street and Oxford Street to the Park, to go in by the Marble Arch and wait near the Victoria Gate until Mr. Carnthwacke who had been out for the night came from Paddington Station to join them. As it happened he was at the meeting-place first. When the car stopped he was amazed to see Mrs. Carnthwacke lolling back in a sort of crouching position against the side of the car. At first he thought she had had a fit of some kind, but there was an odour to which he was unaccustomed hanging about the car and then he discovered a piece of cord twisted tightly round his wife's throat. He cut it in a frenzy of fear and for some time they thought she was dead. But they drove straight to some doctor they knew close to the Park. He tried artificial respiration and brought her round to some extent, and then before they took her home, phoned to Scotland Yard for me."

"What was the motive?" Steadman asked quietly.

The inspector raised his eyebrows.

"Only one person saw Mr. Bechcombe's murderer. Mrs. Carnthwacke was a witness to be feared."

"But you say she is not got rid of! She is alive?" Mrs. Bechcombe interrupted hysterically.

"At present," the inspector rejoined grimly. "Mr. Steadman, if you could come—? As I said before, Mr. Carnthwacke is most anxious to have your advice with regard to what steps should be taken to discover the would-be murderer. And there is no time to be lost."

"I am at your service, inspector." Steadman turned to the door. "You shall hear further particulars as soon as possible, Madeleine."

In the taxi outside John Steadman looked at the inspector.

"Is this the work of the Yellow Dog, inspector?"

"It is the work of Mr. Bechcombe's murderer, sir," the inspector replied evasively.

"You have some grounds for this conviction, I presume," John Steadman rejoined. "At first sight it looks as though it might be an entirely independent affair. An attempt to steal any jewels that Mrs. Carnthwacke might be wearing. Or her money."

"You wait until you have talked to Mrs. Carnthwacke, sir. You won't feel much doubt as to her assailant's identity then."

"But is Mrs. Carnthwacke able to speak?" John Steadman questioned in great surprise. "I understood from what you said—"

The inspector looked him full in the face and solemnly winked one eye.

"It suits our purpose that the outside world and particularly Mrs. Carnthwacke's assailant should think her dying. But, as a matter of fact, when Mrs. Carnthwacke had rallied from the effects of the strangulation, except that she feels weak and ill from the shock, she was practically as well as you or I. She is perfectly able to discuss the matter with us, though by my advice she is keeping to her own rooms and it is being given out that she is still unconscious, lying between life and death."

At No. 15 Blanden Square, they were received by Cyril B. Carnthwacke himself. He was looking pale and worried, but he greeted John Steadman warmly.

"Say, this is top hole of you, Mr. Steadman," he exclaimed. "Come right away to my sanctum and I will put you wise as I can about this affair."

He led the way to his study, a large room at the back of the house on the second floor. When they were inside he locked and bolted the door, somewhat to Steadman's surprise.

"Now," he said, going to the opposite side of the room and unlocking another door, "we are going right away to Mrs. Carnthwacke and you shall hear what she says, Mr. Steadman."

The door he opened led into what was apparently his dressing-room with a communicating door into Mrs. Carnthwacke's apartments. In this a couple of women dressed as nurses were sitting. They rose. Furnival murmured:

"Female detectives to guard Mrs. Carnthwacke. Even her own maid is not admitted."

One of them opened the farther door and ushered them into Mrs. Carnthwacke's room. In spite of Inspector Furnival's report, Steadman was surprised to see how well she looked. She was lying back in a capacious arm-chair; some arrangement of lace concealed any damage there might be to her throat, and beyond the fact that she was unusually pale—which might have been put down to the absence of make-up—and that one side of her face was a little swollen, he would have noticed no difference in her.

He went forward with a few conventional words of sympathy. Mr. Carnthwacke drew up three chairs and motioned to the other men to be seated.

"Now, honey," he said persuasively, "you are just going to make us all wise once more with what happened this morning."

"I will do my best." Mrs. Carnthwacke closed her eyes for a moment. "It is such a horrible ghastly thing. But—but I know that to let such a man be at large is a public danger. So I must tell you though every time I speak of it I seem to live through it again. Well, I left home this morning just as well as ever, Mr. Steadman. And really you wouldn't have thought I *could* be in any danger in my own car with two men on the front; now, would you?"

"I certainly should not," John Steadman agreed.

"Such a thing never entered my head," Mrs. Carnthwacke went on. "But first, perhaps, I had better say that I wore no jewellery that could possibly attract anybody's attention. None at all, in fact, but my wedding ring and the diamond half hoop was my engagement ring that which I have worn as a keeper ever since. I haven't even worn my pearls out of doors lately, because I thought it best to be on the safe side. Well, I went to my tailor's in New Bond Street. It was an awful bother getting there, because as you know Bond Street is up—any street you want to go to is always up—and we had to go very slow in the side streets because all the vehicles which turned out of Bond

Street were crowding up in the narrower streets, and the traffic was generally disorganized. I was just hoping we should soon get out of the crush when the door of the car was opened and a young man got in. In that first moment I was not really frightened, for he looked like a gentleman and smiled quite pleasantly."

"One minute, please," Steadman interposed. "In what street were you now?"

"I don't know. I didn't notice. We didn't seem to have left New Bond Street very long! I really thought for the moment in a half bewildered way that he must be some one I had known very well in the old days when I was in England, and who had altered—grown as it were. He sat down opposite me. 'I see you don't know me,' he said in quite a cultivated voice, 'and yet it is not so very long since we met.' 'Isn't it?' I said. 'No, I don't seem to remember you. Where did we meet?' With that I put out my hand to the speaking tube, for I was beginning to think that all was not right. But he was too quick for me. He caught both my hands in his, then managing somehow to hold them both in one of his he sprang across and sat down beside me. I struggled, of course, and tried to call out, though I wasn't so awfully frightened, not at first, for it seemed unthinkable that I should really be hurt there in my own car in the broad daylight. But when I opened my mouth to cry out he stuck something into my mouth, something that burned and stung. Then in that moment I knew him—knew him for Luke Bechcombe's murderer, I mean. I struggled and struggled frantically, but he was putting something round my neck, pulling it tighter and tighter. I couldn't breathe. And then I knew no more till I was coming round again and my husband and the doctor were with me." She stopped and put up her hands to her neck as if she still felt that cruel strangulating grip.

Cyril B. Carnthwacke's face looked very grim.

"That guy will have something round his own neck soon, I surmise. Something he won't be able to get rid of, either."

John Steadman and the inspector had both taken out their notebooks. The former spoke first.

"You say you know your assailant to be the murderer of Luke Bechcombe. Will you tell us how you recognized him?"

"Because—because that day when I was talking to the man whom I thought to be Mr. Bechcombe, whom we now believe to have been the murderer, I noticed his hands. He kept moving them over the table in and out of the papers in a nervous sort of way, and I saw" Mrs. Carnthwacke's voice suddenly failed her. She shrank nervously to the side of the chair. "You are sure no one can hear me, Cyril?"

He sat down on the side of her chair.

"Dead certain, honey. Come now, get it off your chest and you will feel ever so much better."

"And be ever so much safer," Inspector Furnival interposed. "As long as you only know this secret, Mrs. Carnthwacke, Mr. Bechcombe's murderer has a solid reason for wanting to destroy the one person who can identify him. But, once this knowledge is shared with others, the reason disappears. If Mrs. Carnthwacke is disposed of and there remain others who share her knowledge, he is none the safer. You see this, don't you, madam?"

"Yes, yes! Of course I do," she assented feverishly. "I wish now I had spoken right out at once. But I wanted a big American detective to undertake the getting my diamonds back. My husband had promised to engage him and I wanted him to have this exclusive information. Now, we will have everybody else knowing the secret too."

"Never mind, madam, there will be plenty for him to do," Inspector Furnival observed consolingly. "You were telling us you noticed the hands of the man in Mr. Bechcombe's office."

"Yes." Mrs. Carnthwacke glanced up again at her husband and seemed to gather strength from his smile. "I just looked at his hands mechanically while we were talking, and I saw that though they were nice hands, well shaped and carefully manicured, they had one curious defect, if you can call it a defect. The thumb was unusually long, and the first—don't you call it the index finger?—was very short, so that the two looked almost the same length. It was an odd fault, and I never noticed it in any hand before, until—"

"Yes, madam, until?" the inspector prompted as she paused with a shiver.

"Until this morning in the car," she went on, steadying her voice with an effort. "Just as he caught my hands, I saw his and I knew—I knew beyond the possibility of a doubt that my assailant was the man who stole my diamonds, and murdered Mr. Bechcombe."

"Well, that is definite enough, anyhow," John Steadman remarked thoughtfully. "Were both hands alike, do you know, Mrs. Carnthwacke?"

"Yes, they were," she returned in a more positive tone than she had yet used. "I noticed that particularly."

"Did you recognize him in any other way?" the inspector asked with his eye on his notebook.

"No, not really. I can't say I did," Mrs. Carnthwacke said hesitatingly. "That is, I did think there was something about the eyes, though the Crow's Inn man had his hidden by smoked horn-rimmed glasses, so I couldn't have seen much of them. But there was something about his eyebrows and the way his eyes were set that I certainly thought I recognized."

John Steadman was drawing his brows together.

"Yes, it is a curious defect and I should think as you say an uncommon one, yet I cannot help feeling that I have noticed the same thing in some hands I have seen—fairly lately too, but I cannot remember where," he said in a puzzled tone. "Probably I shall recollect presently."

Was it a warning glance the inspector shot at him? Steadman could not be quite certain, but at any rate there was no misinterpreting Cyril B. Carnthwacke's gesture as he got up from his seat on the arm of his wife's chair.

"She can't tell you any more, gentlemen, and that's a fact. What became of that guy is what we want to know and what we reckon your clever police are going to find out. Now you can't be half murdered and left for dead in the morning without being a wee trifle exhausted in the afternoon, so if you could come to my study—"

"You—you won't be long? I don't feel as if I should ever be safe away from you again," his wife pleaded.

Cyril B. Carnthwacke's reply was to pat her shoulders.

"Sure thing I shan't leave you long, honey. And you just figure to yourself you are as safe as a rock with these gentlemen in the study with me, and these female guys in the dressing-room."

Once more in his study the American's face hardened again as he invited the other men to sit down, and put a big box of cigars on the table before them.

"There's nothing like a smoke to clear the brain, gentlemen," he said as he lighted one himself. "And what do you make of the affair now that you have seen Mrs. Carnthwacke?"

John Steadman took the answer upon himself.

"As brutal and deliberate an attempt to murder as I ever heard of."

"There I am with you," Cyril B. Carnthwacke said grimly. "How did that guy find out where Mrs. Carnthwacke was journeying and when? There's where I should like you to put me wise."

"He may not have arranged anything beforehand. It may have been a sudden thing when he saw the carriage," Inspector Furnival hazarded.

"Don't you bet your bottom dollar on that, old chap!" Cyril B. Carnthwacke admonished, puffing away at his big cigar. "He don't go about with a drop of chloroform and a nice long piece of ribbon handy in his pocket any more than other folks, I reckon. It just figures out around this—some of our folks here must be acquainted with this guy, and put him wise about Mrs. Cyril B. Carnthwacke's movements."

"Yes, I think there can be no doubt you are right about that," John Steadman assented deliberately. "What of Mrs. Carnthwacke's maid?"

"Came over with us from the States," the American told him. "And she is devoted to Mrs. Carnthwacke. No flies on her."

"No young man?" the inspector questioned.

"Not the shadow of one," Cyril B. Carnthwacke told him, leaning back in his chair and watching his cigar smoke curl up to the ceiling.

"No great friend?"

"Never heard of one. Of course I don't say she has no acquaintance, but she is one of the sort that keeps herself to herself, as you say over here."

"Next thing is the chauffeur and footman," the inspector went on. "I should like a talk with them. It seems inconceivable that they should not have seen this man get in or out."

"I don't know that it does," said Cyril B. Carnthwacke thoughtfully. "They are taught to keep their heads straight in front of them—the footman one; and the chauffeur has enough to do in the traffic of London streets, I reckon, to look after himself and his car. However, you can have them as long as you like, but you won't get anything out of them. They swear they saw nothing and heard nothing, and that is all they will say. They were very bothered with the traffic being diverted on all sides, and continually having to slow down, and of course it was this slowing down that gave the guy his chance. He must be a cool hand, that. Say, inspector, do you think it was this Yellow Dog the newspapers have a stunt about?"

"When we have caught the Yellow Dog I shall be able to tell you more about it," the inspector replied evasively. "I will see your men, please, Mr. Carnthwacke. But before they come let me warn you again to be most careful not to allow it to be known that Mrs. Carnthwacke escaped with comparatively so little injury. Continue to represent her as lying at death's door, and let nobody but the doctor and nurses see her. I cannot exaggerate the importance of not allowing it to reach the ears of her would-be murderer that he has failed. We must look to it that not a breath as to her condition leaks out from us, Mr. Steadman."

John Steadman was looking out of the window.

"I quite see your point, inspector. It is most important that we should not allow the faintest suspicion of the truth to leak out among our friends, especially—"

"Especially—?" Cyril B. Carnthwacke prompted.

John Steadman did not speak, but he turned his head and looked at the inspector.

"From the widow, Mrs. Bechcombe," the detective finished.

Cyril B. Carnthwacke stared at him.

"Why Mrs. Bechcombe?"

"Because," said the inspector very slowly and emphatically, "she might tell Miss Cecily Hoyle and—"

The eyes of the three men met and then the pursed up lips of Cyril B. Carnthwacke emitted a low whistle.

"Sakes alive! Sits the wind in that quarter?"

CHAPTER XX

"SAMUEL HORSINGFORTH passenger to Lisbon by the *Atlantic* starting from Southampton seventeenth instant."

Inspector Furnival read the telegram over again aloud and then handed it to Steadman.

"Better get there before the boat train, I think, sir."

Steadman nodded. "I'll guarantee my touring car to do it in less time than anything else you can get."

"Y—es. Perhaps it may, but—" the inspector said uncertainly.

"But what?" Steadman questioned in surprise.

The inspector cleared his throat apparently in some embarrassment.

"I should like nothing better than the car, but that I am afraid that the fact that we are going down to Southampton in her might leak out—and then the journey might be in vain."

John Steadman drew in his lips.

"Trust me for that. My chauffeur can keep a still tongue in his head; and you ought to know me by now, Furnival."

"I ought, sir, that's a fact," the inspector acquiesced. "It is the chauffeur I am doubtful of. Never was there a case in which servants' gossip has been more concerned and done more harm than this one of Luke Bechcombe's death."

"I will take care that he knows nothing of our destination until after we have started," Steadman promised, "but these cold winds of late have given me a stiff arm, and I am afraid rheumatism is setting in. It is the right arm too, confound it! Of course it might last the journey to Southampton all right, but it might not; and it wouldn't do to risk a failure."

"No, we can't afford a failure," the inspector said briskly. "The car then, sir, and you will take all precautions. Have you heard anything of Mrs. Carnthwacke?"

"Lying at death's door. Mrs. Bechcombe has inquired," Steadman said laconically.

The inspector smiled warily.

"We shall have all our time to keep Cyril B. quiet till we want him to speak. Their American detective is here too, butting in, as they phrase it. Ten o'clock then."

"Ten o'clock," Steadman assented.

He was round at Scotland Yard in his luxurious touring car punctually at the appointed hour. Punctual as he was, though, the inspector was waiting on the step for him.

"Got off all right, inspector," the barrister remarked as the detective took his seat and the car started. "Only filled up with petrol at a garage after we left my flat, and I told Mrs. Bechcombe that I might be back to lunch. Chauffeur doesn't know where we are going yet. You direct him to the Southampton Road and then I will tell him to put all speed on."

The day was perfect, no head wind, just a touch of frost in the air. Both men would have enjoyed the long smooth spin if their minds had been free, if their thoughts had not been busy all the time with their journey's end. To the inspector, if all went well, it would spell success, when success had at first seemed hopeless and a long step forward in the great campaign on which he had embarked.

To Steadman it would mean that a certain theory he had held all along was justified.

As they reached Southampton the inspector looked at his watch. "Plenty of time—half an hour to spare!"

They drove straight to the docks and went alongside. The inspector had good reason to expect his prey by the boat train. They had left the car higher up. Steadman waited out of sight. The inspector went on board and ascertained that Mr. Samuel Horsingforth had not so far arrived.

As the boat train drew up, keeping himself well out of sight, Steadman peered forth eagerly. The train was not as crowded as usual, but so far as Steadman could see no Mr.

Horsingforth was visible. Then just at the last moment a man of middle height strolled to the gangway—a man, who, though his face and figure were absolutely unknown to the barrister, seemed to have something vaguely, intangibly familiar about him. Steadman was looking out for a slight, spare-looking man, shorter than this one, with the rounded shoulders of a student, pale too, with a short straggling beard and big horn-rimmed glasses. The man at whom he was looking must be at least a couple of inches taller than the one they were in search of, and he was distinctly stout, and his shoulders were square, and he carried himself well. He was clean-shaven too. He had the ruddy complexion of one leading an outdoor life. He smiled as he spoke to a porter about his luggage and Steadman could see his white even teeth and his twinkling grey eyes. Yet, after a momentary pause, the barrister came out into the open and followed up the gangway. Suddenly Steadman saw Inspector Furnival moving forward. The man in front saw too, and came to a sudden stop; stopped and faced round just as he was about to put his foot on deck, and then seeing Steadman stopped again and looked first one way and then the other and finally stepped on deck with an air of jaunty determination.

Inspector Furnival came up to him.

"Samuel Horsingforth, *alias* John Frederick Hoyle, *alias* Amos Thompson, I hold a warrant for your arrest on a charge of fraud and embezzlement. It is my duty to warn you that anything you may say will be taken down in writing and may be used in evidence against you."

For a minute Steadman thought that the man whose arm the inspector was now holding firmly was about to collapse. His ruddy colour had faded and he seemed to shrink visibly. But he rallied with a marvellous effort of self-control.

"You are making some strange mistake," he said coolly. "Samuel Horsingforth is my name. Of the others you mention I know nothing. I have been backwards and forwards several times on this line and more than one of the officers and stewards know me, and can vouch for my good faith."

The inspector's grip did not relax.

"No use, Thompson, the game is up," he said confidently. "You have made yourself a clever *alias*, I admit; but it is no use trying to go on with it now. You don't want any disturbance here."

Horsingforth, *alias* Thompson, made no further resistance. He allowed the inspector to lead him down the gangway and down to the quay to Steadman's car. Only when the inspector opened the door did he hold back.

"Where are you taking me?"

"Town," the inspector answered laconically. "You will be able to consult a solicitor when you get there—if you want to," he added.

Thompson said no more. He seated himself by Steadman, the inspector opposite.

As they started, another car, which had quietly followed the first from Scotland Yard, at a sign from the inspector fell in behind.

Until they had left Southampton and its environs far behind none of the three men spoke, then Thompson, who had been sitting apparently in a species of stupor, roused himself.

"How did you find out?" he asked. "What made you suspect?"

"A photograph of your daughter, that you had overlooked," the inspector answered. "You had provided yourself with a second identity very cleverly, Mr. Thompson. If it had not been for Mr. Bechcombe's murder you would probably have succeeded."

"I had nothing to do with that," Thompson interrupted with sudden fire. "I swear I had not! Mr. Bechcombe was alive and well when I left the offices. I was never more shocked in my life. You might have knocked me down with a feather when I saw in the paper that he had been murdered, and that I was wanted on suspicion as having murdered him."

"Umph!" The inspector looked at him. "You are a solicitor, or next door to one, Mr. Thompson, I believe. You ought not to need the bit of advice I am going to give you now. As I told you, you will be at liberty to see a solicitor as soon as we reach London. Send for the best you know and tell him the whole truth about this unhappy affair and tell nobody else anything at all."

Thus advised, Thompson wisely became dumb. He sat back in his corner of the car in a hunched up crouching condition. He looked strangely unlike the jaunty, self-satisfied man who had stepped on to the gangway of the *Atlantic* so short a time before. To the inspector, watching him, he seemed almost visibly to shrink, and as the detective's keen eyes wandered over him he began to understand some of the apparently glaring discrepancies between the descriptions of Thompson circulated by the police and the appearance of the man before him. Thompson's teeth had been noticeably defective. Samuel Horsingforth, otherwise Hoyle, had had all the deficiencies made good and was, when he smiled, evidently in possession of a very good set of teeth, real or artificial. This, besides entirely altering his appearance, made his face fuller and quite unlike the hollow cheeks of Mr. Bechcombe's missing clerk. That Thompson had worn a thin, straggly beard, while this man was clean-shaven, went for nothing but Thompson had been bald, with hair wearing off the forehead. Horsingforth's stubbly, grey hair grew thickly and rather low, and though the inspector now detected the wig he inwardly acknowledged it to be the best he had ever seen. Then, too, Thompson had been thin and spare, and though looking now at the man hunched up in the car one might see the padding on the shoulders, and under the protuberant waistcoat over which the gold watch chain was gracefully suspended, altogether it was not to be wondered at that Thompson had been so long at large. Inspector Furnival knew that his present capture would add largely to a reputation that was growing every day. At the same time he realized that he was still a long way from the achievement of the object to which all his energies had been directed—the capture of the Yellow Dog and the dispersal of the Yellow Gang.

Thompson took the inspector's advice for the rest of the drive and said no more. There were moments when the other two almost doubted whether he were not really incapable of speech.

They drove direct to Scotland Yard. From there, later in the day, Thompson would be taken to Bow Street to be formally charged, and from thence to his temporary home at Pentonville.

After the remand Steadman and the inspector walked away together.

"So that's that. A clever piece of work, inspector," the barrister remarked.

The inspector blew his nose.

"All very well as far as Thompson is concerned. But Thompson is not the Yellow Dog."

John Steadman shrugged his shoulders.

"Sometimes I have doubted whether he were not."

The inspector looked at him with a curious smile.

"I don't think you have, sir. I think your suspicions went the same way as mine from the first."

Steadman nodded. "But suspicion is one thing and proof another."

"And that is a good deal nearer than it was," the inspector finished. "The Yellow Dog's arrest is not going to be as easy a matter as Thompson's, though, Mr. Steadman. By Jove! those fellows have got it already."

They were passing a little news-shop, the man was putting out the placards: "Crow's Inn Tragedy—arrest of Thompson." Further on—"Crow's Inn Mystery—Arrest of absconding clerk at Southampton—Thompson at Bow Street—Story of his Career—Astounding Revelations!"

"Pure invention!" said the inspector, flicking this last with his stick. "I should like to put an end to half these evening rags."

"I wonder what his history has been!" Steadman said speculatively. "I am sorry for his daughter—and Tony Collyer too. This will put an end to that affair, I fancy."

"I don't know," said the inspector as they walked on, "Mr. Tony seems to have made up his mind and I should fancy he could be pretty pig-headed when he likes. I sent the girl a letter from Scotland Yard covering one of Thompson's, so that she should not hear of this arrest first from the papers."

"Poor girl! But I think she has been dreading this for some time. Probably anything, even this certainty, will be better, than the state of fear in which she has been living of late."

"Probably," the inspector assented. Then he went on after a minute's pause, "Thompson's is the most ingenious case I have ever come across of a deliberately planned course of dishonesty, with a second identity so that Thompson of Bechcombes' could disappear utterly and Mr. Hoyle of Rose Cottage, Burford, could just take up his simple country life, paint his pictures and potter about the village where he was already known."

"Yes. His fatal mistake was made in putting in his daughter as Mr. Bechcombe's secretary," John Steadman said thoughtfully. "It trebled his chances of discovery and I can't really see his motive. I suppose he thought she could assist his schemes in some way."

"Yes, I fancy he did get some information from her," the inspector assented. "Though I am certain the girl herself did not know that Thompson and Hoyle were one and the same until after Mr. Bechcombe's death. Then I imagine he disclosed his identity to her and that accounts for the state of tension in which she has been living. His second mistake was the leaving of her photograph in his room. That gave the clue to his identity."

"Yes. Well, as you know, inspector, it is the mistakes that criminals make that provide you and me with our living," Steadman said with a chuckle. "And now Mr. Thompson—Hoyle, will disappear for some considerable time from society. And the intelligent public will probably clamour for his trial for Mr. Bechcombe's murder. For a large section of it has already believed him guilty."

"And not without reason," the inspector said gravely. "Appearances have been, and are, terribly against Thompson. Mrs. Carnthwacke's evidence may save him if—"

"Yes. If," Steadman prompted.

"If she is able to give it," the inspector concluded. "But Mrs. Carnthwacke is not recovering from the injuries she received in that terrible assault upon her so quickly as was expected.

In fact, the latest editions of the evening papers, after having devoted all their available space to Thompson's career and arrest, will have a paragraph in the stop press news recording Mrs. Carnthwacke's death."

"What!" Steadman glanced sharply at the inspector's impassive face. Then a faint smile dawned upon his own. "So that, with that of Thompson's arrest, the Yellow Dog will feel pretty safe."

"I hope so," returned the inspector imperturbably.

CHAPTER XXI

"ONE MINUTE, sir. I shan't hurt you!"

With a comical look at the inspector, John Steadman submitted himself to the hands of the little old man in the shabby black suit, who was surveying him with critical eyes in the looking-glass, and who now approached him with a curious little instrument looking like a pair of very fine tweezers, combined with a needle so minute that it almost required a microscope to see it.

They were in a small room at the back of a little shop in Soho, whither the inspector had conducted John Steadman, and where the former had already undergone a curious metamorphosis. The presiding genius of the establishment was this little old man with an oddly wrinkled face that reminded Steadman of a marmoset, and with pale grey eyes that were set far apart, and that seemed to stare straight at you and almost through you, with as little expression as a stone. The room was odd-looking as well as its master. It had very little furniture in it. Nothing on the wall but the big looking-glass that ran from floor to ceiling, and occupied the greater part of one side. Two tables stood near and a very old worm-eaten escritoire was by the window. There were four chairs in the room, all of the plain Windsor variety, one standing right in front of the mirror differing from the others only in that it had arms and an adjustable head.

Inspector Furnival had just been released from its clutches, and now John Steadman was taking his place. A huge enveloping sheet was thrown over him; a brilliant incandescent light was focused upon him, and the queer little marmoset face, with a big, curiously made magnifying glass screwed into it, was submitting him to an anxious scrutiny.

"I shall not hurt you," the soft, caressing voice with its foreign intonation repeated. "Just a few hairs put in—a very few put in, and Monsieur's best friend would not know him."

Steadman thought it very likely his best friend would not as he glanced back at the inspector. But now the lean yellow fingers were at work. From the angle at which the head-rest was fixed the barrister could not see what they were doing, but they were pinching, prodding, stabbing. It seemed to him that they would never stop. At last, however, the tweezers were thrown aside and he felt little, tiny brushes at work, dropping moisture here, drying it up with fragrant powder.

"Monsieur's teeth?" the foreign voice said with its sing-song intonation.

Steadman shrugged his shoulders as he took a plate from his mouth and dropped it into the fingerbowl held out to him.

"Ah, all the top! That is goot—very goot!" Something soft and warm was pressed into his mouth, pushed up and down until at last it felt secure. Then, with a satisfied sigh, the yellow fingers raised the head-rest; the little man stood back, the marmoset face wrinkled itself into a satisfied smile. "I hope that Monsieur is pleased."

Steadman, as he faced his reflection, thought that it was not a question of his best friend but that he himself would not have recognized the image he saw therein. The shape of the eyebrows had been entirely altered. They now slanted upwards, while a clever disposition of lines and hairs made the eyelids themselves appear to narrow and lengthen. His hair, thin in front and near the temples for many a long day now, had actually disappeared, and the enormously broad, high expanse of forehead was furrowed with skilfully drawn lines, and like the rest of his face of a greenish, greyish colour. The nose had become thinner in a mysterious fashion, the bridge had grown higher, the nostrils had widened. But the greatest change was in the mouth, the lips were thicker, more sensual looking. Then, in place of Steadman's perfectly fitting artificial teeth were several projecting yellow fangs with hideous gaps between.

"As the English talk, she, your own mother would not know you, eh?" the silky voice questioned anxiously.

And John Steadman, smiling in the curiously stiff fashion which was all the alterations would allow, said that he was sure she would not.

Both he and Furnival donned queerly designed overcoats that looked more like dressing-gowns than anything else, and soft hats. As they made their way through the streets with their hands folded in front and hidden by their wide sleeves, their eyes masked in blue spectacles, their heads turned neither to the right nor left, no one would have suspected their disguise— no one would have taken them for Englishmen. They got into a taxi and the inspector gave an address not far from Stepney Causeway. Once safely inside, he handed Steadman an automatic pistol and a police whistle.

"For emergencies," he said shortly. "I don't fancy we shall have to use them; but the police are all round the house. At the sound of the whistle they will rush the place."

"Yes, you may depend upon me, inspector," Steadman said quietly.

"Here we are!" said the inspector, drawing a couple of parcels from his capacious pockets. One of them he handed to John Steadman, the other he unfastened himself. He shook out a voluminous, flimsy garment of bright yellow and unwrapped from its tissue paper a small yellow mask. "These dominoes we had better put on here beneath our overcoats, Mr. Steadman, and our masks we shall have to slip on as soon as we get inside."

"You have had the cordon drawn all round as I suggested, inspector?"

"It is as narrow as can be, sir. They will almost be able to hear what we say. Oh, I am taking no risks. But I mean to catch the Big Yellow Dog himself to-night—dead or alive."

"Ay! Dead or alive!" Steadman echoed. "You have been near him once or twice before, haven't you, inspector?"

"Not so near as I shall be to-night," the inspector retorted.

They had no time for more. The taxi stopped and they got out. The inspector paused to give a few low toned directions to the cabman, then he led the way down a side street. From this it seemed to Steadman to spread out in every direction, a perfect network of narrow streets and alleys. It was a veritable maze and the barrister would have been utterly bewildered, but the inspector apparently knew his ground, he wound himself in and out with an eel-like dexterity. At last, however, he slackened his steps and then, side by side, he and Steadman made their way over the ill-kept, ill-lighted pavement, More than once the barrister heard a faint cheeping sound issue from the inspector's lips. Although he heard no response, he knew that the cordon that the detective had spoken of was in its place.

When the inspector stopped again he looked round and up and down, then turned sharply to the right, into a small *cul-de-sac* apparently running between two high brick walls, for Steadman could see no windows on either side. As they were nearing the opposite end to that by which they had entered, however, they came upon a low door at the right. To the barrister's heated fancy there was something sinister about its very aspect. The windows on either side were grimy and closely shuttered; they and the door were badly in need of a coat of paint. What there was upon it was blistered, and so filthy that it was impossible even to guess at its original colour. There was no sign of either knocker or bell, but right at the top of the door was a small grille through which the janitor could survey the applicants for admission, himself unseen. The inspector applied his knuckles to the door, softly at first, then with a crescendo of taps that was evidently a signal. Steadman, with his eyes fixed on the grille, could see nothing, no faintest sign of movement, but for one moment he felt a sickening sense of being looked at, he could almost have fancied of being looked through. Then moving softly, noiselessly, in spite of its apparently dilapidated condition, the door in front of them opened.

The inspector stepped inside, Steadman keeping close to him, and gave the word—"Chink-a-pin," and at the same moment Steadman became aware of a figure veiled in black from head to foot standing motionless against the wall behind the door. The door closed after them with a snap in which Steadman fancied he heard something ominous. They found themselves in a long, rather wide passage down which they proceeded, the inspector still leading; their bare hands held out in front of them, thumb-tip joined to thumb-tip, finger-tip to finger-tip. On the door at the end of the passage the inspector knocked again so softly that it seemed impossible that he should be heard.

However, as if by magic, this door opened suddenly.

Inside, in contrast with the brightness in the passage, everything looked dark, but gradually Steadman made out a faint, flickering light. A soft, sibilant voice spoke, this time apparently out of the air, since there was no sign of any speaker:

"The Great Dane bites."

"His enemies will bite the dust." The inspector gave the countersign.

Once again they moved forward and found themselves in a narrow passage running at right angles to the first. Here, instead of bareness, were softly carpeted floors and heavy hangings on the walls, and a sickly, sweet smell as if of incense. The light, dim and flickering at first, grew stronger and more diffused. Steadman saw that the passage in which they stood served as an ante-chamber or vestibule to some larger room into which folding doors standing slightly ajar gave access. They were not alone, either. At a sign from the inspector, Steadman had donned his yellow mask. In another moment shadowy hands had relieved him of his coat and were gently pushing him forward, and he saw faintly that there were other yellow clad forms flitting backwards and forwards. Between the half-open doors he could glimpse more light, golden, dazzling, while over everything there brooded a sense of mystery, of evil unutterable. In that moment there came over John Steadman a certainty of the danger of this enterprise to which they stood committed, and brave man though he was he would have drawn back if he could. But it was too late. With one hand beneath his yellow domino, clutching his automatic firmly he

paced by the inspector's side into the Golden Room. As the
first sight of it burst upon him he asked himself whether he
could really be living in sober twentieth-century England, or
whether he had not been translated into some scene out of the
"Arabian Nights."

The room was oblong in shape, the ceiling, pale yellow in
colour, was low, across it sprawled great golden flowers and
in the centre of each of them blazed, like some lovely exotic
jewel, a radiant amber light. The walls of this extraordinary
room were panelled in yellow too, and round about them were
ranged twelve golden seats. Ten of them were occupied by
figures, masked and dominoed as he and the inspector were.
The two seats at the end of the room nearest to them were
unoccupied, while at the opposite end stood a raised dais, also
of gold; an empty golden chair, looking like a throne, stood
upon it. Right in the middle of the room stood a great mimosa
in full bloom, its powerful fragrance mingling with that other perfume that Steadman had sensed before. His feet sank
into the pile of the carpet as he followed the inspector to the
unoccupied chairs nearest to them. At the same moment the
hangings at the back of the throne were parted and a tall figure
came through, masked, and wearing the same kind of yellow
domino as all the others. He seated himself upon the throne
upon the dais. At the same moment a sweet toned bell began
to ring slowly.

Steadman had hardly realized that there was any sound to
be heard, but now he became conscious by its sudden cessa-
tion that there had been a low incessant hum going on around.
Then the bell ceased, and the silence grew deadly. The very
immobility of those yellow figures began to get on John Steadman's nerves, though up to now he would have denied that
he possessed any. His eyes were fixed upon that figure in the
chair on the dais. Silent, immobile, it sat, hands joined together in front like those of every other figure in the room; but in
these hands there was a curious defect—the thumb was extraordinarily long, the first finger short, so that they looked
to be of the same length. And, as Steadman noticed this, his
fingers clutched his revolver and felt the cool metal of the po-

lice whistle. Of what use was it, he asked himself, surely no sound could reach the outside world from this terrible room. Suddenly he became conscious of a slight, a very slight movement close to him. Had the inspector moved, he wondered as he glanced round. And then the arms of his chair seemed to contract and lengthen; he felt himself gripped in a vice. Now he knew that the danger he had felt was upon him. He saw the inspector at his side begin to struggle violently. Desperately he tried to bring out his revolver—he was powerless, caught as in a vice. Some hidden mechanism in those chairs had been released, arms and legs were held more firmly than human hands could have held them.

An oath broke from the inspector's lips as he realized the nature of the trap in which they were caught. But there came no answering sound from those waiting, motionless, yellow figures on every side. Their very immobility seemed only to render the position more terrible. And then at last the silence was broken by a laugh, a wicked, malicious laugh, the very sound of which made Steadman's blood run cold in his veins.

CHAPTER XXII

THE LAUGHTER ceased as suddenly as it had begun and, as if by a concerted signal, every light in the room went out. A voice rang out, Steadman fancied from the figure on the dais.

"Arms up! inspector. Arms up! Mr. Steadman." Then another ripple of that horrible laughter. "Ah, I forgot! Our wonderful chairs make all such commands a superfluity! And so, inspector, you are going to have your wish—you are going to meet the Yellow Dog at last! But I fear, I greatly fear that when that interview is over you will not be in a position to make your discoveries known to that wonderful Scotland Yard, of which you have been so distinguished a member." The emphasis on the "have been" was ominous.

But there was no fear in the inspector's voice as it rapped out:

"Be careful what you do, Yellow Dog. He laughs best who laughs last. I warn you that this house is virtually in the hands of the police."

"Is that so, my dear inspector?"

There was another laugh, but this time John Steadman fancied there was some subtle change in the quality.

"But I rather think the police do not know where this house ends, and those of others begin!"

"Shall I supply you with the names of the others? The police know more than you think, you dog!" said the inspector daringly.

"And less than they think," said the raucous voice mockingly, "or you and your friend would hardly find yourselves here, dear inspector."

"Damnation!" Steadman knew that the detective was struggling fiercely from those clutching, enveloping arms.

"In case, however, that there is just the thinnest substratum of truth in your statement, Furnival," the mocking voice went on, "perhaps we had better waste no more time but get on to business."

The silvery bell tinkled again, the light was switched on.

Steadman saw that all the golden chairs were empty, that there was apparently no one in the room with the inspector and himself but that figure on the dais. He saw that the inspector had given up struggling and that by some means he had managed to tear the yellow mask from his face, which was unwontedly scarlet from his efforts to free himself.

"Strip!" ordered that voice from the platform.

In an instant a dozen hands had seized Steadman. It seemed that there were countless, yellow-masked men in the room. He had not even been conscious of their coming, until he had felt them and those ruthless, yellow, claw-like fingers catching at him on all sides at once. The gripping arms of the chair had released him, but it was in vain that he sought to release himself—he was conscious, vaguely, that the inspector was fighting too. But neither the inspector nor Steadman was in fighting condition. Both of them were elderly men who in their young days had not been athletic, and their efforts now were hopeless. Their garments were rent from them, the contents of their pockets were passed to the man on the platform, who commented upon them sarcastically.

"Automatics! Dear, dear! And you never had a chance to use them, either! Shows how differently things pan out to our anticipations, doesn't it, inspector? And police whistles? If we were only to sound one how the scene would change! You did not neglect any precautions, did you, inspector?"

And while the jeering questions went on the grasping yellow fingers were going on too, until the prisoners stood mother naked before their tormentors, their bare limbs bound round and round with cords.

"So now we come to grips," said the masked man, and this time Steadman thought he caught something faintly familiar, and one question that had troubled him of late was answered for ever. "I hope you'll not be much inconvenienced by this return to a state of nature," the man on the platform went on. "I fear you may be rather cold, but it is unavoidable under the circumstances, and it will not be for long. Then I feel sure you will neither of you be cold any more. Now, now, inspector!"

For a while John Steadman stood motionless, his short-sighted eyes peering at that yellow-clad figure; the inspector was swearing big strange oaths.

"You do look so funny, you know, inspector"—and this time Steadman could almost have fancied there was a feminine echo in that vile laughter—"and your language is too dreadful. But this outrage, as you call it, had to be. Clothes are so identifiable, as I am sure you have learnt in your wide experience, my dear inspector. But now this conversation, interesting as it is, must end. And I think we must silence that unruly member of yours, inspector!"

The silver bell tinkled sharply. In an instant those soft hands had seized the two men and gags were thrust into their mouths, and tied with cruel roughness. Then bandages were bound over their eyes and rougher, harder hands held their pinioned arms on either side and pulled them sideways.

Steadman felt certain they were being taken out by the door by which they entered, and very carefully his trained legal mind was noting down every slightest indication of the direction in which they were being taken. A farewell laugh came from the platform.

"So this is really good-bye. I trust, I do trust that your poor bare feet may not be hurt by the path along which you have to travel. But in case some injury should be unavoidable let me assure you it will not be for long, that much sooner than you probably anticipate the pain will be over."

Steadman could have fancied that there was something hysterical in that last laugh. But he had not time to think of it, to speculate as to the identity of the figure on the dais that the yellow domino and the mask concealed. He was being hurried along at a rate that did not give him time to raise his naked, shackled feet. They dragged helplessly along the stone pavement, for, once they had left that sinister yellow room, there were no carpets. Two or three times Steadman felt wood and guessed they were being taken through rooms, and several times for a few paces there would be oilcloth. Once his knee was banged against something the he felt certain was the corner of a wooden chair, once from the wood a splinter ran into his foot. It was evident that either they were being taken in and out or that many of the houses in that neighbourhood must have means of communication, and must necessarily be in the occupation of members of the Yellow Gang.

At last there was a pause, a door was unlocked and they were pushed inside a room with bare plank floor. They were propped up against the wall; something was thrown on to the boards; the bandage over Steadman's eyes was pulled roughly off. A voice with a harsh, uncouth accent, singularly unlike the soft purring voice that had spoken from the dais in the yellow room, said abruptly:

"The Great Yellow Dog has sent you these two rugs. They will serve to keep you warm. He regrets very much that you will be kept waiting. But unfortunately it is low tide and the river is not up yet."

Then the door was closed, they heard the key turn; the captives were left alone in their prison. Steadman's eyes, aching from the tight bandage, were full of water; for a few minutes he could see nothing. He would have given worlds to rub his eyes, but he could not move his arms one inch upwards. However, as the mist before his eyes cleared he saw that they were both propped up against a plain whitewashed wall, in a room that was absolutely bare, except that a fur rug lay at his feet and another at the feet of the inspector farther along.

Steadman could turn his head, almost the only movement that was free, and he saw that the poor detective had fared worse at the hands of their capturers than he had himself. Furnival's face was grazed on the forehead and cheek. It was flecked with blood and slime. As Steadman watched, his fellow-sufferer sank on the rug at his feet with a muffled sound of utter exhaustion. Steadman was not inclined to give up easily and, leaning there, he tried to work the knot of the string that tied his gag, but in vain, the members of the Yellow Gang did their work thoroughly. He looked round the room. It was absolutely bare of furniture and indescribably dirty. It was lighted dimly by a small window set rather high and guarded by iron bars. As Steadman's dazed faculties returned he became aware of a lapping sound and realized that the river must be just outside. The full meaning of that last message from the Yellow Dog dawned upon him now.

As Steadman gazed round the room and then at his exhausted companion, the conviction forced itself upon him that, as far as all human probability lay, their very moments were numbered. Try as he would he could not free his hands. There appeared to be no possibility of escape except by the door or window, and he had heard the door locked and saw that it was of unusual stoutness, while the iron bars across the window spoke for themselves. In his present helpless condition what gleam of hope could there be?

He followed Furnival's example and dropped on the rug at his feet, finding the fall unpleasantly hard even with the rug over the floor.

As he lay there trying to rest his aching bones, while his eyes watched the particularly solid-looking door hopelessly, he became aware of a faint, sliding, grating sound. With a sudden accession of hope he glanced around him. The inspector,

lying on his rug, apparently heard nothing. For a few minutes—they seemed to him an eternity—Steadman could see
nothing. He was telling himself that the noise he heard must
be that of some mouse or rat gnawing in the woodwork, when
his eye caught a faint movement under the door. Hope sprang
up again as he watched.

Yes, there could be no mistake, something was moving!
There was just a narrow space under the door; had there been
a carpet it would have been useless, but, as it was, that sliding,
scraping sound continued and presently he saw that it was the
blade of a knife that was coming through, a short, sharp blade
it looked like, and he guessed that it was the handle that was
proving the difficulty. Presently, however, it was overcome,
and with an apparently sharp push from behind knife and
handle both came through. Something white, a piece of paper,
was fastened on to the latter. Steadman lay and gazed at it.
The distance between him and the door, short though it was,
seemed, in his present state, almost insurmountable, and yet
in that knife and bit of paper lay his only chance of life. And
there was so little time! Not one tiny second to be wasted. By
some means he must get possession of the knife.

The door was on the same side as that on which he was lying and the distance from the edge of the rug to the knife was,
as far as he could judge, something like six or eight feet, more
than double his own height. Bound as he was he could move
neither arms nor legs to help himself. Common sense told him
that the only way he could reach the knife was by rolling towards it. And rolling would be no easy matter. Still, it was not
an impossibility and as long as he was on the rug not particularly painful. But crossing the bare boards was a very different
proposition, dragging his naked feet inch by inch across the
roughened dirty surface was a terrible job.

More than once he told himself that he could not do it, that
he must lie still and give up. But John Steadman was nothing if not dogged. He had not attained the position he had
occupied at the Bar by giving way under difficulties, and at
last his task was accomplished. He lay just in front of the door
with the knife close to his side. But his difficulties were by no

means over yet. Unable as he was to move his hands, how was he to cut the strong cords which bound him. Fortunately for him his hands were not fastened separately, but his arms were tied round his body tightly, the cord going round again and again. It was a method very effective so long as the cord was intact, but Steadman saw directly that, if he could cut it in one place, to free himself altogether would be easy enough. The question was, how was the cord to be cut in that one place? Steadman lay on the ground tied up so that he could not even free one finger, and the knife lay close to him indeed but with the blade flat on the ground.

He lay still for a moment, contemplating the situation. He saw at once that his only hope was in the handle. At the juncture where this was entered by the blade, the blade was, of course, raised a little from the ground. Now if he could by any means push the knife along until he could rest his arm on the handle, thus tipping the blade up, if only a trifle, work the cord against it, he might fray the cord through and thus free himself. It was simple enough to recognize that that was what ought to be done, however, and quite another matter to do it. Time after time Steadman rolled over imagining that this time he must be on the handle, only to find that he had inadvertently pushed it away. With the perseverance of Bruce's spider he at last succeeded. Arms, back and sides were grazed and bleeding, but the knife blade was at least a quarter of an inch from the ground. To get the end of the cord against it, to wriggle so that it was brought into contact with the blade forcefully enough to make any impression upon it was anything but easy, but it did not present the apparently insuperable obstacles that he had successfully grappled with in reaching the door and turning the knife round, Strand by strand the cord was conquered and at last Steadman was free. Free, with bruised and bleeding skin and stiffened limbs, and naked as he came into the world.

Escape, even now, did not look particularly practicable; but the barrister had not been successful so far to give up now. The first thing to do was to free the inspector. Scrambling up from the sitting position to which he had raised himself he found Furnival lying on his rug regarding him with astonished eyes, and making vain attempts to wriggle towards him. At the same moment his eye was caught by the folded-up piece of paper which was attached to the knife handle by a piece of string, and which he had noticed when he lay on his rug. He caught it up in his hands and unfolded it. Across the inside was scrawled a couple of lines of writing:

"The window looks straight on to the river, the bars across can be moved upwards. Jump out into the water at once. It is your only chance. If you delay it will be too late—from one who is grateful."

CHAPTER XXIII

STEADMAN READ the note over twice. Was it possible that they had an unknown friend in this haunt of the Yellow Gang? Or was it just another trap laid for them like the other communications that the inspector had received?

However, there was no time for deliberation. He turned to the inspector, knife in hand. To cut the bonds that bound the detective was an easy matter, even for his stiffened hands, in comparison with the difficulty of freeing himself. Then, taking the gag from his mouth, he saw that the lips were bruised and swollen both inside and out, and the gag had been thrust in with such brutality that the tongue had been forced backwards and several teeth loosened. As the inspector began to breathe more freely the blood poured from his mouth. But there was no time to be lost.

Steadman left his fellow-prisoner to recover himself while he padded across to the bars. In a moment he saw that his unknown informant was right. The bars would move upwards in their groove, easily enough. Evidently this window was used as a means of egress to the river. Inconvenient things could be pushed through and lost too! When the bars had gone, the window frame was quite wide enough to let a man get through. He leaned out. The moon was shining brightly, and he could see various small craft riding at anchor. As he spoke he heard the splash of oars and realized that at all hazards they must get into the river while the boat was about. Therein lay their hope of safety. He turned to the inspector, who had just struggled to his feet.

"Can you swim, Furnival?"

"Got the swimming medal at the Force Sports in 1912," the detective replied tersely. "I haven't quite forgotten the trick."

"I wasn't bad as a young man," the barrister said modestly. "We must do our best, you see." He held out the note. "There is no time to be lost."

"If we are to turn the tables on the Yellow Dog," the inspector said, speaking as plainly as his sore mouth would allow. He looked at the note. "Who wrote this?"

"I haven't the least idea," Steadman replied truthfully.

The inspector stooped stiffly and picked up the knife. Then he looked at the door which opened inwards.

"We might keep them back for a bit with this, perhaps." He went back and stuck the knife under the door, so that anybody trying to open it would inevitably jam it on the handle.

In the meantime Steadman had twisted himself, not without difficulty, on to the window frame. He peered down. The water was still some distance below them, and it looked particularly dark and gloomy, but at any rate it was better than falling alive into the hands of the Yellow Dog. He tore the note into tiny fragments and let them fall into the river. Then he called out:

"Come along, inspector. Pile up the rugs. They will give you a bit of a leg up."

Furnival pushed them along before him.

"Now, Mr. Steadman, are you going first?"

"I suppose so," said the barrister dubiously. "You had better look sharp after me, inspector. They may hear the first splash, and then—"

At this moment they became aware of steps and voices in the passage. The inspector almost pushed his companion off and hoisted himself in his place on the window frame. Steadman had no time to dive. He went down, it seemed to him, with a deafening splash and a roar of churning paddles. The inspector came down at once almost on top of him. The water felt bitterly cold, but after the first shock it braced their jangled nerves; their bruised bodies were grateful.

The two men came up almost together, and moved by the same impulse struck out for the middle of the river. The moonshine was lying like silver sheen on the surface of the water. Steadman realized that their heads must afford a capital target to any members of the Yellow Gang who were in the house they had left. The thought had barely formulated itself before a shot rang out and he felt something just rush by his ear and miss it. There came another shot and another, and a groan from the inspector. Steadman realized that he must have been hit, but the injury must have been slight, for the inspector was swimming onwards. Meanwhile the shots were not passing unnoticed. From the small craft around, from the houses on the bank there came shouts; lights were flashed here, there and everywhere. Steadman became conscious of a familiar sound—that of the rhythmic splash of oars working in concert. He trod water and listened.

There came a gasping shout from the detective.

"The police patrol from the motor-launch down the river! They have heard the shots."

He struck out towards the on-coming boat, Steadman following to the best of his ability. The inspector's shout was answered from the boat. It lay to and waited, and the two in the river could see the men in the boat leaning over peering into the water. There came no more shots, but as the inspector swam forward Steadman knew that the police boat had sighted them, and in another moment they were alongside.

Willing hands were stretched out, and they were hauled up the boat's side. The inspector's first proceeding as soon as he had got his breath was to order the boat to lie to so that he might locate the house and if possible the window by which they had escaped. The police officer in charge looked at him curiously; it was evident that he resented the authoritative tone; and as he met his glance Steadman at any rate realized something of the extraordinary figures they must present in his eyes. Stark naked, bruised from head to foot, with faces bleeding and in the inspector's case swollen out of all recognition they looked singularly unlike Inspector Furnival, the terror of the criminal classes, or John Steadman, the usually immaculately attired barrister.

But they were being offered overcoats; as the inspector slipped into his, he said sharply:

"Inspector Furnival, of the C.I.D., Scotland Yard."

The police officer's manner underwent an instant modification.

"I beg your pardon, sir. You have been conducting a raid down here?"

The inspector would have smiled if his bruised face had allowed him.

"I fancy the raid has been rather the other way about," he said ruefully. "We have been trying to make some discoveries about the Yellow Gang, laying a trap for the Yellow Dog, but unluckily we fell into the trap ourselves, as you see. Now, will you give me a bit of paper, officer. I want to take the bearings of this place. It is evidently one of the outlets of the Yellow Gang."

He looked across; on that side for quite a considerable distance the buildings abutted right on to the river. Farther along there appeared to be small boat-building businesses, just here there seemed to be only tall warehouses, and in almost every case the doors and windows were barred. Look as they would neither Steadman nor the inspector could identify the building from which they had sprung, and curiously enough no one in the boat had seen them until they were in the water. Some little time was spent in making fruitless inquiries of the small craft at hand. Though it would seem impossible that their plunge had been absolutely unseen yet to discover any witnesses would evidently be a work of time and time was just then particularly precious to the inspector. Giving the search up as useless he had the boat rowed back to the police launch. Distinct as the C. I. D. is from the River Police, the different branches of the service are frequently brought into contact. Inspector Furnival found friends on the motor-launch at once, and he and Steadman were soon supplied with clothes and everything they needed. Then, declining the police officer's offer of rest, the inspector asked to be put on land. It was still dark but for the moonlight, but their various adventures had taken time. It was later than the inspector thought, and all along the river bank the various activities were awaking.

The inspector chartered a taxi; when they were both inside he turned to Steadman.

"I believe I owe you my life, Mr. Steadman. But I think I shall have to defer my thanks until later—I am out to catch the Yellow Dog and I mean to have another try this morning before he has had time to get away."

"I am with you," John Steadman said heartily. "And as for thanks, inspector, why, when we have caught the Yellow Dog we will thank one another." The inspector had directed their taxi to drive to Scotland Yard, but half-way there he changed his mind and told the man to drive to the scene of their late experience.

They got out as nearly as possible at the same place, but from there the inspector only went a little distance before he blew his whistle. It was answered by another and a couple of men in plain clothes appeared.

"Ah, Murphy, Jackson," said the inspector. "Well, what news?"

The men stared at him in a species of stupefaction, then the one whom he had addressed as Murphy spoke with a gasp:

"Why, inspector, we have been round the house all night— every means of egress watched. And yet—here you are!"

"Umph! You didn't see me come out, did you?" the inspector said gruffly. "Never mind, Murphy, you are not to blame. What have you to report?"

Murphy saluted.

"Nothing, sir. No one has come in or out since you were admitted last night."

"Good!" The inspector turned to Steadman. "Now, I think we will go in again by the front door, sir. And come out the same way this time, I hope. Murphy, bring six of your best men along, and post others all round the house. We shall probably have to rush it."

He and Steadman walked on, realizing to the full how stiff and bruised their limbs were as they went. Once the inspector spat out a couple of teeth. Steadman's sides and back felt absolutely raw. His borrowed clothes chafed them unbearably.

The *cul-de-sac* looked absolutely quiet and deserted when they entered it. The inspector's thunderous knock at the door roused the echoes all round, but it brought no reply. In the meantime Murphy and his men had marched in behind them.

The inspector knocked again. This time as they listened they heard lumbering steps coming down the passage. There was a great withdrawal of bolts and unlocking of locks and the door was opened a very little way, just enough to allow a man's face, heavy, unshaven, to peer forth.

"Now what is all this 'ere noise abaht?" a rough voice demanded.

The inspector put his foot between the door and the post.

"Stand aside, my man!" he commanded sternly. "I hold a warrant to search this house."

"Wot?" The door opened with such suddenness that the inspector almost fell inside. "Wot are you a goin' to search for? We are all honest folk here. Anyway, if you was King George 'imself you will have to give my missis and the kids time to get their duds on, for decency's sake."

This eloquent appeal apparently produced no effect upon the inspector. He stepped inside with a slight motion of his hand to the men behind. Four of them followed with Steadman, the others stood by the door in the *cul-de-sac*. The man who had opened the door backed against the wall, and stood gazing at them in open-mouthed astonishment.

Meanwhile the inspector was looking about him with sharp, observant eyes. He threw back the doors one on each side of the passage. The first opened into a small room with a round table in the middle, a few books that looked like school prizes ranged at regular intervals round a vase of wax flowers in the middle, and an aspidistra on a small table in front of the window, from which light and air were rigorously excluded by the heavy shutters.

With a hasty glance round the inspector and his satellites went on, speaking not at all, but with eyes that missed no smallest detail. Not that there was any detail to be observed, as far as Steadman could see. This commonplace little house was absolutely unlike that other which had been but the threshold of the headquarters of the Yellow Gang—as unlike as its stupid-looking tenant was to the silky-voiced, slippery-handed members of the Yellow Gang. The passage into which that first door of mystery had opened had been much longer than this, which was just a counterpart of thousands of houses of its type.

The passage, instead of lengthening out as that one of Steadman's recollection had done, ended with the flight of narrow stairs that led to the upper regions and over the balustrade of which sundry undressed and grimy children's heads were peering. The barrister began to tell himself that in spite of the certainty the inspector had displayed they must have made a mistake. Doubtless in this unsavoury part of the metropolis there must be many *culs-de-sac* the counterpart of the one in which was the entrance to the home of the Yellow Gang. The master of the house began to rouse himself from his stupor of astonishment.

"This 'ere's an outrage, that's wot it is," he growled. "Might as well live in Russia, we might. No! You don't go upstairs, not if you was King George and the Pope of Rome rolled into one."

This to the inspector who was crawling up the staircase as well as his stiffened limbs would allow. He looked over the side now.

"Don't trouble yourself, my man. I have no particular interest in the upper part of your house at present."

Something in his tone seemed to cow the man, who opened the kitchen door and slunk inside.

The inspector beckoned to the man behind Steadman.

"Simmonds, tell Gordon to come inside, then send a S.O.S. message to headquarters." Then he hobbled downstairs again. "This grows interesting, Mr. Steadman."

The barrister looked at him.

"It seems pretty obvious to me that we have made a mistake. And I can't say that standing about in cold passages at this hour in the morning is exactly an amusement that appeals to me; especially after our experiences in the night."

The inspector looked at him curiously.

"You think we have made a mistake in the house?"

The barrister raised his eyebrows.

"What else am I to think?"

For answer the inspector held out his hand, palm uppermost. It was apparently empty, but as Steadman, more short-sighted than ever without his monocle, stared down at it he saw that in it lay a tiny yellow fragment. For a moment the full significance of that bit of silk did not dawn on John Steadman, but when he looked up his face was very stern.

"Where did you find this?"

"Wedged in between the stairs and the wall," the inspector answered. "There is a larger piece higher up, but this is enough for me."

"And for me!" Steadman said grimly.

"Gordon is the best carpenter and joiner I know," the inspector went on. "We keep him permanently available for our work. He will soon find the way to the yellow room and then— well, some of the Yellow Gang's secrets will be in our hands at any rate."

As the last word left his lips Gordon came in with another man. Both carried bags of tools. The inspector gave them a few instructions in a low tone, then he pointed to the staircase.

"Last night that was not there. Where it stands an opening went straight through to the next house."

Gordon touched his head in salute.

"Very good, sir!" He looked in his basket and chose out a couple of tools—chisels, and a strange-looking bar, tapering down to a point as fine as a knife, but very long and several inches thick most of the way to the other end. Then, apparently undeterred by the magnitude of his task, he walked up to the top of the staircase and sat down on the top step. His assistant followed with a collection of hammers ranging from one small enough for a doll's house to the size used by colliers in the pits. They held a consultation together, and then Gordon inserted his chisel in a crack. The other man raised one of the mighty hammers and brought it down with a crash that rang through the house. It did not rouse the master of the dwelling, however. He seemed to have taken permanent refuge in the kitchen. There were no children's heads hanging over the banisters now. The house might have been absolutely deserted but for the inspector and his party. Presently the inspector went up to the couple on the stairs and after talking to them for a minute or two came back to Steadman.

"The whole staircase is movable, Mr. Steadman. They have loosened it at the top. Stand aside in one of the rooms in case it comes down quicker than we expect. No doubt the Yellow Gang had some way of opening it which we have not discovered, but this will serve well enough."

"What about the children upstairs?" Steadman asked.

The inspector smiled in a twisted fashion.

"Little beggars! They will be taken care of all right. The parents were well prepared for some such eventuality as this, you may be sure."

Steadman said no more. He stood back with the inspector, while the others of their following went to Gordon's help. There was more crashing, quantities of dust and a splintering of wood, and at last the staircase came suddenly away. Behind it a locked door the width of the passage blocked their way. To open it was only the work of a minute, and then the inspector and Steadman found themselves in the scene of last night's exploits. The yellow room looked garish and shabby with the clear morning light stealing in. The chairs in which they had sat had gone, otherwise everything looked much the same.

But time was too precious to be spent in examining the yellow room, interesting though it might be. The inspector was out to catch the members of the Yellow Gang; but, though, once the staircase was down, to get from one room to the other of the perfect rabbit warren of small houses which had been devised for the safety of the Yellow Gang and its spoils presented little difficulty, the inspector, standing in that room by the river, had to acknowledge that the Yellow Dog and his satellites had outwitted him again. The only member of the Gang that remained in their hands was the man who had opened the first door to them. Not a sign of any other living creature was to be seen. Even the wife and children had disappeared.

But, as Furnival and John Steadman stood there talking, a tiny wisp of grey vapour came floating down the passage, another came, and yet another.

"Smoke!" the inspector cried.

And as the two men turned back, and heard the clamour arise, while the smoke seemed to fill everywhere at once, and over all sounded the crackling of the flames and the ringing of the alarm bells, they realized that the Yellow Gang was not done with yet.

CHAPTER XXIV

THE COMMUNITY HOUSE of St. Philip was *en fête*. Not only was it the name day of its patron saint, but its young Head had just been rendered particularly joyful by the receipt of a telegram from Burchester stating that at a further hearing the magistrates had dismissed the charge against Hopkins, and that he would reach the Community House the same evening. A special tea of good things for all members of the Community was in full swing in the Refectory. Mrs. Phillimore was presiding at the urn at the centre table, and friends of hers at the tables at either side. The delectable pork pies and plates of pressed beef and ham had been carried round by Todmarsh and a little band of workers comprising several of the clergy of the neighbourhood and several West End friends, Tony Collyer, who had been unwillingly pressed into the service, among the number.

Now the first keenness of the men's appetites seemed to be over. Down near the door they were even beginning to smoke and quite a thick mist was already hanging over the tables. The young Head of the Community was looking his best to-day. The rapt, "seeing" look in his eyes was particularly noticeable. The relief from the long strain he had been enduring with regard to Hopkins was plainly written in his face. The bright, ready smile which had been so infrequent of late was flashing, here, there and everywhere, as he greeted his friends and acquaintances. He alone of the members of the Confraternity was not wearing the habit of the Order. His grey lounge suit was obviously the product of a West End tailor, though in his buttonhole he wore the badge of the Confraternity with the words that were its motto running across: "Work and Service."

Just as the meal seemed about to end a telegram was brought to Todmarsh. He read it and then, with it open in his hand, hurried up the room to the platform at the end. As he sprang up, a hush came over the room; every face was turned to him in expectation.

"Dear friends," he began, "my comrades of the Confraternity. This"—holding out the telegram—"brings me very glad news. Hopkins, our friend and brother, has started from Burchester by car. He may be here almost any moment now. What could be happier than the fact that we are all gathered together in such an assembly as this in order to welcome our friend and brother home? Now, tonight, I want all of us, every one of us, to do all that lies in our power to give Hopkins a rousing welcome, to make him feel that we know he has been wrongfully accused, and that his home, his comrades, his brothers are only waiting and longing for an opportunity to make up to him for all that he has suffered."

It was not a particularly enthusiastic outburst of cheering that was evoked by this speech. For a moment Aubrey hesitated on the platform as though doubtful as to whether to go on, then he jumped down and turned towards Mrs. Phillimore. Tony intercepted him.

"Well done, old chap," he exclaimed, giving Todmarsh a rousing slap on the back."

"Jolly glad you have got old Hoppy back, since you are so keen on him. Shouldn't have been myself, but, there, tastes differ."

Todmarsh winced a little. "You would have been as pleased as I am to have Hopkins back if you had known him as I do. The difference it would have made if I had been speaking of some one else and he had been among the audience. His face was the most responsive I ever saw—calculated to rouse enthusiasm above all things."

"Um! Well, in some folks, perhaps," Tony conceded. "But he doesn't enthuse me. I can never get over that pretty fish-like habit of his of opening and shutting his mouth silently. Tongue always seems too big for his mouth too. Seen him stick it in his cheek and chew it, as some folks do a piece of 'bacca."

Todmarsh looked annoyed. "What a thing it is always to see the worst side of people. Now, I try only to look at the best—"

He was interrupted. A man came to him quietly. A car has stopped before the front door, sir, and I think—"

"Hopkins!" Todmarsh exclaimed, his face lighting up.

"I believe so, sir!"

Todmarsh waited for no more, but hurried off. Tony looked at him with a grin on his face. Then somewhat to his surprise he saw that John Steadman had edged himself in by the door at the upper end of the hall, and seemed to be making his way towards Mrs. Phillimore and her friends. Tony joined him.

"Didn't know Aubrey had rooked you into his schemes, sir."

"He hasn't!" Steadman said shortly.

It struck Tony that there was something curiously tense about his expression—that he seemed to be listening for something.

Meanwhile Todmarsh was hurrying to the front door. He opened it. A closed car stood just outside. He could see a man leaning back—crouching down rather, it seemed. Todmarsh waved his hand. "Welcome home, Hopkins!"

Seen thus in the sunset light waving his greeting, there was something oddly youthful about Aubrey Todmarsh's face and figure. Always slender, he had grown almost thin during his time of anxiety about Hopkins. His face with its short dark hair brushed straight back and its strangely arresting eyes looked almost boyish. Watching him there one who was waiting said he looked many years younger than his real age. But it was the last time anyone ever called Aubrey Todmarsh young looking.

The car door opened. The man inside leaned out. About to spring forward, Todmarsh suddenly paused. Surely this was not Hopkins!

At the same moment he was seized sharply from behind, his arms were pinioned to his sides, men in uniform and men out of uniform closed in upon him, and while he tried to free himself frantically, wildly, he felt the touch of cold steel upon his wrists, and Inspector Furnival's voice rose above the hubbub.

"Aubrey William Todmarsh, *alias* the Yellow Dog, I arrest you for the wilful murder of Luke Bechcombe in Crow's Inn, on February 3rd, and it is my duty to warn you that anything you say will be taken down in writing and may be used as evidence against you."

Quite suddenly all Todmarsh's struggles ceased. For a minute he stood silent, motionless, save that he moved his manacled hands about in a side-long fashion. The inspector's keen eyes noted the long thumb, the short forefinger. At last, swift as lightning, Todmarsh raised his hands to his mouth.

"Escape you after all, inspector," he said with a ghastly smile that dragged the lips from his teeth.

He swayed as he spoke, but the inspector did not stir.

Instead, he surveyed his prisoner with an ironic twist of the mouth.

"I think not. You may feel a little sick, Mr. Todmarsh, that is all."

"Cyanide of potassium," Todmarsh gasped.

"You would have been dead if it had been," the inspector said blandly. "But your tabloids are in my pocket, and mine, just a simple preparation with the faintest powdering of sulphate of zinc, have taken their place in yours."

"A lie!" Todmarsh breathed savagely.

The inspector did not bandy words.

"Wait and see!" Then with a wave of his hand: "In with him, men!"

Todmarsh offered no further resistance, nor was any possible, surrounded as he was. He was hurried into the waiting car and the inspector followed him, just in time to see him slip to one side with a groan.

"Ah, makes you feel rather bad, doesn't it?" the inspector questioned callously.

The inspector heaved a great sigh of relief. "So at last we have been successful almost beyond my expectations. It had begun to be regarded as hopeless in the force. The men were getting superstitious about it—the capture of the Yellow Dog!"

"Ay! And yet there he was just under our noses all the time if we had but guessed it," Steadman said slowly. "When did you first suspect him, inspector?"

The two men were sitting in the little study in Steadman's flat. Both were looking white and tired. There was no doubt that their experiences at the hand of the Yellow Gang had tried them terribly. But, while Steadman's face was haggard and depressed, the inspector's, pale and worn though it was, was lighted by the pride of successful achievement. He did not answer Steadman's question for a minute. He sat back in his chair puffing little spirals of smoke into the air and watching them curl up to the ceiling. At last he said: "I can hardly tell you. I may say that, for a long time, almost from its inception the Community of St. Philip was suspect at headquarters. Taking it altogether the members were the most curious conglomeration of gaol birds I have ever heard of, and no particular good of Todmarsh was known. He had never been associated in any way with philanthropic work until he suddenly founded this Community and loudly announced his intention of devoting his life to it. We looked into his past record; it was not a particularly good one. He was sent down from Oxford for some disgraceful scrape into which he said, of course, that he, innocent, had been drawn by a friend. Henceforward, how he got his living was more or less a mystery save that his small patrimony was gradually dissipated. Then came the War when, of course, he was a conscientious objector. After that, he lived more or less by his wits, was secretary to several companies, none of them of much repute. At last, suddenly, with a flourish of trumpets, the Community of St. Philip was founded. Where the money came from was a puzzle, probably to be explained by the loss of the Collyer cross."

He was interrupted by a sharp exclamation of surprise from the barrister.

"By Jove! Of course. And that explains old Collyer's curious conduct. He had found the young man out and wanted to hush it up for the sake of the family."

The inspector nodded. "He had found something out. Probably we shall never know what, but I am inclined to think something that led him to suspect who was Mr. Bechcombe's murderer. I went down to Wexbridge the other day, but I could get nothing out of him. He is merely the shadow of the man he was. Have you seen him lately, sir?"

The barrister shook his head. "Not since he went back to Wexbridge. But I have heard frequently of the change in him. Still, you must remember that Mr. Bechcombe and he were great friends; the murder must have been a terrible shock, quite apart from his guessing who was responsible."

"Quite so," the inspector responded. "But, all the same, it is very strongly my impression that he made some discovery the last time he called at Community House."

At this moment there was a tap at the door and Tony Collyer looked in. Seeing the inspector, he drew back.

"I beg your pardon."

Steadman looked at the detective, then, receiving an almost imperceptible sign from him, he called out:

"Come in, Tony. We were speaking of you, or rather of your father."

Tony came in and took the chair Steadman pushed towards him.

"You told me to call to-night, you know, sir. Perhaps you had forgotten."

"I had," Steadman said penitently. "But I am very glad to see you, my boy. How is your father?"

"I hardly know," Tony said slowly. "He is rather bad, I am afraid, poor old chap! You see he suspected the truth about Uncle Luke's murder and it has pretty nearly finished him off."

The inspector glanced at Steadman. "What did I tell you?"

"He saw a line or two in Aubrey's blotting-book telling him that Mrs. C. would be at Crow's Inn with the twinklers at a quarter to twelve," Tony pursued. "He will tell you himself just what it was. He sees now that he ought to have come to you at once, but he did not know what to do, the poor old governor. He had taken rather a fancy to Aubrey lately, though he never thought much of him as a kid. But, naturally, one doesn't like to try to hang one's nephew, or half-nephew by marriage. You know his mother was my mother's half-sister."

"And Luke Bechcombe's," Steadman said. "Well, no one can help what one's nephews, or half-nephews do!"

"The first direct line we had to Todmarsh came from you, though, Tony. When you told us your suspicions of Mrs. Phillimore, you know," replying to Tony's look of surprise.

"Knew she was a wrong 'un first time I saw her," Tony acquiesced. "Carnthwacke was the same—'bad little lot!' he called her. Pretty well bust up the rich American widow business for you, didn't we?"

"You did!" the inspector said with a grin. "And a detective from Boston, whom we wired to, finished it. He recognized her as a woman that they had wanted for years; been in that crook business ever since she was a kid. I wasn't thinking she had turned reformer over here."

"Not precisely!" Tony said with an answering grin. "Pretty well gave the show away when you arrested her, didn't she?"

"Wanted to turn King's evidence," said the inspector, "but we weren't having any. Hopkins will do for us! By the way, sir," turning to Steadman, "I found out this morning to whom we owed our escape from the Yellow Dog's clutches."

Steadman raised his eyebrows interrogatively. "Indeed!"

"Hopkins's wife," said the inspector. "It was the Hopkinses' child you rescued from under Mrs. Phillimore's car on the day of Mrs. Bechcombe's lunch. You sent it to the Middlesex Hospital and sent your own car to fetch Mrs. Hopkins, and take her there like a lady, as she phrased it. Then you sent the child sweets and toys and this completely won the mother's heart. She acts as housekeeper to the Yellow Gang at the house by Stepney Causeway. If she had not been"—he shrugged his shoulders—"well, you and I would have been in kingdom come, Mr. Steadman."

"Good for her!" said Anthony. "And I suppose my precious cousin's anxiety about Hopkins was lest the beggar should give him away to save his own skin, and not out of love for the gentleman at all. I should always distrust a chap that keeps on opening and shutting his mouth and chewing up his tongue,"

Tony added sapiently. "Mrs. Phillimore, too. Carnthwacke told me he was slick sure he had seen her walking about with his wife's maid."

The inspector nodded.

"Sometimes she was mistress, sometimes maid, and part of the week she was Fédora, the great fortuneteller, and this way she was able to pick up information for Todmarsh. If she had been spotted—well, it was her taste for philanthropy."

Tony got up and walked about the room. "But it is an awful thing, whichever way you look at it. We shall have to keep it from my poor mother. She never cared for Aubrey, but he was her half-sister's son, after all. I don't think he meant to kill Uncle Luke, you now, Furnival. I think it was done in a scuffle."

The inspector shrugged his shoulders. "Didn't care whether he did or not, if you ask me. According to Hopkins, he went disguised, taking chloroform with him to render Mr. Bechcombe unconscious, and wearing rubber gloves, so that his finger-prints should not be recognized. Then, while Mr. Bechcombe was unconscious, he meant to impersonate him and get Mrs. Carnthwacke's diamonds. But Mr. Bechcombe had struggled much more than he expected, and in the struggle recognized him. Then the game was up as far as Todmarsh was concerned and Mr. Bechcombe's death followed instantly. The rest of the programme was carried out as arranged, only that Mr. Bechcombe lay behind the screen dead, not unconscious!"

"Brute!" Tony muttered between his teeth; "deserves all he'll get, and more! Poor old Uncle Luke—" blowing his nose. "He was always good to us when we were boys. It won't bear thinking of!"

Anthony Collyer was sitting in the library at Bechcombe House. A letter from his father lay open on the table. To him entered Cecily Hoyle, looking as attractive as ever in her short black frock, low enough at the neck to show her pretty rounded throat, short enough in the arms to allow a glimpse of the dainty dimpled elbows, and in the skirt to reveal black silk stockings nearly to the knees, and suede-clad feet.

"Tony, you have heard?"

Tony got up, pushing his letter from him. "I have heard that you are not Thompson's daughter after all—"

"No. I was mother's child by her first husband, Dr. James Hoyle. So I am Cecily Hoyle after all. Because Mr. Thompson adopted me and then took my father's name, but he isn't related to me at all, really—not a scrap!" explained Cecily lucidly.

"So I have been told," Tony assented.

As Cecily drew farther into the room he drew a little back, and rested his elbow on the mantelpiece.

"I—I thought you would be pleased, Tony," the girl murmured, just glancing at him with sweet, dewy eyes. "Because, you see, it makes all the difference."

"Difference—to what?" Anthony inquired in a stiff, uninterested tone.

"Why—why, to us," Cecily whispered with trembling lips. "I—I said I couldn't be engaged to you any longer, Tony. But—but if you ask me again, I have changed my mind."

"So have I changed my mind," Tony returned gloomily. "You said you would not let me marry a thief's daughter—well, you see, I have some pride too. I will not let you marry a murderer's cousin!"

"Cousin! Pouf!" Cecily snapped her fingers. "Who cares what people's cousins do?"

"Well, you would, if they did brutal murders and got themselves hanged," Tony retorted, taking his elbow from the mantelpiece, and edging a little farther from Cecily, who was betraying an unmaidenly desire to follow him up.

"I shouldn't really—not a half-cousin," the girl contradicted. "And he was mad, Tony. His father had been in an asylum more than once, only your aunt didn't know when she married him."

"Half-aunt," corrected Tony, "I'd like you to remember that half, Cecily."

"Well, I will!" the girl promised. "And, Tony, I want to tell you that I hadn't the least idea that Thompson was the man that I thought was my father while I was at Mr. Bechcombe's. It seems he put me there thinking to get some information he wanted through me, and which I am thankful to say he didn't.

I never recognized him, he looked so different. Then after the murder when he told me, though he said he wasn't guilty—I couldn't help doubting."

"You might have trusted me," Tony said reproachful.

Cecily burst into tears. "You might trust me now."

Tony's heart was melted at once. He drew the sobbing girl into his arms. "I would trust you with my life, sweetheart—but I—"

"Ah, you shall not say but!" the girl cried, clinging to him. "You do love me, don't you, Tony?" lifting her face to his.

"You know I do!" said Anthony, his sombre eyes brightening as he looked down at her.

"Then that is all that matters," said Cecily decidedly, "isn't it, Anthony?"

And Anthony, capitulating as he kissed her eyes and her trembling lips, confessed that he thought it was.

THE END

Lightning Source UK Ltd.
Milton Keynes UK
UKOW06f0935191116
288021UK00024B/616/P